Tales of the
Mystery Shopper

Taken from the Mis-adventurous
Casebook of his Stupefied Apprentice

Tales of the Mystery Shopper

Taken from the Mis-adventurous
Casebook of his Stupefied Apprentice

Michael Forrest

iUniverse, Inc.
New York Bloomington

Tales of the Mystery Shopper
Taken from the Mis-adventurous Casebook of his Stupefied Apprentice

iUniverse books may be ordered through booksellers or by contacting:

iUniverse
1663 Liberty Drive
Bloomington, IN 47403
www.iuniverse.com
1-800-Authors (1-800-288-4677)

ISBN: 978-1-4401-5369-3 (pbk)
ISBN: 978-1-4401-5368-6 (ebk)

Printed in the United States of America

iUniverse rev. date: 6/29/2009

For my parents

Contents

Acknowledgements

A deeply appreciated "Thank You" to Mary Lou and Lynne for their input on the stories contained herein … and the editing. Definitely the editing. All remaining mistakes are the author's sole responsibility.

The Mystery Shopper

Proclaimed amongst the information on the company's brochure was this, and I quote, 'I Can Make Your Day!' (*Mystery Shopper, USA*). My friend and employer made this his mantra, and pursued its fulfillment with a talent and gusto that has never been equaled, much less seen before, in the Mystery Shopper (at times, hereafter: MS) industry.

His given name was Joe Lopp. The names which he gave himself were, amongst others, Nathan Broadhurst, Colin Throckmorton, and Lamont Baskerville. It all depended on which agency he was working for at any given time. He liked to refer to 'the agency' whenever he was 'on assignment'.

In his younger days he had adopted the personae of such characters as Billy Ray Lester, complete in a wife beater, tight jeans, and cowboy boots or, another favorite, Sid Carpoli, in shiny suits, wide collars, and gold chains.

I had first met Joe as Billy Ray Lester, when I was still in my teens. I was a directionless youth, on the verge of manhood, but astray in outlook and attitude, since I had lost my parents at the age of six. They had run off with a cult, the Ordination of the Silver Seal, about which I, from my largely unsuccessful researches over the years, have only managed to turn up a

1

minute amount of information. And of these sparse crumbs, I found only meandering references, mere whispers really, to some half-assed doctrine of transmigration of either body or soul through either aluminum foil or Indian head nickels. I could never quite figure which. One can well imagine what they must have been imbibing.

At any rate, when I was old enough I ran away from the home of my aunt and uncle where I had been living since my parents had abandoned me. There was no real reason, other than the hopelessly misguided delusion of youth, the one that tells all teens that they actually know everything, and what the world's all about. *My God, what a fool I was!*

Anyway, I flopped around for almost a year with some willing, and many unwilling, friends, one after another. This, hanging out on the streets, and doing some part-time pizza delivery, were my daily routine.

But it was on one of those seemingly endless days of wandering my urban environs, lounging about the coffee shops, loitering in arcades, aimlessly doing a 'whole lotta nothing', that I encountered Billy Ray. It was at the Diamond Disco Roller Rink, it was the eighties, and he was weird. I had seen him on any number of occasions over the couple of years I had been haunting the joint. In those days he was hustling all the kids there in pool, air hockey, pinball, you name it and he played it. Most of the kids there just considered him a freaky old dude (he must have been about thirty by then, though I've never been able to get his real age out of him), hanging around with adolescents and teenagers, scamming them out of their pocket change. No big deal, there are all kinds.

I had never spoken to him before, trying to keep my distance, and my money. So it was with some surprise that he ambled up to me one evening, thrusting his pelvis and stomping his booted heels to a popular tune of the time. I was admiring a particularly 'cute ass', skating through the swirling dots of light out on the floor, weaving through the heat and crush of the bodies all moving to the throbbing rhythms of Billy Squire, pantingly exhorting, *"Stroke—Me, Stroke Me!"*

"Hey, man," he said, as he cocked a cowboy hat back off his forehead, further exposing sideburns down to his jaw line, "you got a smoke?"

"Don't smoke." I eyed him warily.

"Good thing. I see you 'round here a lot. What's up with that?"

"What d'ya mean?"

"Well, you never play me. Afraid of losing?"

"None of those are my kinda game." I really didn't play games, so that made me stand out more than a little. I didn't realize this at the time.

"You wanna play something? You name it," he said.

"Naw thanks, man."

He stretched, flexing his bare arms in a sleeveless t-shirt which had a 7-Up slogan on the front: 'Never Had It, Never Will,' he was particularly fit back then, "You wanna get outta here? Kinda slow tonight."

"You a perv or something?" I edged away.

"No, I'm Billy Ray." He stuck out his hand, "Billy Ray Lester."

He waited patiently with arm outstretched as I prevaricated on whether I wanted to have anything further to do with this dude. Finally, for some reason I have never been able to understand, I reached out and grasped his hand in my own. "Stanley Greene. Stan," I said.

"Well, Stan my man, let's boogie." And with that unfathomable jolt of inspiration, no doubt in the form of a little devil whispering in my ear to take a chance, I began what was to become my lifelong calling: being Joe's closest friend, confidant and apprentice.

We talked a great deal that evening and I came to understand that all he was really looking for was someone he could call a friend, and boss around. But our age differentials made that only natural. I also eventually learned his real name, if not his real self. *That* would only reveal itself to me after many years, and may never be fully understood, even by Joe himself. Over hot dogs and sodas from a vendor's weinermobile, and a great deal of strolling about the city streets, yukking it up within the bubble of our own private joke at the expense of the crowds we milled about, we came to know one another as we shared our secrets and bared our souls that fateful day.

The decade was still young and people reflected a split personality, with holdover attitudes and styles of the Jimmy Carter, polyester, and disco 70's. Upon reflection, I must say Joe fit right in. He was truly a product of the culture, and its changing times.

He regaled me with a great many tales of his adventures, most of which I could not immediately credit to him, though I subsequently came to find out were, in fact, largely true. Joe was to become something of an older brother to me, and I was to become … well, you'll see. But my apprenticeship (I know, it seems hopelessly outdated, but considering the man I was dealing with, anachronism was practically the order of the day, every day. In Japanese jargon he would be the senpai to my kohai, a mentoring master/apprentice relationship, in other words), didn't really begin until one day when we came to the shocking realization that we were both homeless orphans.

What happened was this, we had been out and about when Joe needed to stop by the place where he lived with his grandmother to pick up something or other. But when we approached his apartment building, we came upon heaps of clothing, and other scattered and shattered, possessions, strewn about the sidewalk. He stopped, and dropped suddenly, fingering some of the garments, picking up the pieces of a broken 45.

"*Barry Manilow,*" he said in a strained voice barely above a whisper. Then, "Grandma!!" His scream reverberated up and down the valley of the street. A window on the fourth floor came up, and a large head and torso leaned out.

"Back so soon?" The great, round head sounded scorn down upon my new friend.

"What've you done?" He was on the verge of tears.

"Sendin' your no good, free-loadin' ass packin', that's what!"

"But, but—why?" Joe's jaw quivered.

"It was your dead-beatin' that killed your mother, and it won't be me next. I can't take it any longer!" She began to withdraw, closing the window.

"I'm not a deadbeat!" The window continued to close, "I work! I'll make good! You'll see!" Joe fell down on his knees, flung back his head and howled, "Grandma!!" And with that I could hear the window firmly meet the sill, the curtain was drawn, and the light went out.

I helped him up, patting his back, but he was inconsolable. I had no idea what to do about it, except try to reassure him that he had someone to lean on, as I lent my arm and supported him down the sidewalk and into the growing dark of evening. That was to become a posture I would grow accustomed to holding for my friend, through good times and bad, as the years wore on. It was then that we truly became kindred spirits and would spend the intervening years quite closely involved in each other's lives and work. And it was also during that time in which the transformation of my friend, from virtual Vaudeville penny performer into the virtuoso maestro he was to become, reached its maturation stage.

Since those, his younger days, however, he had abandoned all plebeian trappings, such as his grandmother had rained down upon that long ago sidewalk, and began clothing and carrying himself in a style more suited to his presumed station and profession. Also, he was becoming more than a bit long in the tooth and thick of limb for the kind of attire he once wore so proudly. This was a touchy subject with him. Many's the morning I would catch him unawares, through a crack in an imperfectly shut lavatory door, standing before the mirror staring down sadly at the ever increasing follicles accumulating in the bristles of his brush. I mourned with him for what he must have felt was the fading of his prime into dotage.

But his abilities, like a mellowed, yellowing page, did not diminish, and surely became more precious with the passage of time. He carried himself with a dignity that projected to people the style and wisdom of another, more genteel, tintype era. This served him very well in hoodwinking the unwary, which consisted of almost everyone who happened across the path he trod with ponderous footsteps.

"So, where to tonight?" I asked.

"Tony Roma's." He rubbed his hands together in anticipation, then added, "I've been pining for some ribs lately."

"That's a new name," I remarked idly. We hadn't dealt with them before that I could recall. Yet, taking a cue from Joe's last comment, I did seem to recollect that this Tony entity occupied a portion of the barbecue sector of the food services industry. "What's this one about?"

"The Agency has been contacted by this new client, regarding the overcharging of some of their customers at the particular location we shall be paying a visit to this evening."

He rose and strode deliberately across the room to take up a stance in front of the crackling fireplace, hands clasped behind his back. There was a chill in the air. He stood there for a spell, head bowed deep in thought. Of a sudden, he let out a great sigh, his large round shoulders rising and falling, before moving to the side of the fireplace opening, and resting an arm on the mantle piece. He idly picked up a brochure from the stack he kept piled on the mantle under a cubic zirconia-encrusted tortoise paperweight, next to the Museum Store replica of a clock from the Versailles Palace that always ran to the wrong time. No matter the amount of winding. They clashed horribly, but Joe wouldn't hear of separating them.

I remained silent, letting his thoughts work their way out. The brochures were from a diverse collection of businesses engaged in a bewildering array of endeavors, and their presence on the mantle reflected the reputation Joe's versatile talents had earned him. He was bombarded with succulent offers from desperate companies of all kinds, in need of his peculiar services to uncover and solve some, usually elementary, problem that had been confounding them.

"Hmm, the Six Flags am*uuuu*sement park." He drew out 'amusement' as if it were anything but, thoughtfully tapping the brochure against his chin, "They've been trying to entice me for years with their flash 'n fun." He tossed the brochure into the flames. It took and began smoking. Joe picked a stick of kindling from the grate and held it to the end of a partially smoked cigar he recovered from the mantle. Puffing the stogie to life, he negligently flipped the stick back into the fire, "Not the right season for merry-go-rounds," he continued to puff, his head soon wreathed in smoke, "and roller-coasters only inflame my gallbladder."

What doesn't? I wondered. But whatever his reasons, he just shrugged off these corporate pleadings as being, oh, what was his phrase? Ah yes, "Too common for even the common man."

"And the assignment is ... ?" I tried bringing him back to the evening's business.

He chuckled, his belly shaking, "Why, Stan, to find the culprit, of course. Teffer," he called over to his doorman lurking in the foyer.

Teffer stuck his head in the room. "Sir?" He looked furtively from Joe to me and back again, "What are you doing?"

"Talking." Joe looked steadily at Teffer, "What are you doing?"

Teffer had made the acquaintance of Joe as Sid Carpoli, way back in the days when he used to bowl in numerous leagues around town, and made a pretty good living at it, too. He also did a bit of minor bookmaking on the side, a pastime which the local wise guys discouraged him out of, but that's a story for another time. Teffer suffered from paranoid melancholia (not to be confused with paranoid schizophrenia: a delusional persecution complex), which caused him to be morosely suspicious of everyone. But Joe, being the generous spirit that he is, took Teffer under his wing during team play one season, and Teffer has been in his employee ever since, serving as a kind of Jack-of-all-trades in the roles of doorman, butler, and even chef (though he has no particular aptitude for it).

"Oh, right," Teffer straightened, "what will be your pleasure, sir?"

"Ring around to Tony Roma's, would you?"

"I don't believe they take reservations, sir," Teffer said.

"I don't want to make a reservation, Teffer," Joe said, with forced patience. Teffer wasn't the brightest bulb in any room. "I merely wish to ascertain whether they have that delightful hot Smoky Mountain BBQ sauce I like so well."

"Oh, quite so, sir. Right away, then," he ducked back out again.

Having been driven from his former 'occupations' by a combination of his guilt-tripping grandmother and wise guy mafioso's, Joe eventually found his way into the burgeoning MS industry, where his talents could be displayed on an entirely different stage. Joe worked for more than a dozen different agencies, all told, on a regular basis, not to mention numerous others, which I can scarcely keep track of, on a more needs-based, special commission footing. And all at the same time. It was really quite astonishing, and totally unprecedented in the industry for a mystery shopper to be as prolific as Joe. But he had aliases enough to cover all the agencies that hired his services. And then some, I've no doubt. When made aware of the numbers involved, he would simply reply, "Ah, my dear fellow, aren't they all really one 'Agency'?"

It's important to keep in mind that many MS agencies frowned upon the employment of shoppers, or as Joe would have it, 'agents', who were otherwise employed as mystery shoppers for other agencies. The same person circulating around the same assortment of places was bound to raise suspicions, especially amongst the more furtively lazy and bad tempered employees in the retail world. The point of the exercise was to catch them unawares in their natural surly state. But ability and a hard earned reputation could easily overcome such a discrepancy, when it came to my friend.

"When do we go, Joe?" I asked.

"Uh-uh," he tut-tutted me, "Nathan."

"Sorry, Nathan." So it was Broadhurst, tonight. That one would fit the bill nicely for this shop, I thought. Joe's choices in matching aliases to various kinds of assignments was uncanny. Of course, his aliases were all created with just this in mind.

"Not at all. As to time," he took out the pocket watch that was attached to his vest by a silver chain, with Monopoly game tokens dangling from it. The top hat was unmistakable, a gift from a grateful former client "ETA at our drop off point, hmmm, let's make it seven-thirty. The staff is usually more generous with their servings in the evening." He snapped his watch shut with some vigor, "Or else, they had better be. And, Stanley, could you make arrangements for our conveyance this evening?"

"No problem," I reached for the bus schedule.

He stared off into the distance with a certain gleam in his eye that I had come to recognize, whenever he expected trouble. I silently prayed that this wouldn't be the case, but one could never tell. His cases often took the most peculiar twists and turns. For instance, one of his more mundane, and unlikely, assignments had turned into an entirely unexpected chain of events, with repercussions far beyond what either of us could have imagined. Now let me say right off, I know I shouldn't indulge his more off-the-wall whims, but I have always been a follower, and for most of my life, --his follower. Old habits are broken only with great difficulty, and I hadn't yet learned the trick at that stage.

It began, as all his capers do, with an assignment—a 'case', in his investigatorial jargon. The business to be investigated and rated was a women's clothing store. Here I'll withhold, or change, the name of the establishment and the various persons involved in order to protect the innocent, which my friend happened to be, this once.

I've never known a great deal about my friend's past personal life before I came along. As far as I've ever been able to discern he was a lifelong bachelor. No mention even of a casual lady friend, much less a significant other, for that matter. He has mentioned his mother fondly from time to time, and I've even seen pictures of her, lovingly framed, next to cast photos from his child actor days, when he starred in such productions as *Oliver Twist* and *The Hobbit*. Though what has always stuck in my mind is the uncanny resemblance he bears to his mother. Meaning, they're both large of person, somewhat stout with great heft. Joe bald, but his mother somewhat less so. And, this is the truly odd thing about them, they both resemble the late thespian Sydney Greenstreet (a.k.a. Kasper 'The Fat Man' Gutman), of *Maltese Falcon* fame, to a startling degree. Even his grandmother bore the same stamp, through whatever dominant gene accounted for it. Who knew how far back it went in their family?

It was from those early years on stage that he learned the art of make-up, of costume, and disguise. It wasn't so much that he applied this craft to altering completely his appearance, Lon Chaney-esque, rather he made the most of more casual changes, by giving each of his many and varied alter-egos different dress and personae, that served to allow the same man to morph imperceptibly from one character role to another. Thereby, he thwarted detection, even though, for all intents and purposes, he was the same physical person. He has always been a marvelous method actor.

At any rate, what kinds of successes and failures he endured in his personal relations, and scars they've left, I cannot say. But I've always felt, in strictly *needy* terms, he was still building towards something, and only appeared to stagnate until the time was right. On whose timetable this was based, I couldn't fathom, but more of that in a bit.

Now, it may seem strange that my friend, considering his, um … condition, would be given an assignment of casing a women's store that catered mostly to young ladies. And you would be right to wonder, and question the wisdom of such a posting on the part of that particular agency. But somehow, through whatever channels he prowled out of sight of prying eyes, he managed to wheedle, bribe, or threaten the agency's schedulers (or, 'handlers', as Joe preferred to refer to them), into throwing the case his way. Again, I've no idea *why*, he must have just felt the urge, as it were.

"We shall be in need of fine lingerie for a special lady friend of mine," he had replied, when I asked him how in the world we were to pull this off.

After all, he, a rotund man of late middle age, and myself, a tall, thin, gawky man (it pains me to admit the truth), of still somewhat youngish years, would not readily present themselves as being credible customers in this particular case. At any rate, on the day of the 'mission', we were deposited by yellow cab at the curb of the store's entrance, promptly one hour before closing time, at five p.m.

Joe was always such a cool customer, which made him so successful at what he did. He didn't bat an eye as he marched through the ranks of plastic females, sporting the latest, in using the least to reveal the most, while robbing people at the cash registers.

"May we have some assistance in choosing particular delicates for a female of my acquaintance, please?" He asked the young woman behind the counter.

She blew a bubble and tossed the hair out of her eyes, "Say what?"

"Lingerie," I added helpfully.

Sizing us both up, she said, chomping her gum, "I'm on counter duty right now, but I'll take ya to the department and get ya someone." With that, she led away to the far corner of the store.

"Not a good beginning, I'm afraid," Joe muttered to me. "If things do not improve considerably and quickly, this young lady, and perhaps the entire staff, will find themselves out on the street, once my report is filed."

I knew him to be true to his word every time. The list of employees, and even businesses, he had forced under was long and impressive. An entire organization of professional white collar crooks could not inflict more damage on a company than a single detrimental report by Joe. And he was relentless in the pursuit of his goals, as unfolding events were about to demonstrate.

"If you guys'll just wait here, I'll send Nina over," she said, and left us. My friend snorted, tapping his cane in a discordant rhythm on the floor.

Fortunately, we didn't have long to wait. A woman strolled over, hair piled high above plucked eyebrows, heavy mascara, and ruby red lipstick. She was nearer Joe's age than my own, if appearances didn't deceive. Dressed in a black leather miniskirt, low cut blouse exposing abundant cleavage, and stiletto heels, she appeared to me a streetwalker. Joe was painfully unprepared for this. But it was too late for any evasive course of action.

"Heart's delight," he murmured, enraptured.

"Joe, stay on target," I whispered with a smile in my voice, at that point not attuned to any sense of impending danger.

Personally, I couldn't quite figure his fascination, but I had to remember that this was a man who was about as romantically inclined as a shoe horn. Which is to say that he didn't go out looking for it, indeed seemed to actively avoid it. But, what can I say, if the pollination is swirling about in the air, any bit of it could alight upon even the most unwilling recipient, with no effort on the receiver's part whatsoever. So Cupid's random arrow struck my friend in his fat ass, and he was hooked. She just didn't know yet that she was holding a line, much less that all she had to do was reel.

I must say, it was rather shocking for me, nonetheless. This was entirely out of character, especially for the role of Colin Throckmorton, if I remembered his modus operandi correctly. I immediately noticed a rise in temperature, and quickly realized that it was emanating from my friend. There was an instant kindling of a flame in his heart that would end up burning brighter than a sun, before going supernova and nearly burning him out entirely.

But, I skip ahead. It was there in the lingerie department that it all began.

"How can I help you, gentlemen?" She asked, looking from one to the other. Joe just stood there, struck dumb.

I tried to pick up the slack, "We need --,"

He came to, and quickly cut in, "We are in need of some dainties, some delicates, some, uh, duh ....," He actually blushed, stammering.

"Would you prefer panties, low rise, thong?" She asked, letting it hang there, as an uncomfortable silence settled over us.

"Er, um, well now, you must see that ... oh," Joe was totally at a loss. I had never seen him so completely out of his depth. Rest assured, it was not the subject matter of the shop. He had always scrupulously studied such things beforehand, and his professional acting abilities were beyond question. Here, however, he was unable to avert his eyes. Frozen like a deer in headlights, he took out his handkerchief to pat his sweating brow.

She recognized this for what it was, adopted an appropriately coy smile (oh, how I groaned inwardly when I saw this!), and began the reeling. She sought indulgence, my friend obliged.

"How about I have one of the girls come over and model some of the different styles?" she asked. He gulped. She eyed him critically, "Or would you rather I did it myself?" He nearly fainted. I quickly lent an arm to steady him.

"Not necessary, dear lady," He managed hoarsely, "Stanley, here, can rustle up some samples for us."

"But, I don't know anything –," I tried to protest.

"Now, now, Stan. Be a good sport," he motioned me off. I just stood there. He had already devoted himself completely to the appreciation of Nina. When he bothered to take notice again, he was surprised to see me still hanging about. "Let's be about it, Stan," he clapped his hands briskly. "We haven't all day."

Joe flattered and courted her from that day forward. Scarcely a look or expression would pass from her face to his attention, before her every need or whim was met. He fawned and cooed after her like a pet partridge, and she lapped it up.

You must understand, and, I hope, sympathize with my friend's situation. For all his bravado in playing the roles that he felt life had assigned him, he was just about the furthest thing from a lady's man that you could reasonably hope to find. I know I belabor the point, but it's only because I know him so well. Still, he came alive for yet another new part, but with a significant difference this time—it was a real part. Tragically, I don't believe, by that point, he was able to distinguish between reality and fantasy.

Their relationship can only be characterized as one of intense—oh let me try to find the right word here ... how about 'passion', and we'll leave it at that. *Oh all right!* It was the most blatant example of disgustingly indulged eroticism I have ever had the misfortune of witnessing!

I saw relatively little of Joe during those months, only in passing, really. But when I did happen to catch up with him between costly dinner dates and weekend trips, he was always in a jolly mood.

"I see you're taking another, um, vacation?" There were a couple of suitcases standing by the front door, one day when I dropped by. Teffer milled about by them uneasily.

"Why, yes, Stanley," Joe was straightening his tie in the foyer mirror.

"Where to this time?"

"Paris," he said. I picked up a couple of Greyhound tickets, from beside his wallet and keys. The destination was printed on the front,

"Paris, Texas?"

"Ah yes, Nina still has family in those parts." He turned around and held himself erect, "Well, how do I look?" Teffer made a move to fuss over him, but Joe batted his hands away, "No-no, I'm asking Stanley."

I approached him, never taking my eyes from his, hoping for some sign that Nina's spell could be broken by my intense concentration alone. When the dream clouds failed to clear from his vision, I could only sigh and tell him, truthfully, "You look great, Joe."

A part of me, which had been dying inside ever since their affair began, gave up the ghost at that moment. It did indeed feel like a death in the family. I so wanted to weep for, what I considered, the loss of my dearest friend.

Some afternoons, following a rollicking tryst, they couldn't even bother dragging themselves out of his flat with their clothes on. I've walked in on them more than once—*Yeesh!!!* I'm fortunate not to have become a suicide. Or lost me eyesight, at the very least. It was many a late afternoon, once they'd departed for an evening out, that I, as his dutiful apprentice in the trade, was tasked with picking up after them. The amount of adult toys and devices that had accumulated in his flat was mind-boggling. The place reeked of oils and incense, and was saturated with the unmistakable odor of carnality that was impossible to air out. I have a rather well-founded suspicion that some of their outings were mystery shops to adult entertainment establishments. In fact, many. If the accumulated inventory had ever been properly cataloged, they could have opened their own store. But my friend was still on top of his game. He had never looked better, if a little fatigued, with an ever present spring in his step. I suppose I should have been happy for him, but why was I not?

It could have had something to do with the startling discovery, as I tried to balance his accounts (one of my other duties), that his savings had been draining away at an alarming rate. It could have been the increasingly erratic behavior of Teffer who, given his own issues, had certain fairly harmless habits which were turning more and more bizarre. A perfect example is the day that I found him straining his toenail clippings in the tea infuser. He denied any knowledge of his actions, claimed a migraine, and promptly barricaded himself in his room.

Or, my suspicions could've been raised when two FBI agents stopped by the flat one afternoon, while Joe was out with Nina.

They wondered when he might be back. I told them I didn't know.

They asked if I knew anything about his work. I told them, "a little."

They inquired whether I knew anything about one "Nina Etheridge McCoy, her profession, or her family in Paris, Texas"—I told them to leave.

When the door had closed on their backs, I put mine up against it and slowly sank to the floor in a cold sweat. What the hell had Joe gotten himself into?

It turned out what Joe had gotten himself into was one of the largest organized shoplifting rings law enforcement had ever seen. And his lady love? You guessed it. Her family in Paris, Texas, were the ring leaders, while Nina herself served as the chief in charge of operations for the particular region in which we lived. This all came out over a relatively short span of time. When the horror of it finally dawned on my friend, it was over. I have never learned what exactly happened to Nina, but, apparently (this from an incredibly reluctant and shattered Joe), over espresso and chocolate truffles one day, she announced her intention, under close questioning as to her activities by my friend, to move on. And she did.

As far as I could ever learn from either the FBI or local law enforcement, Nina had either gotten away, or was dead. All that these sources would divulge was either, "We cannot discuss ongoing investigations," or "We have no information about such a person." Whatever, it was a dead end, perhaps literally.

And my friend? Well, he was not the same after that for quite some time. It wasn't just that his heart had been broken, it was the professional outrage and humiliation accompanying it. She had used him in so many ways; physically, emotionally, financially (he was flat broke by the time it ended), but she had also used him as cover for her family's criminal enterprise. Imagine the bonanza of landing a mystery shopping legend, and using that as entree into any store she liked. He spent the next several months fairly isolated from the rest of the world, with only my gentle ministrations and feedings, not to mention Teffer's dark mutterings, keeping him going. Teffer would eventually settle back into what passed for a normal routine, for him.

But what could I do for Joe? He was my best, indeed only, real friend. So I virtually hovered over him, like a concerned little mother hen, until he was able to face the world again. It was only fortunate, as well as hard and desperate work on the part of Joe and myself, that his affair with Nina was able to be concealed. The consequences for his career would have been disastrous, had it been made known. But, by calling in many years' worth of favors from agents, shoppers, and enablers, who worked in or on the edges of the industry, he had orchestrated a rather skillful, if slapdash, cover-up.

"Have I ever explained the properties of Beryllium to you, Stan?" he asked me, bringing me out of my reverie in the armchair, where I sat in his flat. I checked my watch, Tony Roma's was soon. My stomach rumbled.

"Not to my knowledge."

"Well, then, it's important to keep in mind that Beryllium has one of the highest melting points of all the light metals... "

" ...but my point is," he continued, once we'd ensconced ourselves in a booth at the restaurant, "you can't use it any longer in fluorescent lighting tubes, because it causes Berylliosis in the workers handling it," he chuckled, taking another sip from his Tom Collins, drained it, and motioned to the waitress for another. "Time her again, would you, Stan?"

"Do you think they may get the wrong idea, if I keep fiddling with my watch?" I asked.

"What, are you double-o seven now?" He flung himself back in laughter, "More like Agent 86. *Aaa-haa-haa, hee-hee!*" I waited for his chortles to subside, before duly starting the timer on my wristwatch for the third time that evening.

The bus dropped us off a couple of hours earlier. We had dined on mounds of ribs and barbecued chicken, and were now involved with our after dinner drinks. Joe generally needed considerable time to allow for his food to settle. The report, at this stage, looked relatively good for the establishment.

We had been seated promptly upon arrival, our orders politely taken, and food served still hot, and our table cleared promptly upon completion of our meal. There's nothing more offensive than having the waiters attempt to clear a table while the diners are still dining. So, all had gone well. Joe was merely timing the staff at this point, more out of habit than anything else. And, as long as our final bill corresponded with my calculations, there would be no problem. Joe seemed contented, and was more than likely to forego any further tests for the serving staff, in an effort to trip them up. They would pass, this time.

It was at this point of the evening, with a mission well done (perhaps overdone, we had really run up quite a tab), that Joe became expansive, settling into a contented mood, from which, it seemed, nothing could pry him from.

He was a man full of facts, a man overflowing with knowledge both mundane and arcane. He was the kind of person who, if he had had a different personality makeup, could have accomplished most anything he set his mind, and often lagging energies, to. But he accessed the world primarily through such sources as A&E and The History Channel, which caused enough separation between himself and the real world, that I often had to explain to disbelieving ears that life was not so easily fitted out for a facts and figures mold. He would listen patiently and smile indulgently, then proceed to expound upon whatever he had recently picked up from The Discovery Channel.

"You remember the scam where that fly-by-night outfit tried to get you to rob a jewelry store for them?" I asked. It was always a pleasure to reminisce with him about notable past shops.

"I do, indeed." His eyes took on a faraway look, thinking back to the time, though he had had a fair amount to drink as well. "And then they intended to do me in to cover their tracks. As I recall, you saved my life on that one." He reached across the table and squeezed my arm. "How did that all come about? My mind slips a bit." He was setting me up, I knew, but I relished reliving the case as much as he.

Mystery shopper scams were the bane of all specialists like Joe. And it was often only with the utmost diligence and cunning that such doyens were able to avoid being ensnared. Usually such cons are easily spotted and evaded. Some scams require potential shoppers to pay them in advance, and then walk away with the shopper's dollars. Child's play, that. Others are more prankish in nature, conducted entirely online, sending duped shoppers to certain businesses to spend their own money with the promise of reimbursement afterward, only to find no one home at the other end of the URL, afterwards. Since this last took advantage of a common transactional arrangement between shoppers and agencies, it was easy to fall for. In fact, some notorious businesses set up their own scams along these lines in order to drive up their sales. Joe had a run-in with such an unscrupulous company some years ago, and the proprietors are undoubtedly still trying to pull themselves out of both individual and corporate Chapter 7 bankruptcy.

But the incident I was about to relate was of a very different nature. One which Joe has always referred to as one of the most sinister of his career.

"Let's see, as I recall, business had been a bit slow for some time," I began, warming up, "the occasional case, but nothing of any moment. It was a routine contact that set things in motion. An agency neither of us had ever heard of made the call. Looking back, we should have been more cautious. It was certainly out of the ordinary. Yet, they managed to sell us on the assignment through the simple expedient of bringing up some of your past cases. You must admit, they had the details down to a point. How in the world they found out that information I have never been able to uncover."

"I found out," he said, with a rueful expression, but didn't elaborate.

"After you had accepted, they sent the contract, instructions, and credit card to be used in the operation. You had decided upon, oh, let me see, yes, Rutherford DuMonde, as your cover."

"Ah, Rutherford," he said, wistfully, "I still miss him." He had been forced to retire that persona, after the caper was uncovered.

"It may not have been necessary, if the police hadn't become involved," I pointed out.

"No, my friend, the masterminds of the heist would have been able to hound my steps until they either caught up with me, or I dropped dead from exhaustion trying to elude them."

"You're probably right about that," I conceded to my friend's superior experience, "though it's easy to forget that --," I stopped, suddenly looking upon my friend with some concern. The first hint I had that something was wrong, more like a shovel to the forehead, was the expression he had taken on. His eyes were glazed, intently focused on some spot behind me. He blanched and his mouth hung slack. He remained this way for some moments. I feared he would begin to drool. I immediately thought it was indigestion, then I feared something more serious. I sprang from my seat and came around to his side, taking his clammy hand into my own. He didn't move.

"Joe, sorry, *Nathan*, what's the matter?" I asked, panicked now. "Was it the ribs, the hot Smoky Mountain flavor sauce? Oh dear God, say it's not your heart!" He made no reply, only continued to stare ahead. *"Nathan, say something!"* At this, finally, he grunted and jutted his chin in the direction of the front doors. I followed his gaze, and gasped. A couple had just entered. The man was of medium height, slim, in coat and tie, and just taking off his fedora. He had a cigarette dangling from the corner of his mouth. But it was his female companion, who had caused my friend's distress, it was-- .

Joe had a way of spreading his lips and baring wide teeth and gums, when he searched his mind for just the right word:

"—*Her!*" Suddenly the life came back into my friend. He flushed, grinding his teeth, and ground my hand in his grip in the process.

I painfully extricated it, "Oh, dear." Her back was to us, so she was unaware of our presence. But it was definitely Nina. To Joe, she is always *the* 'Ho.

Hmmmph! Alive and well, it would appear, and walking free, to boot. How had she managed that? "Now Nathan, please, don't do anything rash." I didn't really try very hard, it's true. I just knew it would do no good.

"Waitress!" Joe bellowed, "Another round. No, make it three!" At this, Nina turned around to search for the source of the sudden outburst. When her eyes alighted on Joe, they flashed dangerously, as the color drained from her face, but she quickly recovered (*ooohh, she was good!*), and turned back to her dinner companion.

Joe was not to be consoled, try though I did. He dove into his drinks and did not surface again, until he had consumed several Tom Collins, numerous shots of tequila, and a full carafe of wine. At the end of which, he lurched to his feet. Staggering dangerously, he made his way across to where they sat, as I sank further into my own seat. He stopped at their table, saying nothing for a time, only glaring down at Nina, before turning his attention to her table mate.

"You. Meet me in the bar in five minutes," he said, his drunken voice carrying to all corners of the place. What was he doing? He should've been turning his ire on *her.* "We'll settle this like gentlemen. Or should I clarify, and say that at least one of us shall."

"Joe, *dammit*, get over it!" Nina hissed, livid with embarrassment. "We - are - through! Can't you understand that? And if you say anything about ... stuff, I'll see that you regret it."

"I don't know how you got away with it?" Joe was shaking his head.

"Hey, doll, who is this joker?" Her companion cut in with a nasally, tough guy voice.

"No one, honey," then she turned her gaze back up to the swaying figure of Joe, and bit off venomously, "And I do mean, *No! One!*" She spat it out and turned away.

Joe, much to his credit, did not bite back. Instead, he turned again to her companion, "You, sir, have only four and one half minutes left." And with that he spun, losing his balance, he crashed into a nearby table, but managed to keep his feet. Straightening himself, he marched through the room's doorway into the adjoining bar. I followed, as I always did. He was my friend.

Joe had stationed himself in the center of the room. It was moderately full of customers, half at the bar, the other half sparsely populating scattered tables. He stripped his suit coat off and flung it aside, I missed the catch, as he rolled up his sleeves, and took an old fashioned boxer's stance.

"*Nathan, please!*" I pleaded, but he ignored me. The other customers had taken notice that something was up, and, hoping that it would be some form of entertainment, gave Joe their full attention. Sadly, they were not to be disappointed. Of a sudden, he began to roar at the top of his lungs:

"I Gave My Love,
My Love, To Thee
Oooooh, Woe's My Pity
For All To See!!"

"Joe," I heard Nina's voice from the other room, "we're leaving now." Then I heard an exasperated sigh, "Why don't you get a life?" I could hear them rise and gather their things, then their footfalls depart, at which point my friend broke down utterly. With an enormous wail, he began to heave wildly, careening into the bar, and bouncing off of barstools, like some great, deranged bumper car.

I went to him then, catching his great bulk in my arms, as he slid to the floor underneath the bar, sobbing piteously.

I laid his head against my shoulder, and just held him, as the other patrons laughed and jeered. I, eventually, managed to get him into a cab, where he vomited after a block, and passed out in the back seat, cradled, like a snoring, stinking child. I may as well have been his own mother then. Certainly, I was all he had in the world.

How we navigated the trip from the cab to the elevator, and then into his flat, is a further mystery even to me. But I finally got him beached on his own bed, where I labored to undress him (failing that I merely undid his collar and rolled him on his side, so he wouldn't choke on his own vomit should it come to that, again), and tucked him in, before turning out the light.

Needless to say, he was finished in the industry after that unfortunate night. Whether it was the manager of Tony Roma's, or Nina herself, who reported him to the agency, who can say? But word of his behavior while on assignment, as well as his connection to Nina, finally surfaced and spread. His description passed from one agency to the next, and before we knew it, all of his contracts had been terminated. He sunk into another deep depression after that, this time worse than the initial one, following the discovery of Nina's true nature. It was going to be rough sledding for some time to come, I knew. But we would survive, he and I. And what with his emerging interest in Reality TV shows, better times were almost surely on the way.

Post Script - It has been some months since I set down in writing the above events in the life of my dear friend and employer, Mr. Joe Lopp. It was a very difficult period in the aftermath of what I have to come to term 'the situation,' more so for Joe's peace of mind, than my own. I use that euphemism, as I still try to shield him from as much emotional recall of his romantic and professional disaster as I am able. And it has worked, by and large.

Joe paid me a visit at my own small apartment earlier this very week, and we were able, finally, to bury the late trauma, once and for all. Or so I hope. This is what happened: he came to my door one day, knocking, but in typical fashion, did not await my opening the door for him. Instead, using the key I had given him, he flung the door open, and breezed through the doorway, with all the delicacy of a force gale. It so startled me that I jumped, but was relieved to see he had regained much of his semi-dilatory energy.

I had been down on hands and knees arranging my collection of cephalopods. I had all kinds: octopi, squids, and cuttlefish, and they came in various forms: stuffed animal, blown glass, ceramic, and more. I had so many that they had to be arranged all over my shelves and along the floor at the base of the wall. It is a collection I still possess to this day.

"Good afternoon, Stanley," Joe greeted me, tossing his hat and cane on a low divan, before plopping down in a chair. Instantly, he made a face and reached underneath him to extract a crumpled Peewee Herman doll. That was another little hobby of mine. "The Peewees seem to be breeding, Stan," he noted, seeing the numerous new ones I had acquired. Please don't ask how I grew attached to both Octopi and Peewee. Not even my therapist has been able to unravel that tangle. Joe looked the one he held in the eyes, "Ah, Peewee, you were framed, poor fellow," he told the doll, before negligently flipping it aside. "Stan, I've come to have a word with you."

"About what?" I was wary, but hopeful.

"About the recent, ah, 'situation', as you identify it."

"Oh?"

He took a deep breath, then let it out in a single blast, before replying, "Stan, I just want to say thank you, from the bottom of my heart. You really saved my bacon this time. No, no," he raised a hand to halt my response, when I opened my mouth, "I know that oftentimes I don't say it enough, considering all that you do for me. For us. But it had to be said, and so I've said it. If in future you find me seemingly ungrateful for your efforts, you just give me a swift kick in the pants, to let me know I've been a dunderhead."

I smiled, then laughed, "Joe, thank you. You're my dearest friend, as well as employer and mentor. I've never had cause to regret anything I've ever done for you, or your response. You're really more giving in your gratitude than you credit yourself for." And he was, at times.

"Well, humff," he looked around quickly, not for anything in particular, it was just that his eyes had suddenly brimmed. I looked away, too, so he could have time to recover with some modicum of privacy. At last, he said, "It was a close call, that's for sure."

"You made it through all right. Not *too* the worse for wear," I noted.

"A bit of scarring of the heart, yes, but in exchange, I wear a thicker skin and carry on my shoulders a wiser head." I'd always thought he had the hide of a walrus to begin with, but he was right about being wiser now in matters of the heart. "I must say, Stanley, love is a cruel mistress. While she can be intoxicatingly beautiful at night, in the full light of day, she is a green face cream masked shrew in tattered bathrobe and fuzzy slippers, with rollers in her hair. Anyway," he rose, moving towards the door, "I've said my piece, now I must be off."

"What's the hurry?" I rose to my feet.

"I've an appointment."

"An appointment? How come I hadn't heard of this?"

"Because you didn't make it," he chuckled. "Actually, it's more of an audition." He read my quizzical expression, adding, "Yes, it seems a fellow in town is starting up a new series for the local public access TV station. He hopes to call it 'Life with Lopp,' as do I. It will be reality based, following me about my daily routine, letting the run of the mill folks out there have a glimpse inside the life of a legend. That sort of thing." Life with Lopp? How much persuading had that taken? Well, leave it to Joe...

"But Joe, if by legend, you mean as a mystery shopper, ummm," I tried to be delicate. It was hard to find the right words, "Your status in the industry is, uh, up in the air, still?"

"Oh, *ho-ho*," he guffawed, "not to worry about that. I expect, and fully intend, to be reinstated very soon."

"How are you going to manage that?"

"I have my ways, Stanley. The ways of a legend may seem mysterious to all but those of a similar stature, almost magical and mystical, but, in truth, it's much more down to earth. I'll say no more on it right now, but rest assured I'll let you know when it happens." He scooped up his cane and plopped his hat down on his great bald dome, at a rather jaunty angle, too, I noticed. "Now, I'm off. Wish me luck."

"Good luck, Joe."

"This is just the beginning, you know, Stan," he paused at the door. "I'm merely getting my feet wet with this local production. After this, I'm going national, maybe even global. People will be fascinated by me, you'll see. The sky's the limit!" And with that he gusted back out the door, letting it slam behind him with a hollow boom, seeming to suck all the vitality and air out of the room with him.

That was just like him. He always brought a larger than life presence everywhere he went. People were drawn to it, fed off it. And he off them. It was symbiotic, and not usually harmful, though at times Joe engorged himself overly, and that's when innocent bystanders had to be cautious. I could only smile and shake my head. Who knows? Maybe he could make it big. He certainly had the skills: creative adaptation to practically any environment, high-level BS communications, and an unwavering confidence in his own abilities. Yes, this could definitely work.

The Reaper Bowl

I had never known my friend, Joe Lopp, to be a particular enthusiast of the more popular forms of sports, nor of the popular culture of society, in general, for that matter. So it was with some surprise when he sprang upon me, one dreary fall day, the particulars of our next assignment, or 'case', as he preferred.

"Well, Stanley, we have quite an outing to prepare for," he said to me.

"Oh? What's this?" I asked, normally channels along which potential clients pursued Joe's services tended to run through me, as his apprentice and personal secretary, so this was indeed coming from out of left field.

"Why, our newest case, of course. And this one will be a bit out of the ordinary."

"How so, Joe?"

"The clients, for one thing, will be new to our rolls."

"Are you going to fill me in?" I was going along as I always did. Joe's theatrical background and nature caused him to draw out dramatically such moments as this. Whenever he had interesting news of any kind, it was easy for me to get swept along in the wake of his own enthusiasm.

"We have not one, but two, new clients. They are working in tandem on this particular venture." This was not unheard of in the mystery shopper industry, though somewhat uncommon.

"Who are they?" I pressed him, "Names, man, names. And what's the case?"

Joe chuckled, holding up both meaty paws in a gentling gesture, "Whoa, Mr. Greene, pull up, please. One thing at a time."

Still rumbling with mirth, he hoisted himself from the depths of his vinyl armchair next to mine, and waddled across the fine Samarkand reproduction rug to the fireplace. Grasping the poker, he prodded the burning logs in the grate to renewed flame, the dancing light flickering about the walls and ceiling of Joe's study.

"First off," he began the slow drip-drip of information leaking, always so reminiscent of Chinese water torture, "our client tandem." He seemed to be choosing and savoring his words here, resting an arm on the mantelpiece. I nestled back in my own chair, watching, waiting. "The first name may be unfamiliar to you. They are the General Consolidated Vending Corporation. Based in Michigan, I believe you'll find in your researches as we prepare for this case."

"Sounds somewhat familiar," I mused.

"They put the vendor into vending, supplying the food and beverage courts at various sporting and entertainment venues around the country."

"Of course, with such a generic company name, they'd almost have to be in that line of work," I remarked.

"Just so. And the other client and partner to GenCon in this endeavor is a somewhat more well known, dare I say prestigious, entity." He smiled down at me.

I sighed, "Who, Joe?"

"The Mid-Mountain Athletic Conference, otherwise known far and wide by the acronym: MMAC." He drew out the 'm' sound as, "*mmm.*"

"The MMAC?" I, too, drew it out in imitation of him. I sat up in my chair, shaking my head. Was I supposed to know this name? "Who are they?"

"A college sporting conference, Stan," he replied, with some exasperation, "They're quite well known for their athletics and business success. A model conference and member of the NCAA. FYI Stan, they are the governing body for college athletics in the U.S. The MMAC and it's member schools are looked to by other conferences and their members, for tips and guidance in running a profitable college sporting concern. Honestly," he turned his back, shaking his own head now at my ignorance.

Not a great sportsman myself, I felt somewhat helpless in the face of this minor dressing down. What could I say? I really didn't give a hoot about such past times. Still, from the way Joe was talking, this definitely sounded like a big fish in a big pond. I had heard of the NCAA, of course. I wasn't entirely stunned that he would land such a big client, at this particular point in his career Joe was *the* best in the business. The mystery shopper everyone tried to emulate, and it was to be the most productive period of his illustrious career. Truly, 'The Golden Years'.

Yet, for all that, if I had never been much of a sportsman, Joe was even less so. How would he relate to such a testosterone-induced industry? It must be noted here that Joe's sporting experience (and, yes, Joe did regard himself as a great sportsman), was almost totally devoid of much physical exertion. His games and diversions largely consisted of card and parlor pursuits, as well as board and puzzle games. Some darts, arcade, pool and bowling in his youth, to be sure. But, nowadays, croquet and a rare round of golf were all he was up for, when not on a case, or enjoying an evening out at a touring Broadway show, or barbershop quartet rehearsal (where his occasional catcalling had gotten him ejected more than once, I can tell you).

"Indeed," he continued, "they sought me out specifically. By name, I might add," he *was* that good, "yes," he actually bounced up on the balls of his big, flat feet, preening himself, "they knew me by reputation." Then he looked over at me a bit sheepishly, recovering himself. "Obviously, Stanley, you've had a great hand to play in my success, to date." He proferred a small, bobbing bow in acknowledgment.

I laughed and stood, stretching. I moved over to the sideboard to pour us a couple of whiskey sours. "Not at all, my friend. I'm a mere mite in your shadow. But, pray tell, what's the case that would bring together these eminent entities to seek your services?" I asked.

"Well, as to that ..."

On a cold, overcast Friday, during the early hours of October 30th, less than a week after Joe had explained the details of the assignment to me, we boarded an Amtrak passenger liner headed south to the coast. *We* would not be traveling all that way, however. Our stop was the next afternoon at a mid-size university town in the Appalachian mountains. After we were taken to our sleeping quarters by the porter and settled in, it dawned on me that tomorrow we would find ourselves at an evening college football game on Saturday, October 31st--

"--Halloween?" I blurted out loud.

"What's that, Stanley? Er, oh yes, tomorrow is the date of that quaint folk holiday. I hadn't thought of it, frankly," Joe was wrestling a bag into the overhead rack.

"This will be my first football game, and on Halloween, even," I remarked.

"Now don't get superstitious on me, Stanley," he finally managed to secure his luggage. Heaving a great sigh of relief, he collapsed into a seat, where he took out his handkerchief, flipped it open so that it billowed like a sail, and proceeded to mop his streaming face.

"I'm not superstitious, Joe --."

"Morgan, please," he corrected. "Morgan Bellevue, remember?"

"Yes, I remember. Sorry," I took a seat opposite him. He often took on one of his numerous personnas whenever on assignment, the better to misdirect those who may have had contact with him in the past, or even heard of him by name alone. Make no mistake, that was a constant danger with a professional as prolific as Joe.

"Think nothing of it," he declared magnanimously.

Let's see, as I recalled, the character of Morgan Bellevue was a -- , uh-oh,

"Uh, Joe, I mean ... look. Isn't Morgan an ex-football player?" That is, *if* I remembered the background info on this particular alias correctly.

"Not just *any* ex-player, Stanley," he raised an instructional finger. "Morgan was a star, a true B.M.O.C.. That would be 'Big Man On Campus', to the uninitiated."

"At what position?"

"Er, *hem*, well a quarterflanker or, or a, uh, running end."

"Which one?"

"Oh, you know, one or the other," he waved this aside as just so much chaff.

"It's rather important to know this, *if* you are determined to play this character," I pointed out. "I really hadn't thought you'd use this particular personna around others, who would be so knowledgeable about the game." I was chastising a bit at this point, but it was one of my tasks to keep Joe centered, and undercover.

"I, too, am quite knowledgeable about the game, Stanley," he retorted with some exasperation.

"Have you ever been to a game?"

"Of course, I have."

"When?"

"It was a long time ago," he prevaricated. "We'll talk about it later. But right now let's go over what you've learned in your researches." Which wasn't a great deal, and what I did manage to glean was pretty damned tedious, and depressingly petty, grasping, and ... I guess beside the point at this stage.

So, let me try to lay out the situation as clearly and succinctly as I can. The schools playing the upcoming football game belonged to a conference, the Mid-Mountain Athletic Conference, which was trying to take control of the concessions business. Heretofore, the individual schools had controlled their own concessions contracts, but the MMAC and GenCon had hatched a scheme, whereby they claimed to be able to generate more revenue for all of the conference member schools, by running the operations much more efficiently. The member institutions were skeptical, but willing to give them a chance to see if it panned out as predicted.

This was a lucrative gig for Joe, and would involve taking a comprehensive pulse of how the operation was faring. For all that, however, it was more taxing than complicated, thus my presence would be essential for much of the 'leg' work. If only the assignment had turned out to be as straight forward as that. It's only when the most improbable events crop up at the most unexpected times and places, to throw a wrench in an otherwise flawless operation, that one has to remember never to take anything for granted. But let me not get ahead of myself.

"So our clients' angle is this," Joe paused to sip his wine, nodding the waiter away, satisfied with the chaptalized vintage. We had taken seats at our table in the dining car at 7:30, very nearly the first in line, at Joe's insistence, "They need, *desperately,* I'm sure you've grasped, to prove that GenCon can administer the concessions at these collegiate sporting events, more efficiently and profitably than any other such concessions vending companies in the nation." Joe paused again as our dinner salads were laid before us.

"The profitability factor is not our concern," he continued, once the waiter had retreated. "The sales receipts will speak for or against GenCon in the eyes of the conference schools, once the final results have been tallied and presented, at a full conference meeting at the end of the season."

"But, Morgan, how can mere results exert enough pressure on the member schools to abandon their own profitable concessions contracts, and sign over their sovereignty in this area to the MMAC and GenCon?" I asked.

"Stanley, please keep in mind, not all members of the conference need sign on, only a bare majority."

"And our role?"

"The other side of the equation is the customer service angle, and that's our gig."

"Customer service is our bread and butter," I noted, as Joe wolfed down a buttered dinner roll, "but how can our report on quality of service have any impact on the final decision of the schools, as to whether they buy into this scheme?"

"Stanley, *tsk-tsk*," Joe shook his head sadly. "After all this time with me, you still underestimate the power of a shopper's report? The absolute functional importance of customer service to our livelihood is but a metaphor, for the importance it holds with all consumers. CS is of vital import. Never lose sight of that." CS was Joe's shorthand for Customer Service.

"Morgan, I never --,"

"I know, my friend." He speared another roll with his salad fork, depositing it on my plate. "What our clients hope to prove is not just profitability, but customer service excellence. After all, the decision to 'switch sides' is never entirely in the hands of an institution, such as a university."

"Oh?" I was intrigued, where was he going?

"Not at all. The aforementioned entities survive and thrive through their own customers, and in this context such customers are known as fans."

"Ahhhh."

"Precisely. Bad to mediocre, or merely good, service, and the MMAC and GenCon can kiss their scheme of vending hegemony goodbye. But very good to excellent CS may well save the day, and tip the balance in favor of our clients."

"But this vending concession has been going on with this particular conference and its teams all season. A season which, incidentally, is half over," I said.

"Quite so. And from what I can gather, things to date, CS-wise, have been fair to good, by all accounts. Accounts given, I might add, by none other than my predecessor," I quirked an eyebrow, Joe filled me in, "who was none other than Adelbert Doge."

I gave a low whistle. Doge was perhaps Joe's chief rival in the MS industry. Sure, Joe had had others, even some flat out enemies, but he'd bested them all, over the years. Only not Adelbert, who, while still trailing Joe, reputation-wise, liked to pretend that it was a neck and neck race. He might not have been too far off at that, though Joe took the attitude that he was light years ahead. An attitude which was not necessarily born out by the thriving business Doge conducted.

However, Joe was far the superior performer, at least in my eyes. Oh, there were stories to tell about Joe and Adelbert going head to head, but this account is neither the time nor place. Yet, it did raise the stakes for us.

Joe continued, "Let's see if we can't one up ol' Adelbert with superior flair." He gave me a wink. Doge was not of the theater, as was Joe. As I recalled, he came from more of a techie background, accounting or some such. "Doge has always been a stickler for detail, anal to the extreme," Joe remarked. "And while I appreciate detail as much as the next geek, a command performance will trump pocket protectors and scientific calculators any day of the week. In any event, our clients have taken the feedback they've received from 'Bert, processed and addressed all identifiable problem areas, and are just now rolling out the upgrades to GenCon's operations."

"Tomorrow will be day one, then?" I asked.

"You have it pegged, Stan. Oh look, here come our entrees." We paused as our dinner was served. Joe took up again as the waiter departed once more, "I must say, the service on this train is really quite good. Have we done them before?"

"Oh yes, don't you remember?" Then I thought better of it. Best to keep him on target. "Um, never mind, another time. C'mon, back to business, Morgan."

"Yes-yes, ok, then. The clients want immediate feedback on the overhauls GenCon has made. This game tomorrow could well make or break their scheme, and they want to know which way this particular worm will turn, right away."

"What part will this home team's administration and the conference play in events at the game, then?"

"We'll get into that *after* dinner. But right now let's not allow this delicious looking meal to get cold." And with that, he practically dove into his steaming meatloaf, and I could get nothing further from him until he surfaced again, which was some extended time later.

We were relaxing after dinner, with a couple of creme de menthes, when I felt I could draw Joe back to tomorrow's business.

"To wrap this up," I began, "what of the school and conference officials? Will they be helping, hurting or out of sight at the game tomorrow?" It was ever a situation to guard against, a client's interference in an ongoing shop. Oftentimes they were just trying to be helpful, and just as often they loused up the operation. Mystery shoppers had been known to be driven from the ranks of the employed by overzealous clients. It was a general rule that clients were informed to keep a respectful distance, so that a shopper could complete his business unimpeded. Yet there were also instances where middle to lower level management tried to rig the shop, in an effort to improve their district or individual store's score. This had happened to us from time to time over the years, the most heinous example being the ignoble Banana Republic Bungle, as I believe I entitled it in my notes somewhere.

"Non-existent, if we're lucky," Joe said sourly, "though I don't intend to leave our mission all to chance." He was getting that certain mischievous gleam in his eye that bespoke either a coming stroke of genius, or disaster.

"Do the officials know when we're coming?" I asked.

"Oh, they know all right."

"What are you planning?" I was getting suspicious, nervous, trying to contain my rising alarm.

"Nothing terribly complicated," he replied, lounging back smugly in his chair, hands clasped comfortably across his vast mid-riff. "No doubt you'll recall that I'm something of an expert at disguise," he commented sardonically. Oh no, this particular train could be heading off the tracks if Joe got too creative on the morrow. "Some may even call me a full-fledged master," he chuckled, "but enough of that for now."

I raised myself in my chair, hoping to pursue this further, but Joe raised a cautioning hand, "Tomorrow, Stanley, to--," he was suddenly interrupted by the loud clang of the dining car's rear door being flung open, through which poured, what looked to be, half a dozen persons concealed in black hooded cloaks, white skull masks peering from the shadowed cowls.

"*Happy Devil's Night, Suckers!!*" They screamed, then unleashed volleys of water balloons at the diners, who were suddenly jolted from their after dinner torpor into a bedlam of actions, such as ducking and diving, trying to avoid the attackers and their projectiles. All within a din of shouts of indignation, and the repetitive chant of, "*Devil's Night! Devil's Night!*"

One of the dark clad attackers began squirting shaving cream on the horrified diners, while another was splashing red paint (I hoped), on diners and windows alike, where it ran like blood and dripped from the table linens. Once they had reached the far end of the dining car, mayhem in their wake, the trailing vandal, with an excited giggle, pulled out a roll of toilet paper and set it alight, rolling it down the center aisle, before following his fellow rioters out of the car, with the door banging closed on their heels.

The flaming TP unrolled almost perfectly, leaving a flaming and smoking trail of bath tissue in it's wake, as it traversed the length of the car, only to be stomped out by a waiter, who had just come through the far door, with several burly porters in tow.

"*My God,*" I heard the waiter say to himself in a low voice, surveying the dazed and damaged patrons and property, as I crawled out from under our table.

I pointed the opposite way down the aisle, "They went that way." I was shaken, myself. The waiter motioned for the porters to pick up the trail, and pursue the hoodlums, which they did, hurrying from the carnage of the dining car with looks of relief. The waiter, with more arriving, set about assisting the diners. I managed to deposit my jangled self back in my chair, with a great exhalation of relief. I looked across the table—Joe hadn't moved. He sat stiffly upright, staring straight ahead, a squiggle of shaving cream crawling up the side of his head, and splatters of red paint across his chest. I waved my hand before his eyes. He didn't blink.

I grew concerned, "J—Morgan?"

And then he spoke, slowly but clearly, "I'll - Have - Their – Heads."

"Now, Morgan, they're just kids," I tried to mollify him. He was having none of it.

"Stanley, kindly assist me to our quarters. I've had quite enough for one evening." So I escorted a badly shaken Mr. Bellevue back to our sleeping berth, where I was required to explain the vandalous nature and history of Devil's Night, to a sulpherous (in his own right) audience, before being allowed to extinguish the lights, for a, hopefully, undisturbed rest.

We departed the train at the station shortly before noon. Joe insisted on a brief word with the conductor, before collecting our luggage on the platform. The conversation was one-sided, and more of a tongue lashing, dealt by Joe, upon the hapless fellow, concerning the events of the previous evening. The conductor, I must say, conducted himself with appropriate humility, and was profusely apologetic, in the face of Joe's steamed diatribe, which was laced with such keywords as 'barbarism', 'foul report', 'bloated superiors', and 'floggings'. I finally managed to steer Joe away from the poor man, left standing by the idling locomotive, wringing his cap in hand.

Upon arrival at our hotel, having enjoyed a pleasant drive through this relatively small, rural, college town, we only bothered to clean and refresh ourselves, before catching a much needed nap, in an effort to recharge before the game. The events of the previous evening, coupled with the motion of the train, in the past always so lulling, caused Joe and I to find only fitful rest.

"Joe, that was the front desk," I called to where Joe was in the restroom. "It would seem that both school and conference officials have managed to track us down."

"I'm not at all surprised," I heard his muffled voice from behind the door. "Desperation causes people to do desperate things ... such as making complete nuisances of themselves." I heard the toilet flush, water running from the tap.

"I told the woman at the desk to tell them we weren't taking calls," I said.

The door opened, and Joe strolled out toweling his hands, "And you did register us under the name Morgan Bellevue?"

"Of course."

"Then all is proceeding according to plan."

"What plan?" I retorted a bit testily. "They'll undoubtedly be waiting to intercept us in the lobby."

"Undoubtedly," Joe concurred succinctly.

"Then how do we get past them?" I nearly cried out.

"Stanley, do be a good fellow and retrieve my cosmetics bag," he waved off to his pile of luggage on the far side of the room, "whilst I ready my wardrobe for the evening."

"If I'm not mistaken, kick-off is in less than --."

"Plenty of time, dear worrier," he said, "plenty of time."

We arrived at the admittance gate to the stadium as the sun was setting. A biting chill had infected the air. A thick white fog was rolling down from the dark, brooding woods of the surrounding hills and smallish mountainsides, that ringed the valley bowl, in which nestled the football stadium.

I pulled my scarf tighter about my throat with gloved hands, huddling closer in my overcoat. Joe, on the other hand, carried himself jauntily in sweatshirt and toboggan, of the home school colors. He fit right in with the likewise attired crowd, his face painted to match those same colors. An old-fashioned pennant waved on its cane pole, like a banner from yesteryear. Joe was old school all the way. The puffball of his cap bounced excitedly, as he bustled through the throng. And, since it was Halloween, many were decked out in a variety of costumes, or a combination of school gear and holiday garb.

We worked our way towards the gate, past vampires, werewolves, ghosts, zombies, and all manner of other monsters, cartoon characters, freaks, and drunken fools, sporting beer bongs, along with glazed eyes, from an entire afternoon of raucous tailgating. As the gate attendant tore our tickets and offered directions to our seats, I couldn't help but smile, as I mulled over our escape/departure from the hotel, and the ditching of the officials lying in wait …

"Joe, you're not serious," I blurted, a daub of face paint on my finger, poised before my friend's broad forehead.

"Never more so, Stanley," he replied pleasantly. "Now, if you wouldn't mind, please proceed with the application." And so I did. I wanted to do only a minimalist job of it, a few stripes of color here and there. Joe wouldn't hear of it.

"All over, if you please," I was instructed, "with parallel stripes on the left cheek up onto my nose of that side. And, oh, how about a Celtic whorl on the right. Yes, I think that will do nicely."

"It's your face, Joe."

"That it is, that it is," he said. As it happened, he blended in far better than myself.

His plan for the evasion of the awaiting officials in the hotel lobby was efficiently simple, as it turned out. Joe merely stationed me in the hallway outside our room, awaiting other game-goers, then departing for the stadium. This was easy enough. After all, this relatively small college town had its population balloon by many thousands on the weekend of a home game, and, well, there really wasn't anything else going on. So any departing groups from surrounding rooms were undoubtedly bound in our direction. The fact that they were attired much as Joe would make it easy to tag along with such a group. Finally, a party of eight or nine exited their rooms just a couple of doors up the hall. I quickly stuck my head inside our door and announced,

"Here's our ride."

Joe snatched up his pennant and declared, "Game time." With that we tagged along and rode the elevator down, safely crossing the lobby under cover of our unwitting group.

The school and conference officials were easily identifiable. In coats and ties, their lapel pins were a dead give away, sort of a modern badge of office. Lapel pins always stirred in me an irritable dislike, for some reason. Anyway, we easily hailed a cab, and took the short ride to the stadium. I had even considered walking, as so many other fans were doing, but I knew Joe would need to conserve his energies for the game.

"Morgan," I tapped Joe on the arm, "would you care for some refreshments, before we take our seats?"

"Indeed I would," he and I veered off from the crush at the gate, and made our way to the nearest vending station. We had already decided to visit each one as part of a pre-game check, before finding our seating section. Besides, Joe had quite an appetite, and I, as well, admittedly.

So in the course of slightly less than an hour (we had planned the time needed to shop each vendor, and reconnoiter the area), we had finished with our pre-game tour. I had been taking notes, and I could tell that Joe was already mentally preparing the opening of the report, as he munched merrily on his third brat of the evening. And just as importantly, we had avoided the notice of any school or conference officials, even though we spotted several of the lapel-pinned underlings roving about. It seemed to me they were looking for something, or should I say, someone. When I remarked on this to Joe, he just smirked and gave me a wink. The disguise was definitely working. It was always gratifying, and relieving, to get a clear indication of this, though I had had no doubt in Joe's abilities.

It wasn't until we reached our seats, that we would have a chance to go over our initial shop run in greater detail. But first--

"—*WAVE!!*" People screamed all around us. The stadium literally roared. Joe was just wiping mustard from his chin, when all the fans in our section leapt to their feet in unison, and flung their arms in the air. We followed suit, but were a second or two slow. We, literally, stood out as the wave rolled around the stadium. That was an entirely new experience for both of us, but no worries, we'd get the hang of it. Joe was truly in the mood now, waving his banner about. With his appetite sated for the moment, and numerous beers in him, he really seemed to be looking forward to the start of the game.

By kickoff, with the stadium filled to overflowing, we found ourselves crammed in amidst quite a gaggle of horridly made-up characters. Here a ghoul, there a ghoul, everywhere a ghoul-ghoul. The game itself proceeded rather apace. I'm probably not the best eyewitness sports reporter. The game was not really my cup of tea. Joe, on the other hand, was definitely getting into the action. His large besweatered and painted figure would burst from his seat, more and more in unison with the surrounding fans, as the game progressed, whenever the home team made a good play.

He caught on to the rhythms of the expected protocol of the event, and even partook of a couple of beer bongs with some nearby youngsters. The beer bong, for those of you, so far uninitiated, as was I, is nothing more than a length of tube with a funnel affixed to the top. The device is then loaded with one or more beers. The recipient places the tube in his mouth, the contraption is raised, the throat is opened, and the whole contents shoot directly down into one's stomach.

"C'mon, Stanley," Joe danced a little jig, after doing one, stopping only long enough to belch thunderously, to which he received rounds of applause and slaps on the back from his new, rowdy drinking buddies. "You simply *must* try one of these!"

I begged off, claiming the nachos and jalapenos I'd had from one of the vendors, were upsetting my stomach. And for this, I was roundly booed by all the revelers about us, as being a party-pooper. I could live with that.

By the end of the first quarter, the home team, whose mascot was a Mountain Man, led the visitors, known as the Hoary Eagles (who I could only hope, contrary to what their moniker suggested, would prove more sprightly than geriatric in the 2nd quarter), by a score of 14-3. And the quarter couldn't have ended soon enough. The fog had crept onto, and across, the field of play, obscuring the action to such an extent, it had become increasingly difficult to make out what was happening on the field.

"Morgan, shouldn't we make another round?" I suggested. "The second quarter will begin soon, and we'll want to shop the vendors in their down time, as most of the patrons will be too busy watching the game."

"Or trying to watch," he whisked his hand before his face, trying to brush aside the fog. "This pea soup is making it nearly impossible to enjoy the game. Very well, old party-pooper," he laid a hand on my shoulder. "You lead the way. I shall keep a hold of you so as not to get lost in this muck." He laughed easily. Sometimes he operated best a bit intoxicated. I only hoped this was one of those times.

By the time we reached the nearest exit ramp, struggling against the flow of the hordes of fans headed in the opposite direction, the second quarter had begun. I caught one glance back at the field, and the players running around were just barely discernible through the thick fog.

The ramp down eventually began to clear the further we went, the atmosphere growing more eerily murky as the lights fought a losing battle to penetrate the ever increasing wall of fog. Occasionally, I would startle, as a dim shape suddenly materialized as a Freddy Kruger or Catwoman, before just as suddenly disappearing back into the fog. I felt Joe's hand, still resting on my shoulder, spasm and clutch once or twice, before loosening his grip, accompanied by a faint snicker.

"Kind of unnerving, eh?" I tried to lighten the mood.

"Kind of," was all Joe said. "Say, Stan, that glow over there almost certainly indicates a vending station. Shall we?"

I led away in that direction, and sure enough, it finally materialized, only after we had advanced to within a couple of feet from it. There was only one young lady waiting pensively behind the counter. She startled at our approach, as if we had suddenly appeared out of thin air. And in a way, we had. With the light inside her stand to her back, and nothing but dark and fog before her, she was practically blind in there. And with the weird echoes, which can be so misleading in a fog, she would be nearly deaf, as well. The young lady relaxed somewhat, as she was able to make us out more clearly.

"Hi," I said, resting my arms on her high counter.

"Hi. Can I hep you?" Her voice was soft, far away, as were her eyes, taking no more notice of us, as she continued to peer out into the fog.

"Umm," I turned to Joe.

"Young lady," he snapped his fingers, bringing her attention back to us, "two burgers and two sodas, please."

"Jes, Jes, o'course," she backed away, fumbling for our order, her eyes continuing to dart back out into the fog at intervals.

"Hmmm, I don't like this at all, Stanley," Joe said.

"Me neither, I'm getting the heebie-jeebies."

"Not that, Stan, get with the program," he chided. "Only one young woman manning the counter? She's clearly out of it, either too timid for this line of work, or high on something, would be my guess. Added to which, I'd like to get a look at some documentation."

"Oh c'mon, Morgan, you don't think she's ..."

"You may have missed this little footnote," he said with some heat. "I'm not surprised, GenCon and the MMAC would definitely like to keep this hush-hush, but there have been numerous allegations, nothing more mind you, of this particular company having the unethical habit of hiring illegal immi--"

"Young lady," now it was my turn to cut him off. I really didn't want our server to overhear, and, besides, this line of questioning simply was *not* in the mandate handed to us by our clients, "are you the only one here?" Joe sniffed and harrumphed at my side. He could get sidetracked more easily than I liked at times. I needed to shorten his leash ... and keep him from being *too* much of a prick.

"No," she said, setting our foil wrapped burgers and soda cups on the counter, "we alway work in two."

"Where's your partner?" Joe asked.

"She go out to feel the katship and mooster. She shool be back now." Then, she quickly leaned down on the counter and whispered fiercely, "*There somting out there.*"

Joe brushed this aside, "Only fog and revelers, my dear," he actually patted her cheek. "No need to worry."

Just then a mind-scrambling scream rang out. *Somewhere* out there, I couldn't tell at all, it was difficult to get a bearing in the fog. Joe and I whirled about, the young vending woman whimpered in terror.

"*Morgan.*"

"Calm yourself, my friend," Joe was working hard to gather himself, I could tell, and was hastily putting on a brave, if ridiculously painted, face, "and you too, young lady. It's nothing but the natural outcome of the drunken revels to which so many of these fans have subjected themselves all this day. Besides, as you have constantly reminded me, Stan, it's Halloween. Are these not the usual shenanigans on this grand spookfest?"

"Morgan, I swear I saw something out there," I pointed of a sudden. "There! Did you see that? It was moving quickly, running perhaps, back towards the direction we just came!"

"Stanley, now you knock this boo-boo twaddle off at once!" Joe nearly bellowed, then pulled himself together. "Pay the lady and let's be off."

I shelled out the necessary funds for our purchases, laid it before the horrified vendoress, who was crouched low, only her eyes peeking above the counter.

As we walked away into the cloying fog, Joe ticked off to himself his revised report, "Undermanned, poor service, horrible skills, and a possible illegal—excuse me, undocumented, worker. This is all working itself up into a very substandard report. And, I do believe, I've lost my buzz."

"Morgan, I really think--"

"*Where in blazes is the God-blasted condiments station?!*" He roared.

"I think it's this way," I said quietly, heading him to the nearest fuzzy orb of light high on its pole. "I think I see it, Morgan." It had taken longer than I had expected, vision distorted by the extremely low visibility.

"I should hope so," Joe huffed, "my burger was barely warm when I picked it up, now it's a veritable ice cube. Yet another negative mark in my report."

I was only half listening to his ramblings, at that point. The concessions area was strangely deserted. Though, as I said, visibility was virtually nil.

"Here we are," I announced. We came upon the condiments stand of a sudden, nearly bumping into it.

"Stanley, will you look at this, there's ketchup smeared all over this station. And that dispenser is way out of line with the others. Regimentation, that's the key to dispenser setup and presentation, like so many soldiers in formation and at attention!" He growled. "By God, an evening which had begun so promisingly for our clients is now turning quite disastrous. I could have sworn that young lady said her co-worker was out here attending to these condiment bars."

I was silent, my vocal chords frozen, jaw unhinged. A slow, creeping horror began at my extremities, and spread with ever increasing urgency, towards my heart, which had gone cold in my chest.

"Morgan, I don't think that's a condiment dispenser," I said quietly.

"Come again?" He fumed. "What *are* you talking about?"

"Hold a moment," I moved closer, and peered down at the messy bar top, gingerly touching a fingertip to the splatter. Its consistency was not that of America's favorite tomato-based condiment. "This isn't ketchup."

Joe moved forward in a rush, nearly knocking me aside. Surveying the scene, his eyes began to bulge in horror, "*My God!*" Stumbling back, his eyes remained locked on the gory vision, as did my own, of the startled dead eyes and gaping mouth of a human head, resting atop the bar, nestled between the mustard dispenser and a receptacle of pickles.

"*It's a woman, Stanley!*" Joe hissed, dropping his burger and soda. He clutched my arm in a numbing grip. I cast my own refreshments aside as well, having, suddenly, little appetite.

"More accurately, her head," I said, trying to relay calm, though not feeling it too much.

"That young lady said her co-worker was out here tending to the stations. Would you hazard to guess we've just found her?"

"Possibly," I said. "She was also convinced there was someone, or some*thing*, out here also."

"Stan," Joe spun me about to face him, holding me firmly by the shoulders, "you said you saw something moving out here, after we heard the scream. Remember?"

"Yes, yes, I know I did. Over that way, I think," I gestured in the direction of the nearest tunnel into the stadium. "It's easy to get turned around in this soup."

"It is indeed. Let's head back the way we came, back to the ramp and access tunnel. *My God of Great Mercy*, there's no telling how many such a beast could kill," Joe was filled with a fervor, livid with anger at what had occurred. This was well outside our normal purview, but Joe and I had stared death in the face before. Mystery Shopping could be an incredibly competitive business.

"And get away with," I said. "In this kind of cover, it could take quite a time even to find the bodies, not to mention conduct a search."

"Too true, my friend," he peered intently at me for a moment. "Are you up for this?"

I took a deep breath before answering. It was usually my task to assist in looking after the daily minutiae of our cases, dotting i's and crossing t's. I really didn't know if I was up for this. But, be under no illusions, when the excrement hits the fan, Joe had the full capacity and resolve to confront any situation ... did I say *any* situation? Well, we'd see. I had faith, and as always I would be there to extricate him if he stepped in it too deeply.

"I am, Morgan. Though this is somewhat outside our mandate, *way* outside, for this particular case."

"Perhaps so, but we've both seen a lot in our time together. And if that poor woman's head is any indication, this could get a hell of a lot worse. As a matter of fact, we could be all that stops this maniac."

"*If* it's only one killer," I pointed out.

Joe took a deep breath, releasing it slowly, "Nonetheless, we must face *it* ... or *them*."

"Then let us, definitely, *not* get separated," I insisted.

"Definitely not," he took a hold of one of the long dangling ends of my scarf. "I shall keep a firm grip of my bloodhound's leash," he patted my shoulder, affectionately, then, "Let's off!"

And with that we retraced our steps back towards the vendor station we had just patronized, but steered clear of it once we could get our bearing from its light. There was no need in upsetting the young woman remaining. Instead, we veered left, away from it, while keeping concealed, moving towards the dark, gaping maw of the tunnel entrance we had so recently exited. It took what seemed like an inordinately long time of groping, hands out in front like blind men, before we made the tunnel entrance. We stopped just outside, resting for a moment under the weak lights, scouting, listening.

"You're sure you saw the ... thing, flee this way?" Joe asked. I nodded, gulping. "Okay," Joe gave a decisive nod, "then let's—*Shhhh*," he put finger to lips, cocking his head, "did you hear that?"

"It sounded like some noise was just, I don't know, stifled. *I'd swear it!*" I said in a fierce whisper.

"I concur."

Then I heard something that caused my stomach to turn, "There's gurgling, Joe!" I admit I was losing some composure, which was obvious, as I let slip his alias. I took some deep, slow breaths trying to stave off hyperventilation.

"I hear it," he wrapped the end of my scarf more firmly about his fist. "Slowly now, let us proceed. But easy does it, the light's none too good in there. A matter which I may have to raise with school officials, after all."

"Forget it for now, would you?" There was clearly an edge of hysteria in my voice, as we began edging up the tunnel's ramp.

"Steady on, Stan."

We moved along, there was nothing, nothing, nothing— then, all of a sudden, *"Aaahh!"* I let out a wail, as I stumbled over something unnoticed on the floor of the ramp, before slipping on a suddenly slick ground, and collapsing in a heap on top of an unidentifiable object.

"It's got me Morgan!" I blubbered, I know. *"Help Me!"*

"Not to worry, Stan!" At that, Joe gave my scarf a mighty yank. I began to gasp and gurgle as the scarf tightened around my neck, cutting off my air supply.

"Can't—huh! -- *breathe*," I croaked, clawing at my throat with now strangely damp hands. Was it oxygen deprivation, or was Joe the killer?

"Oh God, Stan, I am sorry," no, just something of an idiot at times. "Here, let me help."

He suddenly loomed over me, reaching out to assist in loosening the scarf, but then danced back with a yelp, dexterously so for such a large man, I couldn't help but note as an afterthought. "Stanley, up quickly!"

I looked down upon what it was that had caused my fall, and suddenly leapt to my feet in revulsion. It was the body of some ... person, I couldn't really tell. Arms and legs sprawled awkwardly in all directions in a spreading pool of blood. It's face was obscured not only by blood, but paint and a wig as well.

"What--?" Was all I could manage, before realizing that I had a goodly amount of this poor person's life's blood on various parts of my body, my clothing. I looked down at my blood stained hands, "I'm going to be sick." I was in a nauseous cold sweat.

"Here, take this," Joe handed me his voluminous handkerchief, giving me something else to focus on as I vigorously wiped blood from my hands and neck, where I had tried to loosen my scarf. In light of this fact, I frantically unwound my bloody scarf and cast it away.

"It would seem we're on the right track," Joe observed quietly, eyes fixed on the bloody corpse. "Throat cut through, and deeply, I would surmise by the amount of blood."

I gathered myself with some effort, "What now?" I asked with not much conviction, adrenaline was turning to fatigue.

"How do you feel?"

"Better."

"Do we go on? We haven't any weapons, except for this," he stripped the pennant and brandished his cane pole as a sword.

"Let's go," I said. And we were off again.

We encountered nothing more as we ascended the ramp, but for some unspoken reason, despite the abysmal visibility, we increased our pace as we rose, so that we were practically running by the time we burst through the tunnel exit and into the stadium. We were immediately engulfed by the palpably raucous cheering of thousands of fans, the energy of their emotions vibrating over us like an electric current. I tingled from head to toe, all my hairs standing on end.

"We have no idea who, or what, we're looking for!" I had to shout to be heard. Joe nodded grimly, looking about, trying to discern something to pursue. We didn't have to pause for long, a wailing shriek came echoing up to us from down and off to our right. How many rows, it was impossible to tell.

"This way, Stanley!" Joe led off in the direction of the scream, cane brandished before him. I followed closely behind, pushing Joe's broad back with my shoulder to propel him along, bulling through the increasing crush of the mingling crowd. Evidently, many fans had begun to get the inclination that all was not right in their midst.

"Morgan, *Stop!*" I grabbed hold of Joe at the top of a staircase descending to our left. "Down there!" While very difficult to make out anything clearly, as we peered below us, there was definitely every sign of a mass commotion, sort of a vibrating 'rumble' in progress.

"It went this way, it would seem," Joe said. We had a great deal of trouble keeping our balance, much less making ourselves heard in the riotous atmosphere. We had to move, now or never, if we wanted to keep from getting pinned down.

"But who are we looking for? Any ideas at all?"

"It could be anyone," Joe said tersely. "Stay alert. Come!" He plunged down the stairs, I close behind, struggling and shoving to get through this outer rim of the commotion, as we worked our way to the epicenter.

Suddenly—"Morgan, *beware*, there's someone in Snow White drag, to the right of you!" The person was decked out in the garb of the Seven Dwarves' squeeze, frantically scrambling from 'her' row, trying to gain the stairway just to Joe's side. With flashing speed Joe lashed out with his cane, catching Snow White a solid blow to the side of the head, and sending the costumed reveler cracking back into the fans, still in their seats.

"Stanley, Teenage Mutant Ninja Turtle, to the left of you!" I, instinctively, ducked, and heard the whistle of Joe's cane pass directly over my head, ending in another crack, and yelp of surprise and pain. I glanced aside just enough to see the 'turtle' reeling backwards, clutching its forehead.

Joe grabbed me by the coat collar, "Errr, I have a feeling they aren't the ones we're after. Ah well," he shrugged, apologetically, then, *"Let's move!"* We continued down again, working up quite a sweat, steam rolling from us in the frigid night.

Soon enough, we had come upon a third victim, this one was some sort of dinosaur, if I didn't know any better. The poor, um, saurian, had taken a wound to it's side, but was, thankfully, still alive. It lay on the steps, moaning, the horridly horned and beaked head thrashing about, as some others from the crowd tried to offer comfort and staunch the wound with any bits of cloth or costume at hand. We didn't disturb them, but Joe was grinding his teeth in rage, "If it's not a killer asteroid, it's something else. Darn dinosaurs just can't catch a break," I heard him mutter, tension could make him babble on occasion, but he pulled it together, and accosted a stander-by, "Who did this?!"

The fellow, a rather ordinary looking fan like myself, startled, and wincing, in the face of the bloodshed, as well as Joe's painted, furious features, said, "It was some kinda pirate, man." The fellow's voice shook.

"Which way?"

"Down," the man pointed. We were perhaps twenty-five to thirty rows above the field of play.

I looked out, barely making out what I took to be the game still in progress. Then I looked down. A figure was climbing over the railing, separating the stands from the field. It looked back up briefly. I caught sight of a deathly pale, cadaverous face, with an eye patch over the left eye, and head covered in a flowing black head scarf. The creature grinned. It seemed directed at me personally. A gold tooth flashed.

"Morgan, the pirate!" I pointed to the fiend. Joe looked just in time to see the back of the creature, jumping down from the railing, to the edge of the field below.

"C'mon Stan!" Joe was off, barreling over people now. His momentum, as he accelerated, was an unstoppable force. In fact, I'm afraid he was completely out of control. His great bulk was stumbling wildly. The only thing keeping him from tumbling, head over heels down the stairway, was the pack of human bodies holding him upright.

I chased after, hearing a final word of warning from the fan, who had identified the killer, *"Hey, he's gotta sword, man!"*

And then, all was lost to my ears but the beehive buzzing of the crowd, as I strove valiantly to keep up with Joe. Near the bottom of the steps the crowd thinned suddenly, then parted. Joe's large frame shot from the crowded steps at the end of the staircase, propelling forward at terrific speed, he hit the guard rail, and was in the process of toppling over. Only one large arm locked on the top rail prevented him from falling. I was upon him in an instant, struggling with all my strength to keep him up. I caught sight of a shape slipping into a bank of fog just behind the home team's bench, while Joe was slipping from my grasp.

"Let me go, Stanley," his voice was low, steady, even resigned.

"*I won't do it,*" I groaned, straining.

"Stanley, look down. It's only a three foot drop," I looked. I must say I had no idea the wall surrounding the field was so low. I blame it, as with all things from that night, on the fog. And fear.

So, I let Joe go. He dropped, feet meeting the grass at the field's edge, breaking his fall with the cushion of his large rump. He rolled a couple of times, as I climbed the railing, and leapt down after him. I arrived by his side, just as his log-like rolling revolutions came to an end.

"You ok, Morgan?" I helped him to his feet, brushing him off.

"Satisfactory," he straightened himself.

"I saw it head for the field," We both faced into the thick of the fog, having no idea what to expect. We heard shouting and yelling, men's voices coming from the field.

"It's not over yet, I'm afraid." Joe looked down at the remains of his cane. It had snapped into three pieces in the fall from the rail. He sighed, "Come, Stanley, once more we sally forth."

Side by side, we moved further out onto the field, encountering the back of the home team's bench. As we climbed over it, we came upon a group of players, apparently confused, milling about the sidelines area, as medical personnel attended to several injured persons. Two had evidently received slashing wounds, which were being tended and bandaged. The third had suffered a stab wound, up and under the player's helmet, through the bottom of his jaw, and, by the posture of the young man's unmoving form, into the skull itself.

We advanced steadily, coming upon further carnage. Fortunately, much of the players' equipment acted as armor, helping to spare many of their lives, at least. Coaches and referees faced much worse, as we went further. While, due to the fog, we were unable to get a full picture of the extent of the slaughter, we both knew, just knew, from a sort of sixth sense, that it was on the field of play itself that we would encounter the greater part of this night's horrors. Bad as they were, the carnage out there on the field would be multiplied many times over that which we had encountered in the stands and on the sidelines. And, so it was.

It was an experience that I would never be able, entirely, to forget, as I'm sure it lived on as a nightmare, for all those who attended the game that ill-fated night. Joe was shaken, as well, perhaps to the core of his being. I couldn't be entirely certain, because he closed down, raising the drawbridge to the citadel of his emotions.

And what's more, that ghastly pirate creature was never found. Not a trace anywhere. In fact, no three people could even agree on the creature's appearance. A couple of us, afterwards, would give a description of some kind of pirate, though I saw a cadaverous, skeletal creature, while others thought it was more fleshy and gray. Some described this or that bizarre figure, a well known TV weatherman, or a guitarist in a rock 'n roll hair band, were some of the more outlandish. Though we need to keep in mind the amount of alcohol consumed that day.

The game obviously never resumed, and, due to the inclement conditions, it wasn't until the fog began to lift the next morning, that the full extent of the casualties was known. Seven dead, eleven injured. But Joe wasn't waiting until the next morning. He immediately sought out the school and conference officials attending the game, just as soon as the havoc had settled down somewhat.

As I've said, by the next morning, it was too late, certainly, but the search for the perpetrator turned up nothing. Not a clue, not a lead, not a trail. It's my opinion that the homicidal creature never left the stadium. Now don't get me wrong, and I have not one shred of evidence for what I'm about to put forth, but I'm also not suggesting the killer blended into the crowd and melted away, once the fans were allowed to make their way out of the stadium. And that was to be done over the course of the entire late night and early morning hours, as sheriffs and police state troopers called to the scene, arrived to bolster security and managed to process the fans at the exits in a fairly orderly manner. This was no mean feat, considering the many thousands in attendance, and what turned up? Nada!

No, it's my opinion the fiendish creature did indeed melt away, but not into the crowd, rather into the fog itself. I've never explicitly raised this belief in public, before, only vaguely with Joe, on one occasion shortly after the event. But I have always held the view that the creature was supernatural in its make-up. Some concentration of fear, anger, and hate that had dwelt for untold years in those dark, brooding woods, which blanketed the surrounding mountains, overlooking the lonely valley bowl, where the stadium had been built.

Joe sought out and confronted the relevant officials later that very night. I was not privy to what passed between them, having been made to wait outside the official's sky box, once Joe was admitted, after having identified himself. I did get the distinct, sobering impression he was almost turning himself in, what, after having gone to so much trouble eluding them beforehand. He was almost like a schoolboy being summoned to the principal's office. However, with one caveat, this schoolboy was one large, angry bull of a bundle of emotions: outrage, horror, and fury. The only emotion he shared with the hypothetical schoolboy was fear, deeply buried though it was. When he emerged forty minutes later, he was withdrawn, distracted.

It must be said that his interview with, or rather of, the officials had nothing to do with his prescribed mission, which had brought us there, rather it was concerned with what those officials knew about what transpired that night, which had left so many dead and injured, and so many more frightened out of their wits. Some, perhaps, never sleeping soundly again for the remainder of their days, as a psychological assessment by a prestigious institute done well after the events, seemed to indicate.

It was only some time later, before I could get the full details of what passed between them. And Joe did go so far as to intimate he had been rather in accord with my thought processes regarding the nature of the killer. Suffice it to say, the officials were in an advanced enough state of shock to let a few things slip to my friend. It came out in dribs and drabs that there was something of a reputation for hauntings at and about the vicinity of the stadium. There were the occasional apparitional sightings, and other unexplained phenomena, which were never, up to that point, taken at all seriously. And, especially, after the fact, when such things were quickly and quietly swept under the rug.

By the time Joe filed his final report with our clients, the official version of events had it that the perpetrator(s) had indeed managed to slip out with the rest of the costumed fans. No one has ever been arrested for the horrendous crimes, needless to say, and very few 'suspects' have ever even been questioned.

The relevant authorities made checks of all jails, prisons, and insane asylums within a two hundred mile radius of the site, yet no reports of escapees had been logged. Indeed, the FBI was brought in on the case, and their own extensive data banks turned up no known serial killers who fit the M.O. of the monster who ravaged the stadium that evening. Their profilers suggested it was the work of an entirely new, and previously unknown, mass murderer, and hoped to catch him, her, or them, someday. As the reader is already aware, that is a prospect I'm highly dubious of. At any rate, the case remains officially open to this day, a status which I'm convinced it will retain for, oh ... how about, forever.

Joe was rather lenient in his report, taking a measure of pity on all present that dread evening. What our clients and others involved did with the report is hardly even relevant at this late date. My later researches turned up not too much more than what Joe told me, about those things spilled by the school officials that night. There had, it seems, long been legend of frightful events having taken place in that approximate area, at some point in the distant past. Events involving colonists or Indians, African slaves and/or a mysterious group known as the Mellungeons, or even pirate rebels and buried treasure, depending on which source one chose to believe, if any.

The tales and details were as murky as was the hideous fog I'm convinced brought such misery, the night of that infamous game, afterwards earning the moniker 'The Reaper Bowl'. After that night, while never admitting to a rampant superstition, Joe did begin to take a deeper interest in spiritualism and the paranormal. Bolstered, I'm sure, by his later fling with a fortune teller he met, while working a sideshow carnival, on a subsequent case. But that's a story for another time.

The Royal Governor

In the spring of 20--, Josef Lopp, Ph.D., and I, were engaged in a spot of spring cleaning. *Dr.* Lopp insisted that I use the 'PhD' biz in any public or official documents, after he had been awarded an honorary doctorate at the annual convention of the National Association of Mystery Shopper Organizations (NAMSO).

I'm not entirely certain the organization's accreditation was academically legitimate, though they were associated with numerous institutions of higher learning, and many of the members had taught as adjunct professors, including Joe. As a matter of fact, his adventures in academia were still the subject of the occasional research paper and scholarly journal article, many trying to correlate his professional methods with his teaching style, and for the most part getting it wrong. At some point I'm going to have to collect the various published works, and give my own take on events, as a rebuttal to what has been published concerning my employer.

Needless to say, I suppose he was deserving of the honor. He is, after all, one of a select group of professional mystery shoppers, who actually worked outside of the confines of an agency, as well as inside, when the job and salary were right, and could pretty much name his price, at that. Unlike the legions of amateurs, who signed on for the 'spend your own money and we'll reimburse you' end of the business. Sadly, it appeared more and more companies were going this cheap and easy route. Specialists such as Joe were a dying breed. But there were still enough businesses out there who had need of a bona fide expert, when the chips were truly down. And in the current climate of corporate greed, solely interested in the bottom line, that could bode either good or ill for his practice.

We had closed the office early that day, it was such fine weather out. We dismissed our doorman, Teffer, to a free half day to cavort and treasure as he would, and hied ourselves home to the flat I shared with Joe (six-month roommates and counting, fingers crossed!). Neither Joe, nor myself, has ever been of a nature to share his private life with others. But, considering how long we have been associated, it just seemed to make sense, for the convenience of work, and to save on expenses. Besides, when the day arrived, that found my friend too infirm to continue in his profession, and he retired, I had resolved myself to care for him. May that day be long in coming, but that's what friends were for. I have always loved spring cleanings, 'out with the old and in with the new', as the saying goes. Joe, on the other hand – *CRASH!*

"Bloody Buggin' Blastit!!!" Joe's voice boomed. Oh dear, I hoped it wasn't my special mirror.

No, as it turned out, it was an antique Vitriola with a bum leg. When I entered the back parlor, Joe was on hands and knees, sifting through a small mound of debris, which had been dumped from the storage cupboard of the Vitriola's stand.

"Joe, anything broken?" I knelt to assist.

"A set of old records, it would seem," he picked up a couple of dark fragments, his face taking on a wistful expression. "Remember when we were just getting acquainted?"

"I do," I too went back in my mind to that time, we were young then, and …

"Only this time it's not 'Copacabana', only some old Bluegrass," he sifted through some more debris. "I got these during that case involving the antiquarian and the bingo parlor racket, do you recall?"

"Ah, yes, a quirky cover-up that was."

"Just so, have you managed to write that one up yet?"

"Not just yet, only a couple of pages of notes from the time."

"Well, I'm sure you'll get around to it. What else do we have here?" Joe and I delved through the spilled contents of the Vitriola's belly. Only a few of the records had broken, though there was much more than just records in that collection. Memories there were, memorabilia from cases past.

"Hey, Joe, wasn't this the slipper from that enamored ballet dancer, who we helped gain a controlling interest in th--"

"Yes, yes. He was quite smitten with me for some reason," he laughed and shook his head ruefully. "The number of times I tried to divert his affections to you, you'll never know." He laughed, I didn't.

"Joe! How could you?" I was stunned, furiously thinking back to that time.

"Not to worry. He never took the bait, too focused on our enterprise, and me, I'm afraid."

I fished out a leather bound book of some sort, turned it over, a medium sized volume, but no markings on the cover, old though by the look and smell. "Hey, what's this?"

Joe glanced askance at it, about to avert his attention away, before turning back, riveted. "Stanley, hand that over, if you please." I placed the tome in his outstretched hands, he reverently turned the volume over and over, gently dusting here and there, before hugging it to his chest. "Do you have any idea what this is?" he asked.

"Never seen it before," I said.

"I haven't seen this for years, couldn't quite remember where I'd placed it."

"What is it?"

He looked at me, and smiled slyly, "Why don't you rustle us up some tea and sandwiches, and I'll lay a nice little fire in the grate. It's likely still to be a bit chill this evening."

"But, Joe, the ... what is it? A book?"

"A diary, my friend," he struggled to his feet, clutching the diary in one hand, and brushing off his knees with the other. "A journal, chronicling the exploits of one of my ancestors, another great man. I've read and reread this so many times, since my grandmother left it to me in her will, yet, I never tire of it."

"Who was he?" I asked, never having heard mention of this before now.

"He was a Royal Governor in Colonial America, my dear Stanley, and quite the adventurer to boot."

"Is it in his actual hand? That would be rare, and valuable, indeed." Not that our finances were in particularly bad shape, or anything.

"No."

"Was he illiterate? Many were back then," I remarked offhandedly. Joe fixed me with a steady gaze, chewing on words, without opening his mouth. Finally, he said,

"Certainly not! He was a man of great distinction. Sadly, nothing in his own hand has passed down to us."

"Whose diary is it, then?"

"The man's name was Manlius Bizzle. He was my forbearer's personal aide. Actually, he served a role, very similar to the one you serve with me."

"Kind of an apprentice, then?"

"A bit more or less: secretary, confidant, friend," he reached over and gave my shoulder a friendly pat. "Let's call it a day, and settle in my study, shall we? I'll have the fire going by the time you bring the refreshments."

"You see, Stanley, to put it bluntly, he was what had once been quite commonly referred to as a bastard. The offspring of some minor nobleman and a ... oh what's the word for it?" Joe tapped his chin thoughtfully. We were ensconced in our usual chairs in his study, the remains of our snack on the table between us. A fire crackled in the hearth, and the warmth and mellow light put me in a comfortable, drowsy mood.

"Prostitute?" I offered.

He fixed me with a cross look, before biting off tartly, "No, Stanley, *honestly*!" He took a sip of tea to settle himself, before continuing in a tone of forced patience, "She was something along the lines of a scullery maid, but I can't quite think of the precise term. Well, it's of no consequence. Nonetheless, being the illegitimate result of a hasty tryst, left my great-great-great-great-great-great-great-great-great grandfather with nary an option, save one."

"And that was?"

"Why, to come to the colonies, obviously. Make a new life in the New World. And that he did, rising all the way to the position of Royal Governor, as I've said."

"Wasn't that somewhat uncommon, for a bastard, I mean?"

"Perhaps somewhat, but not unheard of. Different rules applied in the colonies than in the old country. Ben Franklin's bastard son served as a Royal Governor of New Jersey, leading up to the American Revolution. The last, in fact."

"Fascinating," I remarked.

"Indeed, but not nearly as fascinating, as some of the tales of my nine times removed, grandfather's adventures, as related to us by his personal aide-de-camp," Joe tapped the book in his lap.

"Of what colony was he a Royal Governor?" I asked.

"Oh, um, it was in what then was known as New Sweden. The, uh, area around which we today call the Delaware River. In parts of modern Delaware, Pennsylvania and New

Jersey, thereabouts," Joe seemed oddly evasive all of a sudden. Professionally he may have been quite the actor, but in private, I could read him like a playbill. I looked at him with increasingly narrowed eyes as I detected the signs: slight flush, light perspiration, darting eyes. My questions were becoming a bit too direct, I deduced, skirting the edge of an area he would rather leave uncovered. But he had brought the entire subject up, so it was no fault of my own. I chuckled inside, he had a way of ensnaring himself in traps of his own design and setting. What gives here? That's what I wanted to know.

"New Sweden, you say?" I asked.

"Yes, that's what I say."

"What years are we talking about, Joe?"

"Oh, I don't know. Somewhere around the late 1650's, I should think," he replied, casually inspecting a fingernail.

"Would an exact date be in that book?" I pointed to the diary.

"Yes," he replied stiffly, with a straight face. "It may have been 1661 or '62, come to think of it. Your pressing questions seem to have jogged my memory."

"So your grandfather, nine times removed, was Swedish?"

"Yes, Swedish, and Sami, on his mother's side. The indigenous people of northern Sweden, you know. Also known as the Lapps. Thus the derivation of our surname."

"Very well," I said, rising from my seat I crossed the room to where Joe's collection of Encyclopedia Britannicas were housed on his cluttered bookshelves.

"What are you doing, Stanley?" Joe's voice had an edge to it.

"What was your forbearer's name?"

"Gustavus Adolphus Lapp. The first two names were in honor of the great King of Sweden, who originally chartered the colony. The last was for my mother. Since he was illegitimate, he couldn't very well take his father's name. The 'A' was changed for an 'O' only later."

I stretched out an arm for a volume, but Joe stopped me in mid-reach. "You won't find him in there," he said quickly.

"New Sweden colony, then?" I grabbed a different volume instead. I hadn't expected an answer, and didn't receive one. Joe sat silently for several minutes, while I read. I caught the movement of him from the corner of my eye, fiddling with some pipe cleaning odds and ends, in an ashtray on the table beside him.

"Just as I suspected," I declared at length, having found what I thought I would.

"What?" It was more an accusation than a question.

"Your claim that your ancestor was Royal Governor around about the year 1660 is entirely erroneous."

"Watch your tongue, mister!" Joe snapped.

"Look, all I'm saying is the colony lost its political independence in 1655. That's when the last Royal Governor returned to Sweden. Oh, they later regained a measure of self-government with the creation of ...," I flipped back to my place.

"The Upland Court," Joe supplied, in a subdued voice.

"Exactly. So, how could your ancestor be a Royal Governor *after* the last one departed?"

Joe thought this over for a moment before replying, "Stanley, history is full of misprints. The record shall be set straight. Just as it shall be when your stories of my exploits are finally released to the public. By the way, when am I going to get to see them?"

"Um, I'm still working on them," I said hastily, "but back to your ancestor."

Joe took a deep breath and let it out slowly. "There were some who didn't recognize the authority of his office," he allowed.

I was speechless. How does one confront such audacious falsehoods? "Are you going to persist in this?" I asked point blank.

"Stan, listen to me very carefully. Simply because my ancestor was not officially appointed Royal Governor by the authorities of his day, who's to say he wouldn't have been, had events turned out just slightly different."

That, at least, made a measure of sense. Still, I couldn't help but try to clarify, "One event in particular, Joe. The Dutch annexation of the colony of New Sweden."

"Filthy Dutch," Joe swore, "what with their rotten tulips, and their confounded clogs, and their infernal dikes!"

"Wait a minute, Joe, this is all very confusing," I said, if for no other reason than to stop his tirade.

"How so?"

"I thought you were Dutch yourself? Or was that English?" I could have sworn he had told me something to that effect at some point in his colorful past. "Yet, now you claim you're Swedish?"

"Stanley, as Americans, we're full of so many bits and pieces of more ethnic groups than you could shake a stick at," he stared up at the ceiling, frowning thoughtfully for a spell, before continuing, "I guess we're more like dogs than anything else. Mutts, mind you, not those stuck up pure breeds ... though some are. Which reminds me, do you remember the dog show we worked that one season?"

"I do, I do." It had been one of Joe's more embarrassing performances, best left out of the annals for now.

"Damn dog shit everywhere," he muttered, then more loudly, "if it had been up to me *no one* would have been awarded prizes. Not one single pooch, upon my word I swear it!" Yes, he remembered the event only too well, as did I. It didn't do to get Joe off on a jagged tangent of reminiscence about disastrous professional episodes. A welcome change of subject appeared just then in the form of Joe's enormous cat, Benji, who chose that moment to stroll into the study, waddling across the rugs like his beloved owner. He mewled lazily at Joe's feet.

"Oh, my big man," Joe cooed, and obligingly lifted the diary clear. Benji pounced up and circled a couple of times, before depositing his furry bulk in a heap on his owner's broad lap. "Of course, I've always been more of a cat person myself," he chuckled, resting the diary on top of his cat, who took no notice, as he'd already drifted off to feline dreamland.

Joe flipped open the diary, leafing through the pages with no real aim. "Well now, where to begin? There are so many great tales in here. All true," he flashed me a warning look, "you can have no doubt."

"Just pick one, old friend. Any will do," I settled back in my chair, stretching my legs out to the fire, and wrapping an Afghan more securely about my chest.

"You haven't the soul of a true connoisseur. Never will, I'm afraid," he chided gently. I just smiled. "Here now, how about this. It's one of my faves. I'll do my best to translate into a modern idiom, though it may be a bumpy go at stages. My facility with this particular language has gathered considerable rust, since the days I learned it from my great grandmother as a small tot." It was difficult imagining Joe as a 'small tot'. "Do not be thrown off, if I leave in certain curious particulars of speech, for purposes of providing something of a feel for the time period." He shifted carefully so as not to disturb Benji, took his reading spectacles from their case, perched them on his plump face, and began thus: "The year was 1662. It was springtime, just as it is now..."

March 21, 1662

His Excellency urged his mount to a canter, just as soon as we broke clear of the tree line. Emerging from that tangled forest allowed me to breathe freely, for the first time since we had entered it. His large, powerful, and, admittedly, rotund frame, sat his horse proudly. The fringe of hair around his bald dome was grown long, pulled back and tied in a pony tail. I spurred my own mount to keep pace. His two hunting hounds,

Rork and Bjork, were out scouting ahead of us. I would not yet have been able to tell them, one from the other, if not for Rork's tendency to gnaw his own nethers, and Bjork's habit of jobbering his privates.

"*Jobbering?*" I broke in.

"*That's the closest translation I could come up with,*" Joe explained, "*but I think you get the picture.*"

I did, "*Yak! What a pair of nasty dogs.*"

"*Quite. Man's best friend, after all, would need be most like man both physically and spiritually,*" Joe sniffed, stroking Benji's lush coat.

"*How do you mean?*"

"*Why do you think cats and dogs don't mix?*" He asked rhetorically. I could only shrug. "*Simply because, cats have a certain aura of divinity about them, recognized millennia ago by our human ancestors. You know the old saying, 'cats have nine lives'?*"

"*Of course.*"

"*Well, dogs can't stand this, drives them utterly wild with envy. As it does man, thereby explaining their close alliance, based on the premise of a shared feline abhorrence. Thus the age-old conflict between the two species.*"

"*I think I see now.*" I didn't.

"*Excellent.*" He turned again to the aged text, "*Now please do not interrupt, Stanley. Disruption of the narrative takes away from the efficacy of the account.*" He cleared his throat and continued:

I liked them not. They were ill-tempered, flea-bitten, and perverse, but His Excellency was ever so fond of them. He preferred to match a bitch with a cur for, as he put it, "the cur for sheer viciousness, and the bitch to keep him in line."

Sadly, his last bitch had been drowned in a bizarre rafting accident, involving the transport of contraband of one sort or another, from either New England colony, or New Amsterdam to the north, or New France to the north of that, in an effort to avoid the Dutch customs. I hadn't been along on that particular expedition, and the facts, as to what verily happened, were sparse weedings from His Excellency. He had claimed that the 'so-called authorities', were unable to decipher his seal, thus forcing him into an act of smuggling, which I considered well beneath his station. When pressed, he confessed they believed his seal illegitimate. When asked why, he would only offer, "damnable Dutch." No doubt because he knew how much I disapproved of any measure which would upset our precarious balance vis-a-vis the Dutch, and I dreaded any hint of such activities reaching the ears of the Upland Court. They would, of a surety, take action hurriedly. However, His Excellency was the Royal Governor of the Swedish subjects, still in our pirated colony, and, thereby, wielded a certain measure of authority, himself.

The land we crossed, once leaving the claustrophobia of the forest behind, had been cleared some years ago in the early days of the colony, and settlement in this area. It had been necessary to provide clear vision, and line of fire, from the village of Tinicum and the Dutch fort next to it, where they sat hard on the banks of the Delaware River.

"Damnable insects," His Excellency swore, swatting at a cloud of gnats, hovering about his head. He needn't have bothered, for they were soon replaced by mosquitoes. It was lowering to dusk, and the warming of the season was making them more and more voracious. The first torches were being lit at the fort's gate. Lights were also popping up in the clustered village.

"I must have a score of ticks taken up residence in me beard alone," I remarked, scratching at my whiskers.

"And I've chiggers galore camped out in me crotch," he gave his vitals a good, brisk rub.

I was still somewhat in the dark as to the purpose of our foray this afternoon. His Excellency had said he was hunting, but he and the hounds did precious little of that. At least for game, I hasten to add. He did seem to be hunting, however, or should I say scouting. But for who or what, I could not say. He was keeping me in the darkness once more, and it made me irritable. It had been seven years since the Dutch had annexed our beloved Nya Sverige. To be sure, they had allowed a measure of self-governance, by allowing the creation of the Upland Court six years past. But His Excellency always felt it was well beneath him, to seek appointment to serve with men, not accustomed to his natural leadership abilities. He had sought a higher office, and had been rewarded with just that, when he was appointed Royal Governor. Yet, often, I wondered why he wouldn't let me see the proclamation of his appointment?

"Should we not make a stop at the fort?" I asked, as he veered away from the gates, heading for the village instead. "My records show we owe Colonel van der Poote the monthly residence tax he has a-levied on the island."

"Manlius, please," His Excellency clutched his chest, feigning discomfort.

"It was the deal struck, when we arrived to take up residence in the Governor's Mansion."

"Your words, lad, your words. Ye must work harder to pick and choose the language ye use more carefully, else someone may misinterpret what ye say, and get the wrong impression."

"Apologies, sir" I could see his gentle rebuke was meant to aid me, in becoming a more effective personal secretary.

Just then one of the Dutch guards called out from his post at the fort's gate. Having recognized His Excellency's personage, he addressed him thusly, "Hey Guv, we sure could use yer monthly rum payment to keep us warm tonight." His Excellency chose to ignore this, and rode on with head held high. "Better come soon, y'hear! Cause if the rum ain't keepin' us warm, yer Governorship is gonna grow mighty cold out of doors." The other guard on duty guffawed coarsely.

It was at this point, His Excellency reined in his horse. "*Enough of this insolence*," he fumed, for my ears only.

Spinning his horse in its tracks, he sat his steed, staring coldly at the smirking guards. Mayhap it was the chiggers in his britches which provided apt inspiration. He whistled shrilly a certain set of notes, at which his hunting hounds dropped what they were doing, which appeared to be worrying at themselves yet again, and shot like two arrows from the same bow. Swiftly to their targets they flew, impacting, with jaws locked on firmly to the groin of each of the guards. I must admit, I wished His Excellency had not taken this course of action. I fretted silently.

The poor fellows never knew what hit them, really, only having time to register the attack with astonished looks, only a tick of a clock before the bites were laid low. At which point, all that was left was the screaming. His Excellency allowed his hounds to hang on for a spell, too long in my opinion, as he gave himself over to a chuckle, whilst the guards whirled and danced, trying to shake the dogs loose. Only when one of them raised the first fist, to try to hammer his passenger off, did His Excellency snap his fingers once, twice, thrice, and the hounds released their grips, and, immediately, came to heel at his horse's hooves.

"Let that be both lesson and warning to ye," he called out to the two figures, curled on the ground, clutching their vitals.

"Was that wise?" I asked him, as we rode away.

"Perhaps, not wise," he admitted, "but necessary, my dear Man. Respect for my office must be maintained at all cost." I mulled this over for a moment or two, before nodding acquiescense. I just hoped the repercussions wouldn't be too debilitating.

His Excellency laughed, and clapped me on the shoulder, "I knew ye would see the wisdom of my ways, however harsh."

"Where be we off to then, if not the fort? The rowboat?" I asked, in all innocence.

A pained expression wore its way onto his features, "The ferry, Man, the ferry. Not a rowboat, for the love of God. And no, that's not where we be headed at the moment. First we have an appointment to keep at the tavern. Giddup." He jangled the reins and spurred his horse, "Time's a-wastin'. It's almost nightfall." I had no recourse but to follow, and no chance to ask anything further. I must admit I was somewhat put out with His Excellency. As his aide and secretary, I should have been apprised of this appointment. He was keeping entirely too many secrets for my liking.

The tavern and stables, where we kept our horses, were a bare stones throw from the Dutch fort.

"Stay," he said, snapping his fingers once, and his hounds immediately sat by the side of the tavern. His Excellency negligently flipped his reins to a drunken tramp, snoring in a heap beside the tavern's front door. "Water and oats for the mounts, my good fellow," he declaimed, as he barged his way through the door.

The tavern was a low ceilinged log construction, with no windows. The fireplace, and scattered lamps and torches, had no real place to ventilate, so the common room was hazy with smoke. Tables and benches were moderately populated.

"Two ales, barkeep," His Excellency called out to a stout man, behind the bar tapping a keg with a mallet.

The man looked up, squinting suspiciously, when he saw who had addressed him, "Let us see some coin first."

"Mark it on me tab," His Excellency returned, a bit grandly, but not totally overdone. He had to display decorum, after all.

"You be overdue," the barkeep shot back.

"My aide-de-camp will see to it," he sniffed over his shoulder, as he headed to a table in the far corner. I sighed, but it had become customary. Unfortunately, I hadn't the necessary funds, never did, to settle the entire account. But the tavern keeper accepted a modest payment on the overall debt, and drew a couple of tankards, with the admonition, "next month." I could only hope, my purse was nearly depleted.

I set a tankard in front of His Excellency, and asked, as I took a seat next to him on the bench, "Sir, who are we meeting?" He waved a hand for my silence. We sat quietly for a time, before my own impatience caused me to cock an eyebrow.

He caught this, "We're waiting for someone else first."

"Not your secret rendezvous?"

"No, the commander of the Dutch fort," he replied complacently. I was about to ask him how he could possibly know this, when the door of the tavern burst open. I could hear the hounds' low growls following the Dutch commander, barreling his way indecorously into the room. Colonel Joost van der Poote scanned the room quickly, before casting baleful eyes upon His Excellency. He strode, clomping his boots, towards us. Two new guards trailed a step behind, with matchlocks shouldered.

"*Ye*," he snarled upon reaching our table, "ye assault me men and refuse to pay yer tax to the Dutch Republic?" It was really more of a statement, an indictment, than a question. By way of answer, His Excellency took a long swallow from his tankard, leaned to one side, and farted lustily. "Ye think ye're funny?" Colonel van der Poote had his hand on his sword hilt in a flash, "I could have ye up on charges, ye realize?"

"And risk an international incident?" His Excellency replied blandly, "I think not. As for refusing to pay tax? Why, not at all. Funds have merely been a mite short of late, what with the long journey here to take up my duties, getting my affairs in order, and whatnot. As for your men, they insulted me office, and were dealt with accordingly. As the representative of the Swedish Crown, it behooves me to uphold my honor, thus the honor of my country, and for ye to instruct your men in proper manners accordingly."

"Yer office?" The Colonel shook his head in amusement. "Ye and this poltroon," he said, jerking his head in my direction, "show up out of the blue not six months ago, and take up residence in the abandoned house of the former Royal Governor of the now defunct colony of New Sweden, without any official explanation, *and ye expect me ta believe ye are legitimate?!*" His voice had been growing louder as he spoke. The other patrons in the tavern now turned to watch the proceedings.

"I have explained all of this to ye before," His Excellency replied coolly. "Ye have seen the official documentation." I only wished *I* had seen the official documentation, I thought, but kept my mouth shut.

"Documents are easily forged," the Colonel said dismissively. "Ye may be interested to know that I've been in contact with our Governor, the Director General in New Amsterdam, and he has, some months past, sent to Europe for word on what a new Royal Governor is doing holding office for the King of Sweden, when this colony was surrendered to the Dutch Republic seven years ago."

"As I have informed ye on more than one occasion, I am the emissary of the King of Sweden to his subjects, who yet inhabit these parts, by the way."

"They be Dutch subjects now!"

"And, yet, they have been allowed self-governance, with the creation of their Upland Court."

"Ah yes, the Upland Court." The Colonel smirked now, "I have been in contact with its members as well."

"Ye've been very busy."

"Indeed. When queried about yer background, do ye know what they had to say?"

"I should venture to say they had nothing positive or negative to input," His Excellency replied airily, taking another sip of his ale.

The Colonel's eyes grew flinty, "Very close to it," he growled. "As for the precious court itself, they have very limited self-governance, I assure you."

"Nevertheless," His Excellency said equitably.

"Where do ye go on yer almost daily jaunts with this character," me, again, "and yer mangy hounds?"

"Hunting, prospecting, visiting the subjects in my charge, what of it?" His Excellency took another drink, hand rock steady.

"Prospecting?" The Colonel asked, skepticism evident in his tone.

"Why yes, perhaps I am attempting to acquire the taxes ye say are owed."

"I don't say, *they are owed!*" the Colonel shouted. "And another thing, I've been receiving reports of smugglers operating in our territory. Would ye happen to know anything of this?"

"Why should I? I am a law-abiding man," His Excellency demurred. "However, I would hasten to add that any interference of a foreign emissary trying to do his due diligence to the Dutch Republic, could have rather serious consequences."

The Colonel stood there for a long count of seconds, eyes boring into His Excellency's own, grinding his teeth, which made his mustaches bristle, finally, "I'll be keeping me eyes on ye, and when news does come of yer fraudulent 'office', I'm going to relish slipping my dagger between yer ribs personally," and with that he spun away, brushed past his guards, and strode briskly to, and out, the door. The sound of dogs barking, and the Colonel cursing, followed. His Excellency chuckled into his tankard.

"He's very angry," I stated the obvious, trying casually to get His Excellency to spill some of the information he was keeping from me.

"He's always angry," he replied pleasantly, as if he hadn't a worry in this world. "It be a by-product of latent melancholia."

Just then, two figures detached themselves from occupied tables at opposite ends of the common room, and made their way towards ours. One was a short European, with a paunch, and considerable whiskerage about the face. The other was tall, dressed in a long coat, and wearing a broad brimmed hat, underneath the shadows of which I could tell he was a native Indian. They sat down on the opposite bench across the table from us, without a word of permission. I was on the verge of protesting this affront to the personage of His Excellency, but was forestalled from doing so by His Excellency, himself. "Well met, gentlemen," he greeted them. So these were his secret contacts? Interesting. I had been put so off kilter by the rantings of the Dutch Commander, I had nearly forgotten the rendezvous.

The paunchy fellow inclined his head, "I be a-hopin' ye're still game, aye?" By his accent, I could readily identify he was English.

"We await, with growing impatience, the delivery," said the tall Indian in precise, plain tones.

"Ye both will get what ye desire," His Excellency said.

"But will ye outfox that old fart?" asked the Englishman, jerking his head towards the door. "He seemeth suspicious, s'truth."

"Never fear," His Excellency assured him. "I can dance circles about that jackanapes."

"Our time will come, then?" The Indian asked eagerly.

"Indeed so, as will yours," he directed this last towards the Englishman. "And ours," he finished grimly.

"When?" The Indian asked.

"Why not the morrow?" His Excellency suggested. "I scouted out spots A, B, and C just today. B seems most fortuitous. Dutch patrols tend to pass it by. Can ye have the cargo at the place by morn?" he asked the Englishman.

"Aye, t'will be done."

"Excellent," His Excellency rubbed his hands together in satisfaction. "Tomorrow, then, and once I get the cargo, it's just a matter of transporting it to your people. Early afternoon acceptable to ye?" he asked the Indian, who nodded once. "Til then," he raised his tankard in salute. I did not. For whatever reason, I was suddenly filled with foreboding.

I waited for the two to depart, before giving tongue to words, "I know the short man be English, but who's the Indian?"

"He's of the Lenne Lanape tribe," was all he offered.

I waited a few moments before speaking again, hoping he would say something further, but, alas, no. The Lenne Lanape had tense relations with the Dutch, unlike the Swedish colonists, who had always maintained good relations with our Indian neighbors. In fact, the Dutch were constantly trying to embroil our people in fights with the Indians, on the Dutch side, of course. But His Excellency, and the Upland Court, and the entire population, were ever resistant. "Your Excellency, may I inquire as to what this is all about?" I had to ask.

He gave me a shrewd look for a moment, eyelids drooping, in what I knew to be a sign of serious consideration, then said, "All will be revealed on the morrow, my trusted aide." And he would provide nothing further.

We departed the tavern, loaded His Excellency and hounds in the 'ferry', and I rowed us across the intervening water to our home on Tinicum Island, situated out in the Delaware River. This was the seat of His Excellency's authority in the form of the Royal Governor's mansion, the Printzhoff. I could make out by moonlight the hulking form of the abandoned Fort New Gothenburg, which shared the island with the mansion. The Printzhoff had served as the residence of the Royal Governors of New Sweden since the first, Johan Printz, commissioned its construction. We found it in a tolerable state when we first moved there, but the fort, sadly, had become somewhat dilapidated in the intervening years, since the Dutch had treacherously captured the colony.

I so wanted to niggle further information from His Excellency, but knew any further inquiries would be met by a stone wall. I also knew I was in for a long night. After all, part of my duty to His Excellency was worrying about his well being, even when he would not. So, like many an evening at the Governor's Mansion, he read correspondence in his study, while I prepared supper.

"*Not* more possum stew," he said with a look of distaste, when I informed him it was ready. What am I to do? Funds are tight, and with increased settlement in the colony, the woodland was receding at an alarming rate, and game was becoming scarcer to find. "I can't bear it!" he exclaimed. "I see them smashed on the cart paths and trails all of the time. Mark my words, one day they will learn, and avoid such dangers." His oaths could be vigorously given, yet blithely forgotten. "I'll just have some bread and cheese, thank you. No more possum, until they put up a decent fight, understand?"

Fine with me. Personally, I can't stand their greasy flavor. But with His Excellency's meager resources, what were we to do for meat? Fish got tiresome, and gave him hives. I suppose I could ring a few pigeons in the village.

After he had eaten, it was his custom to play his oboe, before retiring to his bed. I must say, here, his playing of that accursed instrument was one of the most horrific sounds I have ever heard. It did seem to soothe the cares of his office, however, though it reminded me of nothing other than torture. Only, once he stopped playing, and the hounds ceased their howling, could I, at last, get some sleep.

March 22, 1662

We departed the island before the dawn. I ferried His Excellency and the hounds across the river, dipping the oars in and out of the water as silently as I could. We floated some little distance downstream from the village and fort, His Excellency having informed me, the previous evening, we would be traveling by foot initially. He maintained it would be too risky for us to retrieve our horses from the tavern's stable. When I pressed him, and, yes, I did actually press him, once more, as to the nature of our journey and this mysterious 'cargo', he grew even more mysterious, talking about missions and justice and the like. In further words, it went nowhere, as I expected.

After beaching the boat, and covering it in brush for concealment, we set off with the hounds leading the way. We kept off the main tracks, opting, instead, for game trails, which His Excellency's hounds did a fairly good job of leading us on in the pre-dawn darkness. His Excellency was a passing good woodsman, in that he generally didn't get lost these days, though I had to keep a sharp eye on his steps, and a hand ever ready to grasp his belt, should he go floundering into a bog. You would not think so by looking at him, since he exuded an air of such cultured civility, with a high appetite for the finer things of this world, namely spirits to drink, and vittles to eats a-plenty. Yet he could be a rough-and-tumbler, if the situation required it.

In fact, his very entry into life in the colony had been less that artful. In point of truth, he had been a walking disaster. This, largely due to a lifetime of semi-indolence, as the under-the-table supported bastard of a minor nobleman. Just as an example, in one of his many forays into self-sustainability, he tried his skill as a land surveyor. But, possessing no knowledge of the use of compass or sextant, he quickly sought other trades, barely two steps ahead of angry new landholders, who found their parcels of property criss-crossing one another, in dizzying, higgledy-piggledy fashion. Admittedly, he will never be a true tracker or trapper, either, but satisfactory, for all intents and purposes. Time, and the experience gained thereof, have aided him somewhat admirably.

Dawn had brought its light nearly an hour earlier, when, of a sudden, I was forced to accost His Excellency, by laying a hand to his arm, and drawing him to a halt. I have always, fastidiously, made it a habit of not laying hands to his personage, but simply could not avoid it in that instance.

"What is it, Man?" he asked.

"Is Your Excellency aware we are being followed?"

He gave me a shrewd look, "Are ye certain?"

"Pretty certain," I nodded.

"Well, I think not. The hounds would have picked up on it."

"Not if they stayed downwind, and moved silently," I countered.

"There is no way they could have tracked us this quickly," he insisted.

"Who is 'they'?" Maybe now, I would get an answer.

"Why, the cursed Dutch, of course," he spat. He always did of late at mention of the Dutch, even if he did the mentioning.

"Is Your Excellency going to be forthright with me at long last, and divulge what in the name of seven hells, ye are getting us into?" I was on the verge of losing my temper with him, but I managed to maintain some composure, if with a biting tone. "Or would ye care to create an unsalvagable situation involving a foreign power, with no help from me to guide us over the shoals?"

"Listen, Man, ye will know all soon enough," he gave me a reassuring pat on the shoulder. If it involved the English and a neighboring tribe, then, I knew it involved trouble ... big trouble. But, I let it go for the nonce, and we resumed our hike.

It wasn't but the span of another hour, when I became absolutely convinced we were being followed. Our trackers had misplaced a foot, and broken a stick or fallen branch, with a loud *crack!* The hounds, at once, set off in a fray of loud barking. I grabbed them by their leather collars, to detain them from dashing off after our unidentified shadow. At least, until I received instruction from His Excellency.

"We have company," I whispered tensely to him from the other side of a great oak. I heard him gather up a hasty handful of leaves to finish off his business.

"So I heard," came his reply. He stepped around the trunk, fastening his breeches.

"Shall I unloose the hounds?" They were fighting my hold on them, and they were large creatures, my arms were tiring.

"Let us not give the unwanted snoopers cause to believe we, necessarily, know they are there. Heel!" He snapped his fingers once, and the hounds, immediately, fell silent and dropped to their haunches.

"Feeling better?" I asked.

"Much," he patted his barrel-like belly. "Let us be off. Not much further now."

And he was correct in his assessment. Little more than a quarter hour later, we came to a cart path, which bisected the game trail we had been following. There, waiting for us, was a cart hitched to a particularly sorry looking and broken down old nag. Our Englishman from the tavern was holding the bridle, as we emerged from the woods. A second man sat a horse off to the side, and held the reins of another, obviously intended for our Ingles.

"I was beginning to wonder if ye had lost the stones to show," said the Englishman from the tavern.

"The stones are large and solid. Have ye no fear on that account," His Excellency replied.

"Very good, then."

"Have ye the coin?" His Excellency inquired.

"Aye," the Englishman removed a small pouch from inside his coat, and tossed it to His Excellency, who caught it from the air, gave it a few testing bounces in his palm, which produced a jingling, before tucking it away inside his own coat.

"And this," the Englishman said, offering the nag and cart to us, "is for ye as well. I know she does not look it, but she be a dependable worker." I was unbelieving of that claim. She looked set to keel over at any moment.

"And the cargo?" His Excellency asked.

"All there in the bed, packed and tacked for transport." The bed was covered with a canvas tarpaulin.

"Excellent, excellent." said His Excellency. "It has been a pleasure doing business with ye," he clasped hands with the Englishman, before clambering up into the cart's driving seat.

"Just make sure that cargo gets to our friends," the Englishman said, climbing into the saddle of his own horse.

"That I will."

"To freedom for all!" the Englishman called. Then, he and his companion wheeled their steeds, and galloped off down the cart path.

"What is in the cart, Your Excellency?" I was compelled to ask again. "Mind if I take a peek under the tarp?"

"Not now, Man, all in due time. Once we reach our destination, ye will know all and marvel, for a-surety, at me brilliance." the farther this bizarre caper advanced, the less and less convinced I was of that chance.

"Come," he slapped the seat beside him. "The day be a-wasting." So I climbed up next to him and he shook the reins, and, wonder of wonders, managed to get the nag in motion. We creaked off down the cart path in the opposite direction the Englishmen had taken.

"What of our followers?" I asked, trying to sound casual, but in actuality, trying to grasp for anything at that point.

"If they be a-foot, they will not be able to keep up with old Friskycup, here," he proclaimed, confidently.

"Friskycup?" I could not imagine anything further from reality, at that moment.

"Yes," he said candidly, "I have just named her, or rather renamed her. It's customary. Come ye, Friskycup, let us pick the pace up and put paid to the skepticism of my trusted aide-de-camp and make good your new name. *Heeyah!*" And with that, he snapped the nags rump with the reins, to which she nickered in an annoyed manner, and moved the pace we had been traveling up a whole 'nother notch. Which for her, and us, sadly, was probably no more than an extra one and one-half English miles per hour.

I sighed, and His Excellency, in an effort to boost my spirits, began to sing one of his favorite drinking songs, which involved the antics of a tavern maid, a magical chamber pot that could sing, and a gambling pig. I have never been able to ascertain the purpose of the 'dandy, crowing cock with blue bonnet balls', which character makes a brief appearance in the eleventh verse, though I have heard the tune on a number of occasions. Suffice it to say, I will not be transcribing the lyrics to that particular ditty here in this journal. I assure you, posterity will not be made the poorer by their absence. Likely, future generations will benefit by its total and complete disappearance.

At any rate, it wasn't the song which piqued my ire, but the singing itself. "Had we not better be keeping our tongues quiet in our heads, Your Excellency, what with those who have been trailing us, in all likelihood, still about?"

"Good idea. While I'm quite confident my superior woodcraft gave them the slip-away on our jaunt to meet the English, one can never be too sure," he made the motion of locking his lips and tossing away the key. I nodded, relieved.

Our journey passed in silence for some ways further after that. It seemed as if it were no time at all, though, in truth, must have been near on two hours agone, when I did hear the unmistakable pounding of hooves. That they were horse, I had no doubt. Wild game would not make so defining a rhythm as a horse beridered.

"What be that persnickety racket, woodpeckers?" Posed His Excellency, cheerily.

I was forced, without thinking, to give His Excellency a long, hard stare before I spoke thus,

"Nay, Your Excellency, it's horses. I cannot reckon the number, but by the beat and direction they do be following us, and gaining." His perceptions at times did run into the firm barrier of his own peculiar imagination, "Your Excellency, if those following us are the Dutch, as you let out some time ago, t'would it not be most prudent to leave this path now, and hope for a place of concealment?" He may not have let me in fully on his caper yet, but if he suspected the Dutch of pursuit, a point I did not disbelieve by then, it would stand to reason they were to be avoided. Most likely, because of what we were transporting in the bed of the cart. Said cargo, by the by, which would of a certainty be best left uninspected by them.

He lost himself to ponder this, overlong, it seemed to me, so I gently but firmly prised the reins from his clutches. He did at times like to engage in menial tasks, for, as he was wont to proclaim on such occasions, "it keeps me a-touch with the common folk." I guided our rickety cart, pulled by the equally rickety nag, in between the next propitious break in the tree line, to the right side of the path. Slowing down even further was unnecessary for the turn, as Friskycup was not in any danger of sending us careening out of control. We pulled in, and ground to a halt behind enough foliage, I adjudged, to provide an effective screen.

We awaited, the approaching hoof beats grew louder, and when the riders appeared, my worst fears were at last realized: they were Dutch soldiers. They thundered past us, a full dozen was their compliment, and I bit my tongue as a cold dread crept over me. I glanced to His Excellency, and there he sat, a bemused expression on his features. I realized it was pointless trying to coax him into call this thing, whatever it was, off. When he set his mind to something, trying to divert his course was akin to trying to halt a stampede. However, from here on out, I drove, and played a wearying and nerve-wracking game of cats and mice with the troops.

They would come charging up the path, and I would take as much evasive action with the cart as I could, and dart off the path to hide us amongst the brambles and trees of the forest.

It was easy to discern that these soldiers were not woodsmen, though I aided our cause, by trying to dust out our tracks, whenever we were forced to make a sudden halt and hide. His Excellency did not help overmuch, though he did offer many words of encouragement, and not a few inadvisable suggestions on how best to elude our pursuers. The most notable for its outlandishness was that of a proposed ambush, His Excellency fingering the butt of his cumbersome pistol with one hand, and the hilt of his sword with the other. Though I, too, was armed, such an attack upon twelve heavily armed soldiers was about as close to suicide as one is likely to arrive, without really trying. It should not be supposed that His Excellency is a bloodthirsty man, merely a bit too romance-addled to provide good common sense, in a situation such as the one in which we found ourselves.

I should have realized we were on the approach to the Indian village, by the change in the timbre of the bird calls nearly half a mile before. We must have passed out of the realm of Dutch authority and into the Indian's territory somewhere in between, for I was surely unaware of it. The village turned out to be a neat collection of small domed structures, with supple branches bent to an apex, forming the dome, which frame was then covered in cured hides. All eyes were upon us as we rolled to a halt. The first to greet us was the self-same Indian, who had been at the tavern with the Englishman.

"Greetings, my friend," he extended an arm, and His Excellency clasped it, climbing down from his seat.

"Well met," His Excellency responded, ordering the hounds to lay up under the cart, and safely out of the way, lest they should suddenly desire to test the tastiness of any of the Indian villagers.

"Did you bring the cargo?"

"Aye," and here His Excellency peeled back the tarp, revealing eight long wooden crates, stacked four on four.

"Very good," said the Indian, then spoke a few words in his own language, to which several young, sturdy braves approached, and began unloading the crates.

"Just a moment," I said, determined that mine ignorance should end there and then. Unsheathing my dagger, I slid the tip of the blade under the lid of one of the top crates, and pried it off. Brushing the straw packing aside, what gleamed up to my eyes were a row of freshly minted and polished muskets. "What is the purpose of this?" I demanded.

His Excellency and the Indian contact exchanged a look. "Hunting," His Excellency offered, almost hopefully. He could sense I was angry, even afraid, which further fueled my anger.

"That's a lot of firepower for hunting," I said, not believing it for a moment.

"They are for use against the Dutch," the Indian said, without guile. His Excellency winced. Clearly, he had thought I would take the news of the ultimate plan somewhat more calmly. "They have harried us for the last time!" the Indian declared boldly. I very nearly fainted dead away on the spot. I clutched the side of the cart's bed to steady myself.

At last I managed to find my voice in a hoarse whisper, *"Your Excellency, aiding and abetting an attack upon the Dutch does put our own situation in grave peril."*

"Not if the Indians win," was his simple response, in a situation, where simplicity of thought and short sighted preplanning, would likely get us all killed.

"What if they don't?" I countered, trying to get His Excellency to add some complexity to his outlook.

"We will not lose. They will have no warning," the Indian said confidently.

Another realization hit me just then, "This also explains the English role in all this. Anything that hurts the Dutch helps them. What happens if they take the place of the Dutch? Do you have any guarantees from them?"

"Nothing in writing," His Excellency admitted, a bit uncomfortably, "but we do have an informal understanding."

"What could we possibly hope to gain from this?" I asked, shaking my head sadly, at his folly in trusting the English.

"The colony of New Sweden returned to its rightful owner. Think on it, Man! We will be heroes." His Excellency's eyes shone with the same fervor as our Indian contact, and many others now, who had gathered about us, trying to follow what was taking place, though I do not know what number of them shared the faculty of our language with our Indian contact.

Somewhere in the back of my mind, I had already come to the conclusion that events would turn this serious. I had kept such notions safely locked away there, but no more. I confess I was in a cold panic. Now, all of His Excellency's odd meanderings on our faux hunting expeditions, and his insistence on my *not* reading certain of his correspondences, were made plain the reason, with the cold, clear light of revelation. He had become a weapons smuggler, practically the worst form of smuggling one could engage in, and whose professional outlook was particularly bleak, if captured, due to the fact that such smugglers were generally left dangling from the end of a noose. *And he did it all under my very nose!*

"And if they do win, what of our position? The Colony's?" I asked, trying to gain myself time to digest all of this, and to think of a way out of this brewing debacle.

"A treaty has already been signed between myself, acting in the name of the Crown of Sweden, and the Chief of the Lenne Lanape. Wancho's the name, fine chap," His Excellency explained.

"So it has gone that far, has it?" My God, what would the Upland Court do if word of this reached their ears? The Dutch would certainly take punitive action against them, as well as us. My thoughts on the matter were far too concerned with self survival, at that point, to give a fig about what happened to the Dutch, should the Indians prevail. The haughty little burgermeisters!

"Your colony of New Sweden will be protected," our Indian contact assured me. "We have never had bad relations with your people."

"So those are the terms?"

"Well..." His Excellency looked abashed, lowering his eyes to the ground, and tracing half circles in the dirt with the toe of his boot, like a naughty urchin.

"What else?" I demanded. Now what?

It was our Indian contact who answered for him, "The Royal Governor is to be wed to the Chief's daughter. It will seal our pact." I stared in disbelief at the blushing Royal Governor, as if I had not laid eyes on him before. I had always taken him for a lifelong bachelor, with little interest in the fair sex.

"Colotana's her name, lovely girl," His Excellency said, with forced nonchalance. So now he was getting married, to an Indian Princess? Well, I had to admire his ambition. His Excellency did have a mighty capacity for moving up in the world.

We stayed on in the village til late afternoon, a feast of thanks had been planned in advance of the arrival of the arms. We were cordially met, and dined with Chief Wancho and His Excellency's bride-to-be. She was, as he had claimed, quite lovely ... and far too young for that old conniver. I digress. I toasted their happiness, and hoped privately that someone of his more advanced years would be able to keep up with such a young filly. More often than not, such an age discrepancy lent itself to a great deal of unhappiness and embarrassment for the cuckolded husband. But for now, he seemed to dote on her, even presenting to her an engagement gift of a beautiful golden chain and locket. Upon opening the little locket, His Excellency explained, through translation, that the miniature portrait inside was a likeness of his own mother. All were impressed, and he gave her a warm kiss, having slipped the chain about her neck and clasped it.

How symbolic, two love birds chained together, for life. I really was not envious, merely cautious. God's truth. As we bid farewell to the village, His Excellency had a few private words with the Chief, our Indian contact, whose name translates to Three Shafts, acting as interpreter. It was only once we had rattled away in our cart, with hounds foraging out before us, that His Excellency informed me that he and Colotana would be wed just as soon as the Dutch were defeated. I pointedly asked for the date of the planned attack, but he would not divulge it. Only offering that we should make ourselves scarce for a spell, just to be on the safe side. We had been given assurances that the village of Tinicum would not be harmed, they were only after the Dutch troops. It left me with small comfort.

We rolled into Tinicum as the last rays of the sun were dying. Handing off our new found nag and cart to the stable boy at the tavern, we hiked the distance to where we left our vessel so that I could row His Plump Contentedness and his disgusting hounds out to our island residence. Part of me wished to forgo all protocol, and wipe that satiated smile from his chubby jowls with the back of my hand. But just as that thought occurred, I instantly dashed it away, to be replaced by more modest and sincere thoughts of a concerned nature for the well being of His Excellency, and what grand things could come to pass with the fruition of his labors in this entire affair. He evidently had not been happy, both with his status in the colony, and now seemingly his lonely personal life. It was incumbent upon me to assist him in any way I could.

As we came around a bend in the river, I angled the craft directly toward Tinicum Island. I spied the Dutch fort and a figure atop it's battlements holding what could only be the tube of a spyglass to their eye. The figure pointed in our direction. I alerted His Excellency of this, and he took out a kerchief and waved it gaily at the figure espying us. The spy glass was lowered, and, even at a distance, I could make out the dour visage of the Dutch Commander. He raised a fist in the air and shook it, to which His Excellency whooped with delight. And then the Dutch commander was out of sight, and we were home, safe and sound. For now.

March 25, 1662

I write this late at night. His Excellency and I returned this evening from a three day fishing expedition upriver, so we have been incommunicado with events around Tinicum, since my last entry. This was our 'making ourselves scarce' during the planned attack by the Indians, as well as the need of His Excellency to find some relaxation, after our harrowing evasion of the Dutch, and delivery of the firearms to the tribe. His Excellency had been in fine spirits, well looking forward to his impending marriage, and fretting about his wedding day like a young, gushing bride. So, it is with even greater sadness, that I relate this tragic tale for posterity.

Upon return to the Governor's Mansion, it was already dark, so it was impossible for me to make out what had happened at the Dutch fort: signs of fighting, fire, and the like. There were, however, the usual torches burning, and, from what little I could see, all looked perfectly natural. This was most curious. I dropped His Excellency and hounds off at the island, knowing he would be perfectly safe with them, and rowed to the village to gather supplies for our dwindled larder. I had a bit of the Englishman's coin stashed about me, so I was confident I could fend off our creditors a while longer. And it was in town where I heard the news, which was to have a devastating effect on His Excellency, myself, and the future course of our lives.

On receipt of the disastrous news, I naturally hurried to the boat, and rowed with a will, as if the devil himself were after me. When I found His Excellency tootling about his study, I was suddenly struck dumb. I didn't know how to say it. I'd lost the very power of speech. He spotted me standing in the doorway, mouth agape. I must have been quite a sight.

He laughed and said, "Well, what is it, Man? You have a look, as if you have seen the rising of the dead." And, in a way, he was right on target.

I finally regained my voice and blurted, "Your Excellency, there has been a great tragedy."

"What are you saying?" He demanded, turning serious. My appearance had a sobering effect on him, *"Speak, Man!"*

"Y-Your Excellency," I stammered, "the tribe ... they-- *they have been wiped out ...*"

"What?" He whispered, paling, and seeming to perceptibly age, suddenly, before my very eyes. He stumbled about, before knocking against a chair, and clumsily lowering himself into it, *"How?"*

"It was the Dutch. Apparently, one of the tribe was plied with liquor, and, in his inebriation, unwittingly gave the plan of attack away." It was not uncommon for some local Indians to be hanging about the village and tavern. Tragically, fraternizing with the colonists proved to be their undoing, in so many ways.

"Colotana?" He asked, or rather pleaded.

I shook my head, swallowing hard, "Everyone in the village perished, Your Excellency." He just shook his great head back and forth, back and forth.

After what seemed an eternity, he rose, held himself proudly erect, and, with eyes fixed straight ahead, he walked stiffly from the room. I was forced to jump out of the way, lest he run me underfoot. I resolved to follow him, in case he were in need of my assistance. I grabbed a lantern, and followed him out of the Governor's residence, across the grounds, and into the abandoned fort. Up to the creaking battlements he went, and, directly to the lone remaining cannon left in the place: a rusting six-pounder that hadn't been fired in who knew how long. It was a wonder he did not fall and break his neck in the darkness, but he seemed to have the eyes of a cat. Grief may have made his senses heightened, for such I had heard tell of, but only in old folklore.

"Ready the powder and shot!" he bellowed. I was stunned in my tracks, just having attained the top of the ladder. What in blazes was he about? I shone my lantern on him.

He grasped the canon's leash and gave it a mighty yank, meaning to pull it away from it's sight hole in preparation to load it. The rotted rope snapped, instead, sending him down on his over-sized duff. He scrambled back to his feet with what dignity he could, and set about trying to wrench the canon away from it's aperture with bare hands and brute force.

"What do you mean by this, Your Excellency?" I managed at last.

"This is war, Man! And if you are my loyal aide-de-camp, yet, you will give me a hand with this blasted thing."

"We haven't powder or shot, Your Excellency." It was the first thing that came to mind, so I grasped it. I doubted very much the canon would fire even if we did have. More than likely it would explode, killing the both of us.

"*What?!*" He nearly screamed. I spread my hands in a helpless gesture. "Then get some!"

"You cannot do this, Your Excellency. It would be madness to fire on the Dutch fort." I pointed away across the expanse of river separating our ramshackle jest of a fort from theirs. "They have fifteen odd canon and two hundred men. How can we possibly battle such odds? T'were suicide!" I added some heat to these last words, in hopes of bringing him back to his senses.

"T'were revenge!" he hollered, jaw jutting and eyes fierce, though the trembling of his lip gave this away as a false posture.

"I'll not assist you in making war upon the Dutch, Your Excellency. It's a wonder they haven't arrested us yet, for assisting the Lenne Lanape, and the English, in attempting to make war upon them." And I prayed with great verve that they never found out. This was the very first act of disobedience I had ever registered in his service, "I am sorry, but she is gone," with these final words sinking in, he crumbled and collapsed, heaving and sobbing over the canon's ruined barrel. He was about this torment for some time, before pulling himself up and dashing the tears from his eyes. He now took on the appearance of the oblivious sleepwalker, without recognition, once more, of any of his surroundings. Moving by no discernible volition, he departed the battlements and exited the fort. Again, I followed.

He headed for the river. I hurried my step, presuming he meant to take the ferry, perhaps to confront the Dutch Commander. I hoped not. I would have to see that he were disarmed aforehand. I was prepared to hop in before him, so that I might steady it, and ready to cast off, but he didn't go for the boat. With unwavering steps, he walked directly off the shore of the island and kept on going. As you can imagine, I was horrified. With an entirely undignified yelp, I shed my coat and shoes, and leapt in after him. He had already disappeared under the rushing water, not ten yards from the stern of the ferry. Yet, I feared he would be swept away by the current which was notoriously dangerous, especially this time of year with heavy spring run-offs.

I dove down, again and again, surfacing repeatedly, trying to locate him, but without luck. I was in a panic and exhausted all at once, yet resolved to give it a couple more tries while my strength held. It was the least I owed him. At last, with my strength flagging and my spirit waning of hope, my fingers brushed a rope-like something, deep under the water. I couldn't be sure, but I grabbed ahold and pulled with all my remaining reserves. Surely God is merciful, because a great waterlogged mass came up with it. I had grabbed the pony tail created from his fringe of head hair.

I need not belabor what a struggle it was to raise him. Providence was indeed helping me to buoy his great weight, making it possible for me to reach the shore, swimming against the forceful current, and dragging him to dry land. There is simply no other explanation for how I managed to perform the task. But was I not too late? He was lifeless. I wanted to cry, to scream at the Heavens. I tore the collar from his throat, and rolled him on his side. Using two fingers to clear his mouth, I banged on his back until a great gush of water came spewing from his mouth and he began to cough, and suck in heaving, ragged breaths. Only then did I allow myself to sit back on my heels and take a heartening sigh of relief. He would live.

I had to lend his great husk quite a crutch, just to get him back to the mansion. I tucked him safely in his nice warm bed, with a roaring fire keeping his chamber toasted, and poured the better part of a bottle of rum from our medicinal stores in him, to help him off to slumber and fight any lingering chills. Only now, can I find my own abandonment of this awful day in, what I hope will be, dreamless rest.

March 26, 1662

Early this morning we set out on horseback. His Excellency was past caring if the Dutch spotted us. The trip to the tribe's village passed in a blur, as the day dawned and grew older. When we arrived, it was nothing but a ruin, still smoldering in patches from where the Dutch had put it to the torch. Charred bones were interspersed with charred wood and pottery. I did so want to lead him away from that place, but he was intent on sifting the ashes, looking for some sign of his lost love. I thought it a pointless exercise, yet readily acknowledged it was one he had to go through, even if only for the sake of ritual.

A small cry escaped him, and I thought he had injured himself in some manner. But, he straightened up, holding part of a slim chain, with a tarnished locket attached, scorched mostly black from the flames. I recognized it, of course, as the betrothal gift he had given his Indian Princess. With shaking hands he opened it. I went over to him to take a look over his shoulder. The heat from the flames had ruined the miniature portrait of his mother, burning it as black as the outside.

He closed it, a tear sliding slowly down one cheek, and tucked it away inside his cloak. He took out his snuff box, flipped the lid and cast the contents aside, then knelt and scooped up a handful of ash, filling the box to the brim, before snapping shut the lid and tucking it away with the ruined locket. Who knew if those were indeed the ashes of Colotana. As long as he believed it, that was all that mattered.

"Let us be off," he said, and we made our journey back to the village. He did not turn for the village when we arrived, however, instead guiding his mount directly to the front gates of the fort. "I'll speak with your Commander," he announced coldly, to the guards on duty.

"He ain't seein' anybodies," one of them sneered.

"*Now,*" it must have been the lifeless void in his voice, coupled with his natural air of command, which set the guard in motion, before he even realized what he was about. With a shrug he let himself in through the gate, and motioned His Excellency and myself through. He took us to the Commander's quarters, rapped upon the door, and ushered us into the room, once the Colonel had barked, "Enter!" Then he departed, quietly closing the door behind us. "Well, well," the Colonel said, seated at a small writing table, "just the man I wanted to see."

Without a word His Excellency crossed the small room in three long strides, whipped his riding gloves from his belt, and struck the Colonel squarely across the face. The Colonel was momentarily stunned, hand on stinging cheek, before collecting himself and leaping to his feet, overturning the stool upon which he had sat, *"I could have ye hanged for that!"* He thundered.

"I propose swords at dawn," His Excellency returned calmly, patting the hilt of the one he wore at his waist.

"Why should I give ye the satisfaction?" the Colonel answered shrewdly. "One whistle from me and my men will be here so quickly, they'll blow enough holes in ye to make of ye a sieve."

"Coward," His Excellency spat a great gob on the Colonel's boot. "Just as ye did the Indians," he said in an eerily calm voice.

"They were renegades and savages," the Colonel snarled contemptuously, "plotting war against us. And all with the help of the English ... and *you*."

"Prove it," His Excellency said. "You can prove neither my involvement, nor that of the English. Nor, that the tribe was planning an attack."

"We have the guns, captured when we sacked their village."

"What make?" His Excellency asked, offhandedly.

"Doesn't matter. I had more than enough intelligence on ye and yer cohorts to launch the raid."

"I hardly think so." It was then His Excellency removed his snuff box, took a pinch of the contents and noisily snorted it up both nostrils. I could see the courage rise within him, the mere act of inhaling his lost love bringing forth his passion and pride. Not to mention that was probably the most intimate he had ever been with a woman in his entire life, "I'll see that ye pay for what ye have done."

"I very much doubt that," the Colonel shot back.

"My office--" His Excellency began, but was cut off by derisive laughter.

"What office? Ye are a fraudulent vagabond, who just showed up and took over the residence of the last *real* Royal Governor."

"I'll have ye know that--"

"NO!!" the Colonel boomed. "I'll have ye know this farce be over! I've received word from New Amsterdam that there was no *new* Royal Governor dispatched by the Crown of Sweden," the Colonel gloated. His excellency swallowed hard, and myself? My world reeled, mine knees nearly gave way, I could scarcely breathe. What was he saying? What was happening? "And, furthermore, the recognized owners of that island and all its properties have sold them to a new owner. Ye and yer 'aide' have until dawn tomorrow to vacate the island, or I have orders to expel ye forcefully."

"Just as you did with the Lenne Lanape," his Excellency said quietly, after a moment, as the news sank in.

"Aye," the Colonel hissed. "Sorry 'bout yer Indian friends ... and sorry 'bout yer luck."

We departed the fort without a further word to anyone. The Colonel must have figured us beaten and harmless, and so did not detain us, as his 'evidence' of our involvement was presumably not nearly so damning as he would have us believe. And we were, by that point, truly broken.

We made our final crossing to the island and set about dolefully packing our belongings in silence. I dared not broach the subject of His Excellency's imposture as Royal Governor. Partly out of concern for his mental well being, he had suffered enough traumas for the nonce. Yet also partly due to the fact that I was still trying to digest the news myself. How could I allow myself to be so readily duped? And still, I had to reflect that, if I was duped, which I, of a certainty, was, then it was not from cruelty that it was done. I *had* wanted wholeheartedly to believe it anyway, which made me a full party to the deception. Ah, well, for a time it was my privilege to serve such an august figure, in whatever role I or he could devise.

We were only able to take what we could carry on our backs, and our horses. The residence had been a good home to us, and I would dearly miss it's hallowed halls and all the history of the colony of New Sweden, which it held to its timbers and stones. But, the colony was gone, and with this final act, truly, its very last Royal Governor was gone now, too. It was evident then that the Crown of Sweden had, once and for all, forsaken its former colony, with the sale of the property. How else could such a paltry ending come about? Shameful! I record this in hopes that future generations may understand how it truly came to be, and regard something of the character of this great man, who served to the very end, however unofficially: Gustavus Adolphus Lapp.

Once we crossed back and collected our horses, we pondered where to head next. To the English colonies further north? Or west into the wilds to be woodsmen and trappers? His Excellency, for he would ever be that to me, commended us both to the whims of fortune, chose a random trail, and we followed it off into the gathering dusk, our new lives already calling to us.

When Joe had finished, he reverently shut the journal, leaned his head back, and closed his eyes. I left him like that for a few minutes. The fire had burned down in the grate, and only the ticking of the Versailles replica clock on the mantle made any sound.

At last I spoke, "That was some story."

"My forbearer did get his revenge, in a roundabout way," Joe said, without opening his eyes. "Oh yes, it was when the English took control of the Dutch colony and evicted their governance, in turn, in 1664."

"The character resemblance between yourself and the Royal Governor is remarkable." I noted.

"It's a Lopp family trait, known as 'Lopp Carry-over', to us Lopps."

"I think there's a scientific term for it," I mused.

"You may be thinking of phylogenetic systematics, or perhaps vertical gene transfer, but we Lopps invented it."

"Invented?" I sounded skeptical.

He opened his eyes, "Very well, then, perfected it." I could only smile.

"Is there more in that journal?" I asked, changing the subject, trying to get him down from his high horse. The one that rode up amongst the clouds.

"Much more," he caressed the cover. "But such further adventures will have to await another sitting. Come, it's late, and we'll need all our rest, if we're to shop that musical instrument rental store tomorrow morning."

The Arch-Enemy

During those times in which the Mystery Shopper business was slow, or cases weren't of a sufficient complexity to challenge, and therefore interest, my friend, he often took to piddling about on his computer. Or any other he could lay his hands on. Consider it a word to the wise: never leave Joe alone around an untended computer with internet access. Two of his favorite pastimes were making a bit of extra money by taking online surveys, and visiting internet message boards. He was quite proficient and could generally complete a dozen surveys in the same time, and at the same time, it took him to run his PCH (Post Count/Hour) up to quite astronomical numbers.

Such trolls as Joe were generally considered to have no life, but he did, he really did, as any reader of his exploits can attest. It didn't matter the topic of the forum: art, contemporary politics, or sports. He would be there lurking and ready to vociferously flame on any other poster, who dared disagree with him, whether he knew what he was talking about or not.

If he grew bored even with these pastimes, his antics could run to the truly childish. I once discovered him editing a Wikipedia article on rabbits, wherein every time he encountered the word rabbit he would change it to bunny. What can one say, his creative energies needed an outlet, and it sure beat turning to drugs.

Joe was a highly intelligent person. It was just difficult, sometimes, to get across to him that he didn't possess *all* knowledge. One of his favorite schemes, when signing up with any of the online survey services which had proliferated in recent years, was to register as, say, an Hispanic female, or an Asian male, in order to drive up his survey counts, and the amount the survey services were willing to pay. He discovered early on that 'white' and 'male' tended to be altogether too commonplace, for what most companies were interested in paying survey takers.

From time to time, he would get busted, and whichever account he was using would be suspended, but he had enough different IP addresses, that he could usually evade detection as a poser. Or, in the event his account was deleted and he were banned, he could just start over anew. Joe was very big on fresh starts. He had to be, in his profession. He would even go so far as to use the computers at any number of branches of the local library system, to aid him in his purposes.

On the odd occasions, when I've admonished him on the unethical nature of these subterfuges, he invariably replies, "If these damned companies don't care for the opinion of a middle-aged male Caucasian, then why should I care what they think?" Joe's logic was sometimes skewed, but never entirely bent. Usually. What he failed to take into account was the fact that a company initiating a survey of, say, women, were targeting that particular demographic, because they were selling a line of female hygiene products, for instance. That was all pretty much lost on my mentor, Mr. Josef Q. Lopp. My headstrong friend had difficulty conceiving of a place where he didn't, or couldn't, fit in.

It was during one of these slow periods in which I found him of a day, in between surveys and forums, playing a game of Snood instead. I had been rummaging through the business mail, testily tossing out meager assignment offers, and spam canning the rest, when I came upon the only current job offer that seemed to bear even the remotest interest for my employer.

"These little grey ghoul heads will be the death of me," he said, without turning from the monitor as I entered his study.

"I have a potential shop, to help take your mind from your Snood woes," I announced.

"And that would be?" He continued vigorously moving the mouse and click-click-clicking, while popping handfuls of Chex Mix into his mouth, with his off hand. This continued for some minutes, before, "Aha! Victory!" he proclaimed at last. "You see, Stan, the ability successfully to handle Chex Mix in a tense situation is an indicator of maximum concentration, and ultimately success. Look around," he swept an arm about the area where he sat, "not a crumb on the floor, or in my lap." It was at moments such as these that I truly marveled at the man. What wasn't his elusive mind capable of concocting, and then rendering into a workable stratagem for everyday life? Remarkable!

"Congratulations. Now, about this new mystery shop opportunity."

"Oh, yes-yes. What is it, then?"

"It's the Grand Opening of a new Best Buy."

"I hate those," he said rather petulantly, and even went so far as to fold his arms huffily across his chest, then stuck out his lower lip. If you can imagine a normally dignified older gentleman suddenly taking on the resemblance of a childish, overstuffed, graying meatball, then be my guest. The word 'absurd' comes readily to my mind.

In fairness, Joe had been in something of a slump, at the time, going on a couple of months. He seemed to have lost some of his famous drive which had always served him so well, propelling him on to some of his greatest achievements.

I couldn't be sure whether it was simply his getting older, or if he was slipping back into one of his periodic depressions, which had plagued him from time to time over the years. A common malady of the artistic genius set. I know he insists not, absolutely refusing to take any of his meds. He's even gone so far as to hurl the bottle at our doorman, Teffer, who hastily bolts away in fright, and locks himself in his room, vowing not to come out and fulfill his duties until, "the ogre has been tamed."

"Come on, Joe, it will do you a world of good to get out," I wheedled him. "Besides, along with any grand opening, comes the obligatory G.O.S. (that's, Grand Opening Sale), and I know you've wanted to update your hard drive. This will be the perfect opportunity."

"Possibly," he conceded, somewhat. "Where is it?"

"At the Lime Tree Center."

"Hate strip malls," he muttered, rubbing his chin and casting about for some way out, I could tell. "When?"

"Tomorrow evening, 6 p.m."

"Hmmm, that's better. Because I can tell you," he jabbed a finger at me for added emphasis, "if it had been in the morning, you would never have been able to drag me out of bed." He was right about that, for he was a large man and I a slim one.

"So you'll go?" I wanted his firm commitment.

"I suppose," he picked up a small brass bell, shaped like a cornucopia, and rang it. Some moments later, Teffer appeared, "You rang, sir?" He wasn't the best servant one were ever likely to come across. He wasn't trained to it from an early age, for one, of many, things, but he tried.

"Who else? What's for dinner, Tef?" This was a daily ritual for Joe, though he tended to be disappointed.

"Stew, sir."

"What kind of stew?" Joe asked mildly, examining a cuff link.

"Meat and potatoes, and carrots ... I think." He honestly didn't seem to know, yet presumably he was the one preparing it.

"What kind of meat?" Joe continued, gently prodding him, always training, always bringing his pupils along gradually. Joe could, and would gleefully, spend years coaching and coaxing. He was born to teach, to lead. Besides, he knew, as well as I, that, if his erstwhile doorman/manservant became upset, well, who knows in which direction he might 'go off'.

"Um, I think it's beef, sir," he definitely didn't know, but he couldn't really be blamed for lacking in culinary skills. Prior to Joe taking him on years before, Teffer's idea of fine fare was the daily special at the local greasy spoon.

"Anything else?"

"Garden salad, with your favorite vinaigrette dressing." Joe actually hated vinaigrette.

"Hummm, rabbit food," he mumbled. "Very well then, carry on."

"Thank you, sir," Teffer bobbed his head.

"Not terribly appetizing, by the sound of it," I remarked after Teffer had departed.

"Noooo," Joe drawled, "but it's important we keep his spirits up. We don't want a repeat of that time he tried to bake a Sachertorte Cake, and nearly hung himself when he failed so miserably." I nodded agreement. Yes, I remembered only too well. It was I, after all, who had to support the weight of the body, as Joe cut the rope. So Joe was not *quite* correct. Teffer had hung himself, he just hadn't finished the job of actually dying, thanks to our efforts. I'm still unsure whether he's grateful to us or not, but we were just in the nick of time to save him, and that's all that counts. Sometimes, I wonder whether it was a mercy? Never mind, I'm being uncharitable.

"Stanley," Joe said after some consideration, "I think it best we assign our trusted doorman no less than an hour and a half of Food TV ... three days a week, let's make it."

I took out my pocket planner and made a notation. "His culinary shortcomings are becoming a tad wearisome," Joe understated.

The next evening, we caught a taxi in front of our building, and headed to the grand opening. I would have preferred a nice walk. The Lime Tree Center was barely half a mile from our place, but Joe always made a habit of minimizing his physical exertions whenever possible. He claimed it put too much pressure on the little gray cells, due to gas or toxin buildup, or some such concept. I imagine, however, that he would have preferred to take a rickshaw to the event, or been borne aloft on a litter. For all that he went out of his way to minimize his own physical exertions, he strangely enjoyed watching others exerting themselves. Especially if it was in service to him. I've always suspected him of being an old school closet imperialist, and can at times, only too readily, picture him wearing a pith helmet and snapping a riding crop against his jodhpurs.

The Best Buy was packed when we arrived. Joe had insisted on foregoing getting there early for the ribbon cutting ceremony. He considered such events fit only for novices. We were in time to get our numbers, however, for the drawing of prizes, an activity which Joe considered great sport. He was always very competitive about such things. Once, security were forced to bodily remove him, when he thought he'd won a prize in a similar drawing, only to find out he had read the numbers upside down. Realizing his error, rather than backing down, he had vociferously argued his case to the management, but to no avail. He couldn't really be blamed, with a number like 69, there was bound to be confusion. It was only due to my hasty damage control that the incident went unreported, though he vowed vengeance on the store and swore never to shop there again. A vow, I believe, he's kept to this day, not that the company ever sought out his services again. But still.

"I've heard there are to be a large, albeit unspecified, number of other mystery shoppers here this evening," I said to him. I had to raise my voice more than I would have liked, to be heard over the babble of the crowds, not to mention the blaring music, and video chase scenes and explosions, coming from a myriad of electronic sources, as we wended our way through the store.

I'd always disliked stores such as this, too much emphasis on adrenaline for my tastes. Only BigMart was worse, in my opinion, what with their diabolical system of targeted, and barely imperceptible, strobe light wattage, and inaudible sounds designed to guide the acceptance of subliminal suggestions in their customers. Just think back to how you felt when entering the store, as opposed to leaving it: the heightened dizziness and disorientation, the bleary eyes, and ringing ears, not to mention the loads of crap you just purchased for no apparent reason. Many may disbelieve this, but such had been hinted at for many years, yet nothing had ever been definitively proven until Joe came along. But that's a case whose telling belongs for another time ... if the lawyers can ever clear away the silencing restraints, that is. But here and now, Joe seemed complacently unperturbed. He was the consummate professional.

"Let's play a game, Stan," he said by way of response, flashing a wicked little grin, tight and self-confident. "Can you think of the one I'm going to suggest?"

"You've always been partial to 'amateur turnabout'." I responded. This was a game Joe had devised where a mystery shopper actually shopped other mystery shoppers. It had begun as a relatively harmless form of entertainment, with Joe going out of his way to befuddle less skilled mystery shoppers, in an attempt to force them inadvertently into revealing themselves, particularly in front of the employees of whichever establishment they were shopping. I say relatively harmless, yet, I had seen Joe take it to extremes, if he spotted a mystery shopper being unnecessarily harsh to a blameless employee. Joe could and would come down hard on sloppy and negligent employees himself, but he always favored the innocent.

On one occasion, he actually managed to have a mystery shopper, whom he considered to be disgracing the profession, arrested on the spot, and taken from the store in handcuffs on the charge of shoplifting. I was never able, afterwards, to get a clear admission from him on whether or not he had actually planted items on the unfortunate mystery shopper, but, with his background in magic and sleight of hand, he certainly possessed the ability. The charges were later dropped, when he declined to testify.

Though what began as a game soon turned into a valuable niche profession within the larger mystery shopper industry, that of mystery shopper supervision. And it was Joe who had pioneered its development. However, that was not part of our assignment tonight. We were merely to provide a senior level complement for all the other mystery shoppers who had been brought on board for the grand opening. Joe, with obvious long term tenure in the business, was well regarded for providing a steadying hand at large shindigs, such as grand openings, and was often sought after for just this purpose. The particular agency which had contracted Joe for this event, had informed me that another agency already had someone signed on for the 'supervise', as it was known. It was not uncommon for more than one agency to share double duties for an event of this magnitude, but they wouldn't tell me which agency, or who the supervise was to be, only that it was an industry veteran. I could well pull up half a dozen names off the top of my head, and they were all good professionals, don't get me wrong, just not in Joe's class.

"Close," he said, "but a bit too participatory for my likes this evening. I was thinking more along the lines of 'spot the shopper', with an initial spotting earning one point apiece, identification of what they are doing correctly earning two points, mistakes they are making being worth five points, and detection of any criminality on their part raking in a whopping ten points."

The current MS industry was much better policed nowadays, than it was in its infancy in the 1940's, or even when Joe had first gotten his start. My friend had played a key role in helping establish standards, which served to weed out the unethical or merely inept, but, truth be told, there would always be some bad apples in any profession. It also helped to control the competition, incidentally.

"Sounds fair," I agreed to the scoring guidelines, too readily, as it turned out.

"Then let the game begin," he announced.

Naturally, Joe spotted the first mystery shopper, and the second. The first was an elderly lady kindly soliciting the assistance of a young sales representative. I could just as easily have identified her as someone in the business, but Joe picked her out at a passing glance. It took me a few moments to recognize how she was gently, yet artfully, guiding the young man through a series of questions regarding what appeared to be a small MP3 player. She was evidently not one who was seeking to confuse or trip up the subjects she shopped. I have always greatly respected the truly good-hearted professional, such as the lady we were observing, and conveyed this to Joe as he ticked off the points he had just earned on his fingers.

"What? Oh yes," he commented distractedly, "I've always admired that aspect of her work. Not quite *my* cup of tea, but to each their own."

"You know her?" I sounded surprised.

"Not personally," he shrugged, "I've seen her around from time to time, giving me the opportunity to observe her methodology."

"Who else here do you know?" I was becoming a bit indignant, partially in jest. It shouldn't have surprised me. I myself knew many of the same mystery shoppers as Joe, of course, yet he kept a far longer roster in his head, and was not always forthcoming in the field of attaching names to faces. He claimed it was a need to know security issue.

"Stanley, you would be surprised by who I know and don't know. Take that man, for instance," the man Joe indicated was a short, round man of middle years, gesticulating wildly to a wide-eyed teen sales associate, and another, older man, who was clearly managerial level, "even had I not encountered him before, I couldn't possibly be expected to overlook his hectoring style. How insufferably crass." Joe clucked his tongue in disapproval, "One only involves management as a last resort. I seriously doubt an employee would be so rude or out of sorts during a grand opening, considering the copious training regimen they all, undoubtedly, underwent in the run up to this event. Ah well," he shrugged, "more bonus points for me." He began ticking off on his fingers again.

"No way, Joe," I shook my head emphatically, "people whom you're acquainted with don't count."

"I'm not *acquainted* with either of the ones I've spotted. I simply recognized them professionally." We argued about it good-naturedly for a time. Due to Joe's competitiveness, it required a fair measure of convincing before I finalized his agreement, with grumblings of "I may not score at all" and, "probably know every mystery shopper here." To which I conceded that, if he spotted anyone else he recognized, he could count them, but only at half the points he quoted to start the game. He nodded his assent, curtly.

Now, I had to get busy and put some points by my name on the tally, and very quickly it appeared as if I would do just that. I spotted a customer who was exhibiting all the identifiable characteristics of someone in the business: a sense of self-assuredness bordering on arrogance, a poise of command to make a general blush, and the sly look of someone who holds a secret to which no one else is privy.

"Joe, I think I've got one," I said excitedly. There was no response. "Joe?" I sensed he was no longer by my side. Turning, I found the space beside me empty. I looked back the way I had come and spotted Joe about fifteen feet away. He was standing stock still, utterly frozen in his tracks. His expression in profile was one of incredulity, tinged with a sickly pallor, come upon him suddenly. What could cause such a drastic reaction in my normally unflappable mentor? I followed the line of his gaze, and then froze myself. I must have experienced exactly what Joe had, when I saw what he was staring at ... or should I say *who*. It—it couldn't be. *It just couldn't be!* My mind was dulled in response to what my visual senses were feeding it. Of all the grand opening, in all the cities, in all the world, and *he* walks into this one? He was the last person I would have ever expected to see staring Joe down, there on the Best Buy showroom floor: Marvin Balman, Joe's greatest nemesis.

Marvin moved first, crossing the distance toward Joe with unhurried, almost insulting, strides. Joe still had not moved and looked exceptionally vulnerable, as his old enemy bore down on him. I had to go to his aid and stand by his side, facing this mortal threat together. With a heavy effort, I picked up my feet, as if from rapidly drying cement, and, placing one unsteady foot before the other, crossed the distance to my friend, arriving just as Marvin did. I had Joe's back, he needn't worry on that score.

"Oh, do stop gaping, Lopp. On second thought, continue for a moment longer as I can better savor your bug-eyed, fish out of water astonishment," Marvin barked a laugh.

"You," Joe hissed. It was pure cobra venom.

"Yes, me, Lopp," Marvin said. Now that I had a closer look at him, all I could think of was how much he had changed. He had ever been a large man, as was Joe, but where they had differed in the past was in personal dress and hygiene. Joe had always maintained himself by indulgent grooming and impeccable dress, the dark, three piece pin-striped suit being his uniform of choice. Marvin, on the other hand, had been at least two rungs below slovenly. Put bluntly, the old Marvin was a complete slob, with torn jeans, old faded Iron Maiden T's and flip flops, serving as his wardrobe.

But the new Marvin? He wore coat and tie, which actually remotely matched. His complexion looked healthy, since his raging acne had cleared up, and his full head of hair was glossy and neatly styled. I had always been aware that Joe harbored some envy for that full head of hair (even though in the past it had been long and greasy), where his had vanished save for a fringe. I had chosen never to broach the subject with him out of propriety and the laws of personal space, which were both physical and emotional. Yet, I knew a resentment was there.

"You look as if you've seen a ghost, Lopp. But then, I guess you have," Marvin flashed a big smile of perfectly straight, white teeth. I had to shake myself. The old Marvin had had teeth which looked like a mouthful of Fruity Pebbles. There were legitimate reasons why we nicknamed him 'Messy Marvin'.

"What are you doing here?" Joe was slowly regaining his composure, and he would need it around someone as treacherous as Marvin.

"I would imagine much the same as you, Lopp."

"Shopping?" Joe scoffed. "You can't be, you were banned from the industry five years ago. And it was a lifetime ban." He was right, Marvin had been blacklisted by every known mystery shopper agency and organization in the developed world, and justifiably so. His record of unethical practices and criminal misdeeds was long and varied. If it hadn't been for a consensus amongst the most prominent players in the business, to seal the information away, it well could have wrecked the entire industry. They knew where their bread was buttered, and, since it was Joe who had played a prominent role in having him booted from the MS ranks in the first place, he had reluctantly gone along with the 'loose lips sink ships' policy, though he always privately favored prosecution.

"What's up, beeyotch?" A voice behind me said. I whirled just in time to be elbow-brushed by a wiry little weasel of a man. *Holy Diabolical Double Dipping!* It was Sed Letticus, Marvin's henchman from the old days. Like a faithful hound, he took his place now at the side of the man he had ever called master. For a moment I thought Marvin would pat him on the head. A growl just then escaped my throat. Joe waved me to silence, and I obeyed.

Sed had been a private investigator once upon a time. His specialty? Divorce cases, heavily tinged with adultery. He had been very adept, and thus highly sought after, for his ability to slip under doors, around curtains and through blinds, with his cameras. That particular sub-section of the P.I. profession has ever been regarded as seedy, but, if there is a demand, someone will inevitably rise to supply the fix. Or rather, as is most often the case in the slimy divorce market, someone is always prepared to stoop down in the gutter. Sed, for his part, reveled in literally wallowing in it. He ultimately had his P.I. license revoked, due to his foray into internet porn, making use of pictures and video he had shot for his clients. He had had quite a back stock of material from which to upload. Unfortunately for his little operation, he had done it without the 'actor's' approval, much less their knowledge, so that, when he was found out, it was curtains for his theater of raunch.

It was only after his forced career change that Sed hooked up with Marvin full time, though they had been associated for years. Neither Joe nor I had ever been able to determine when, where, or how they met. No doubt during some back alley deal of nefarious intent. However it was, Sed played a role for Marvin not dissimilar to the one I play for Joe, only much dirtier. I can't say I was surprised to find them together once more, if they had ever parted. Their kind will always carouse together like maggots on rotting meat.

"I've been accepted back into the fold," Marvin said, by way of explanation.

"With open arms," Sed smirked.

"That simply cannot be," Joe insisted.

"Joe's right, you were absolutely disgraced when you were banned from any further mystery shopping activity," I said. "You're lucky you avoided a prison term."

"Things change, people move on," Marvin said, spreading his hands innocently ... *not*. "So nice of you to remember though, *Stan*," he said my name, as he always had, in a whiny tone. I've always been frustrated by not knowing why he did that.

"Looks like this couple hasn't moved on," Sed noted, sneering, "ass hats."

"I don't believe that," Joe declared, ignoring Sed as was his habit. Wish I could say the same.

"Come now, Lopp," Marvin pretended reasonability, "you yourself had a spot of trouble a couple of years back. A spot of trouble named Nina, remember that? Of course you do. Don't bother looking so surprised. I followed the events quite closely at the time. And don't ask me how, I have my sources as well." I winced. Nina would always be an especially sore spot for Joe.

"There was a big difference between what happened with Nina, and what happened with you: I was innocent, you were not."

"Guilt, innocence, it's all a matter of perspective," he shrugged. "The only point of relevance now is that I'm back in business. Deal with it."

"I will get to the bottom of this," Joe promised.

Marvin laughed, "Oh, you do that, Lopp. Then you let me know how you like it at the *bottom*." He said with a snarl, "I spent five years there!" And, then, he dropped his voice to a whisper, "Something I have you to thank for, and I will, in my own time and my own way." I had to put a restraining hand on Joe's arm. He was trembling with affronted outrage, and I feared he would go for Marvin right then and there. He really shouldn't allow Marvin to get to him so deeply and so quickly, as to cause him to do something which might damage his reputation. It took a lot to get Joe so visibly riled, but Marvin, and a seeming threat to his profession, were two good, or very bad, ways to go about it. Taken together they were an elixir of danger, one which Joe was obviously taking very seriously.

I was relieved when Joe forced himself under control. He asked in a clinically detached voice, "Who scheduled you for this event?" Good, he was trying to mask his unease to Marvin. However, the way in which Marvin had always known how to push Joe's buttons, suggested he may have been unsuccessful.

"None of your flippin' business," Sed spat.

"Bring it, beeatch!" I countered. Now I was losing it.

"Stand down, Stan!" Joe said sternly. I took a deep breath, searching for calm.

"It's okay, Sed," Marvin said. "If it's any of your business, I was hired by the firm which was looking to fill the role of the Supervise."

"The Supervise?" Joe was taken aback, again.

"That's right, Lopp," Marvin said casually, almost lazily. The way a cat toys with a mouse, it dawned on me. He removed a small notepad and pen from his coat, and made a few notations, as he continued, "I'm afraid you're unlikely to get paid for this evening, Lopp."

"What do you mean by that?" Joe asked quickly.

"Once I give my Supervise report, your agency is going to be very displeased with your work ethic."

"What *are* you talking about?" Joe was indignant. He snorted and stamped a foot. I recognized the signs, and readied myself.

"I've been observing you and *Stan*," Marvin said, again my name a ninny's whine. I ground my teeth as he went on. "You've done zero work this evening, the two of you. Nothing but wandering aimlessly about the store, and sharing a few inside jokes by the looks of it. Now don't tell me," he paused, and appeared to be mightily racking his brain for something, then pretended to grasp it, "was it the 'who can spot the mystery shopper' game, with bonus points for identifying positives and negatives in their performances?" Joe flushed a deep red and worked his jaw back and forth but never opened his mouth. "You're so predictable, Lopp," Marvin gave a sad, mocking shake of his head.

"We've done nothing wrong," Joe blurted at last, on the defensive. Even I had to admit it was a pretty lame rejoinder.

"Oh, no? What if other non-mystery shopping customers had overheard you? Not to mention, horror of horrors, any of the targets?" By this he meant employees. "What then? You'd have given the entire game away, you great oaf." I sprang then, the moment Joe moved his first muscle. I was on his back, restraining his arms, and trying vainly to halt his advance, as he lunged for Marvin's throat with a howl of rage and outstretched hands.

I hated to do this to him, but I would have hated myself even more so, had I let him go. My efforts proved successful. Joe staggered for a few more steps, before collapsing to his knees at the feet of the laughing Marvin Balman and Sed Letticus. Oh dear, oh dear, oh dear, I hastily scrambled from Joe's back. It was so humiliating! I helped Joe to his feet. Offering my apologies, I set about straightening his coat and tie. I was fortunate in remembering to bring my small, travel delinting brush with me. Marvin and Sed fell about themselves with malicious glee, as a tidied up my patron. Joe appeared dazed, confused. Such physical exertions were trying on a man of his age and heft, and the emotional battering he had just taken weighed more heavily still.

"This isn't finished," he said stonily.

"*Ooohh, aha-ha*," Marvin struggled to bring his laughter under control, "*aah, hee-hee*, you can be sure of that, Lopp."

Joe turned on his heel and stalked away, without another word. I hurried after, but was not out of ear shot before I heard Marvin remark to Sed, "There goes the great Lopp. There's not a situation too insignificant where he won't make a complete ass of himself."

To which Sed added, "Turds."

"Stanley, be a good chap and retrieve the big black book, middle, third shelf," he pointed off vaguely from where he lay on the sofa in his study, an ice bag covering the upper part of his face.

"This one, Joe?" I indicated a large volume wedged in between a book containing a collection of old coroner's death scene photos, and another entitled, *1000 Nudes*, which I knew to be a collection of antique nudie pix. I recall one time inquiring of Joe what his purpose was in possessing such a work, since it seemed so out of interest and character for him. He had replied something along the lines of, "there's nothing like old sex to allow a person to grasp the true meaning of our human nature, and its well spring in the womb." Not being quite sure what he meant by such a sentiment, I inquired about the death scenes collection, to which he responded wryly with, "there's nothing like old death to cause each and every one of us to strive to get right back up in that very womb, never to emerge again." Joe was deep that way, or perhaps it was his feminine side shining through. Either way, the philosophical insights of his keen mind were truly a wonder of our times. I could sit for hours in rapt attention listening to his ramblings, and often did.

Joe peaked an eye out from under his ice pack, "That's it."

I hefted the book from its place, "What is it?" I couldn't recall having ever seen it before. Of course, Joe had so many books, partly for pleasure, and partly due to his dabbling in the used and antique books trade. It would have been easy to overlook.

"It's one of my scrapbooks. The one you hold follows the career of none other than Mr., and I use the term very loosely, Marvin Balman." I knew Joe to be a keen cataloger of all manner of information and minutia, regarding matters relating to his profession, and just about any other subject which caught his interest. In this, he was following in the footsteps of other great authorities who had come before. By keeping detailed scrapbooks and journals, and even publishing monographs for the intellectually curious, these forerunners served to highlight the great mental processes required to track and solve some of the most difficult mysteries. It was not only for his personal reference, therefore, but for the benefit of posterity.

"Isn't this a bit obsessive?" I asked, handing him the book, once he had grunted and heaved himself into a sitting position.

"Hardly. Only once you've sifted and weighed all the evidence, and come to the only logical deduction possible, then you shall see that this was well worth the effort," he said, flipping through the book.

"And that deduction is?" I asked, taking a seat beside him.

"That Marvin Balman is a criminal mastermind of an ingenious magnitude."

"But we already knew that, Joe."

"Ah, Stanley," he said in a tone which carried a hint of pity at what he felt sure would be revealed as my naivete, "you had thought his career ended when I drove him from the profession five years ago, hadn't you?"

"Well, hadn't it?" I bristled, feeling a touch of resentment.

"Far from it. You see, these pages deal with his nefarious career, as we knew it, during our mystery shopper battles leading up to his downfall," he rifled quickly through that section of the book. I caught brief glimpses of photos, newspaper clippings, and other assorted memorabilia, all framed by Joe's sloppy, sprawling hand writing. "But here," he stopped at a section about two-thirds of the way towards the back, "is where my investigations continued to track his movements and doings, even after we last officially dealt with him, and he had been sent to his exile."

"And?"

"Unbeknownst to you and anyone else with an interest, Marvin has been anything but retired this past half decade."

"Oh, come off it, Joe," I said, unbelieving. "Balman's shown neither hide nor hair, since you sent him packing."

"Not so, Stan," he responded gravely. "Undoubtedly, that's what he would like the G.P. to believe."

"G.P.?"

"General Public, Stan. Those not in the know," he supplied. I winced, hating it when he went elitist like that, which was often.

"So what do you *have* there?"

"Quite an interesting collection of clues and anecdotal evidence, all pointing towards one man. For instance, had you ever heard about the pseudo-robbery at the Crazy Clicks Camera store?" I shook my head. "Well, this was the case which first brought to my attention the very real possibility, at the time, that Messy Marvin and Sed the Cuss were still in business, though they'd gone underground. A possibility, I hasten to add, which over the intervening years became a decided probability."

"What was this Crazy Clicks case about?"

"Observe," he indicated a clipping from a newspaper posted to the page. The date atop the piece was just over four and a half years ago, "in this news piece there was related a most curious incident which had occurred at said photography establishment that deals with the sale and rental of cameras and video equipment, as well as the development of film and editing of videos. One week before this piece ran, the store had reported to police a burglary of some of their video equipment. It was not a newsworthy event, being such a commonplace occurrence, so was not reported in the papers initially. What transpired to make it newsworthy was that later that week the equipment had been returned, in perfect working condition. As you can imagine, the equipment was dusted for prints, but it had all been meticulously wiped clean. Now, surveillance cameras in the store failed to catch any after hours intruders. Since there was no apparent evidence of tampering, it has remained quite a mystery as to how the equipment was stolen, much less later returned."

"I'll admit that's odd," I allowed. "Shoplifting theft often takes place in broad daylight, as it seems most probable in this case. But, why return it?"

"To abrogate the fact that a crime ever occurred, perhaps?" Joe's eyes twinkled. He did so love having an insight unshared by others. He was like some smug, devious Santa Claus, preparing to lay the presents beneath the tree, after having raided the fridge. "My subsequent investigations revealed that the very week the burglary occurred, the store was being shopped. I was never able to uncover just who had been assigned the Shop, but it wouldn't have been too terribly difficult for the recently disgraced Mr. Balman, to use his old MS contacts to find this information out, and then pose as a mystery shopper, to carry off the heist ... and the return."

"But, why?" I objected, bewildered. "Why would he do such a thing?"

"Think, Stan. Remember how Sed used to make his living, before teaming up with Marvin?"

"He was a P.I.."

"And do you remember how he ultimately lost his license?"

"Ooohh, *right*," Sed's clandestine video business suddenly popped into my head, and yet, "I'm still not following Joe."

He gave a huff of impatience, "It should be perfectly obvious. Since they were both unemployed, and presumably low on resources, they decided to fall back on Sed's video expertise, and get themselves back into the internet porn business. But they obviously hadn't access to the equipment with which to carry off the enterprise. I spent weeks trolling every internet porn site I could find, trying to catch some trace of them, but came up empty." I suppose I was giving him a very peculiar look, because he returned it with, "What?"

"Um, nothing Joe."

"Let me tell you, it was hard work," he said a trifle pugnaciously. I was trying to recall the time, and it seemed, if memory served, that the period Joe was referring to was one that lasted not weeks, but months, and involved many late nights holed up in his den with uneaten meals, and tissues. I remember wondering, at the time, why he was having Teffer buy so many boxes of tissues. Not that I spy on my patron, but I do keep his accounts, and it's the kind of curious expenditure which would naturally register with me. What can I say, I'm a penny pincher.

"This all seems to be rather flimsy evidence," I commented.

"There's much more where that came from," he assured me, and there was. He proceeded to string together a litany of like odd occurrences as he turned through the scrapbook. To my way of thinking, his 'evidence' appeared to be nothing more than half-baked hunches and flights of fancy. I won't use here the word paranoia, because as Joe always says, "Paranoia does not illegitimate a healthy suspicion." I had always thought it was the other way around, but that's why I was the amateur and Joe was the pro.

"Well, this is all quite fascinating," I said, when, an hour later, he had concluded his briefing.

"Isn't it, though?" he closed the scrapbook and stretched, yawning. "I think a good nights rest will put this all into perspective by morning." I seriously doubted that, but took this as a perfect opportunity to make my exit, and do what I had nearly done several times while Joe was holding forth: fall asleep.

The next morning I found Joe in his study. "Very good then, thank you," he said into the telephone receiver before hanging up.

"What's up, Joe?" I asked, rubbing the sleep from my eyes. He, like myself, was still dressed in pajamas, though he had a dressing gown covered with lions thrown over, and black leather slippers with large, square silver buckles, reminiscent of pilgrim's shoes, on his feet.

"I've spent the morning trying to track down by what means Marvin has managed to get back in the business," he told me. "Or if he even had at all, and was not merely bluffing last evening."

"Any luck?"

"None. Though my sources confirm that he is definitely back in the fold, dismal as it may be." Joe's sources were widespread. He was an old-fashioned man who, while certainly making use of modern technology, preferred to rely on the old tried and true methods of detection, as related to information gathering. His desk had a couple of different landline telephones, and was covered with an oversized calendar blotter, which was littered with notations and doodles, as well as a multitude of paper scraps scattered across the surface. Occupying a full quarter of the desk was a Rolodex, the size of a small automobile tire. It was crammed full of index and business cards, which Joe would spin like a raffle wheel, before expertly stopping it on the contact he desired, with hardly a glance.

"What now?" I asked.

"We wait," and wait we did, though I wasn't sure for what. But, it was only to be for a few minutes before I faintly heard the doorbell ring. I raised an eyebrow to Joe. "Earlier than I had expected," he said quietly to himself.

"Who?"

"Who do you think? Come, let's hurry and get dressed," he sprang from his chair. "Do tell Teffer to show them to the front parlor, and to keep an eye on them while they wait."

It was not five minutes later that Joe and I reunited in the entrance foyer. Teffer was waiting there, just outside the parlor door, occasionally peeking in uneasily. Joe dismissed Teffer before sweeping into the parlor. Marvin and Sed were quietly discussing something in front of the large window, which looked out onto the boulevard fronting our building.

"Good morning, Bals," Joe drawled.

"At least I've got a pair, Lopp," Marvin replied.

"To what do we owe this pleasure?" Joe used the Royal 'We', ignoring his retort. He took up a stance midway in the room. I at his side. I saw Sed mouth the word, "beeyotch," at me from just behind his master's shoulder. I chose not to respond in kind.

"Delivering a friendly notice, Lopp," Marvin told him.

"That's doubtful," Joe said sourly. "Well, what is it? Out with it, man!"

"Just this: I've signed a long term contract with Global Shopping Resources. They've initiated a worldwide review of all agencies which fall under their aegis, which are quite a lot, I'm sure you know. I'm the Supervise for this entire district."

I could feel Joe stiffen. *"This can't be,"* he said in a hushed tone.

The organization which Marvin had mentioned was a relative newcomer to the industry, but had, in a fairly short period of time, amassed quite a lot of power through acquisitions, hostile or otherwise, mergers and partnerships. GloShoR, as they were known, had branches worldwide that directed the operations of their various enterprises, which consisted of private investigation firms, market research labs, merchandising companies, as well as training organizations and companies providing mystery shopping services. It was a generally regarded, unwritten rule, that if a mystery shopper fell afoul of GloShoR they were pretty much screwed in the business, to use a layman's term. Hell, even those in the business used that term. I'd heard of more than one unfortunate mystery shopper having remarked as much, after being downgraded, a sterile bureaucratic euphemism for essentially being unemployable. The more professional slang held that one, meeting such a fate, had been 'gloshored'. If this was true …

"Oh, but it is, Lopp," Marvin spoke in an ominous voice, which oozed gleeful malice, "and you know what *that* means, don't you?" I heard Joe swallow hard. I hoped the others couldn't sense his complete discomfort. He didn't answer, so Marvin did it for him. "You're finished, you great fool. I will be there every step of the way, my red pen at the ready to grade your performance. When I'm done with you, you'll never work in this business again!" he finished with savage delight.

"You won't win," Joe managed to croak at last.

"I *always* win, Lopp."

"I defeated you the last time, when I had you booted from the industry," Joe was beginning to rekindle some defiance.

"That is the only time you've ever won, and for that I will have my vengeance! Ever since that dance contest in 1979, *I've owned you!*" I hadn't heard of this before. Sounds like it was before I met Joe. Of course, I knew he and Marvin went way back before that. I just wasn't sure how far back. Joe had always been a bit vague on the subject.

"That dance-off was rigged," Joe asserted.

"Nonsense. You were just a step too slow and behind the times. 'Better Dead Than Disco', yet you clung to it like a drowning man, while I had already gone Heavy Metal."

"Fool," Sed sneered.

"Tread lightly, little beeatch," I warned him, Joe gave me an admonishing look, shaking his head ever so slightly. What? I was just sticking up for him.

"Would you care to put your questionable skills where your fat mouth is?" Joe asked Marvin.

"What're you suggesting?"

"A duel," Joe hurried over to the coat closet and rummaged around inside, as Marvin shifted uneasily. Good, now he was the one feeling discomfort.

Finally finding what he was searching for, Joe strode back to his previous spot and flung something at Marvin's feet. Marvin stooped to pick it up, "A mitten?"

"It will have to do stand-in duty for a gauntlet, I'm afraid," Joe declared, not at all apologetically, "In any event, it has been thrown. Do you accept the challenge?"

"What challenge?" Marvin seemed taken aback. Joe had *him* off balance for a change.

"Dance til you drop. The loser not only eats massive helpings of crow, but agrees not to interfere with the winner, in any way, ever again."

"I don't think so, *Lopp.*" Marvin had a way of spitting out 'Lopp'.

"What's the problem, chicken?" Joe tucked his hands up into his armpits and began to cluck.

"No," Marvin said. But Joe was paying him no mind. He had begun to prance about the floor in circles, flapping his folded arms and bobbing his head,

"Bok-bok-bok-bok!" He clucked.

"Alright, Lopp!" Marvin snarled. "You'll get your shot. You couldn't beat me then, you sure as hell won't now."

"You agree to terms?"

"Certainly. Dictate whatever terms you care, makes no matter. Sed will stand in as my second."

"With pleasure," Sed said.

"Stanley, will you favor me by standing as my second?" Joe needn't have asked.

"It will be an honor," I said without hesitation, though I was still somewhat unsure exactly what he had planned. I tried to picture what a dance til you drop 'duel' might look like, but couldn't get a clear view in my mind's eye. Other than it undoubtedly involved dancing, *duh*. Yet, the others seemed to accept it as a natural course of events.

"You're goin' down, dawg," Sed puffed up, pointlessly, since he had nothing to puff up. But Sed was a pointless fellow.

"As host, I believe it's my prerogative to choose the tunes," Joe raised an inquiring eyebrow to Marvin.

"Go for it," Marvin agreed easily, way too confident and cocky already, "just let's not have a square dance, okay?" He and Sed guffawed.

"Stanley, by the stereo system, I believe you'll find an old Van Halen cassette," Joe directed me.

"Which one?" Marvin asked quickly, eagerly.

"The first." Joe said simply, eliciting a grudging nod of approval from his opponent. "Side one, track one, if you would, Stanley."

"Runnin' With The Devil," Marvin said in a low voice, his mouth forming a firm, unreadable line. Was this good or bad?

"Let's do this thing," Joe took his coat off and flung it aside. Pulling his shirt tails from the waist of his pants, he removed his tie, and undid the top couple of buttons. Marvin followed suit. They moved to face one another in the center of the room, stretching muscles (what there were), and unlimbering arms and legs. Marvin rolled his neck around, I heard it pop, while Joe cracked his knuckles.

What followed I will try to record as accurately as I can for the reader, though my meager abilities will almost certainly not do justice in conveying the intensity and energy of that titanic duel. While at the same time I will endeavor to abbreviate, whenever possible, for two reasons: firstly, so as not to make it too overlong, and secondly, in an effort to clean up some of the language in order to make this account more suitable as a family read. One could write volumes about every nuance and subtlety of strategy that took place during the encounter, to be sure it had all the ingredients the ancients used in their epic poetry. But for this rendition, brevity will have to suffice.

The music began, the cassette's tape a bit worse for wear, supplying a hint of static at the beginning, and as Van Halen jammed, so, too, did the combatants. Marvin began with the classic head banging motion, throwing his head back and forth, while rocking his body. Joe matched him in good rhythm, the only problem being Joe couldn't match Marvin's full head of hair, snapping with every head flow. His own short fringe encircling his bald dome was no competition, alas.

Sed caught onto this glaringly obvious fact, as well, halfway through the first track. "LMAO @ Lopp and his nekkid egg head!" He shouted above the blaring music.

"STFU Sed!" I countered. Calm, I counseled myself, almost as soon as the words had left my mouth. This was about Joe and his honor, not to mention his likely professional future. The stakes couldn't be any higher. Besides, this was just another facet of Sed's fraudulent personality. If his side couldn't win fairly, he would try to better the odds with taunts in an attempted psych-out. Pathetic, really. Still, I'd love to get a piece of that guy.

As the song wound down, I could tell Joe was in some distress. He was sweating copiously, and his large chest was heaving in search of more and more oxygen. Marvin, on the other hand, was holding up considerably better, for all that he had approximately the same amount of bulk as Joe, and was close in years. No, he was not nearly staggering the way Joe was. This could prove fatal for a desirable outcome. I fretted, but was pretty much stumped, limited as I was to aid my friend. At least I assumed I was unable to give assistance. I wasn't really sure. Why was I assuming there were even any rules?

The song ended and I decided to test it. I grabbed for a blanket on the arm of the couch and made to throw it to Joe, so he could towel off. But Sed stayed my arm, "No interference, beeyotch, or it's disqualification for your boy."

"It's alright, Stan," Joe pulled out his handkerchief to mop his face, once the song had ended. I don't know where Sed got off with his 'disqualification' nonsense. It surely couldn't be in the rules, and what was a second for anyway? What was the proper etiquette for dancing duels, anyway? WTH, I'd never have guessed I would ever be asking such a question. Much less of myself. But such was life in Joe's undefinable world.

At any rate, Joe needed a breather, but the space between tracks one and two was mere seconds, thus affording him no such down time. Lucky for us the next song was "Eruption", which could mean only one thing, *Air Guitar!* Now, Joe had to play this just right, if he were to catch his breath and conserve energy. This wasn't a long number, so every second counted, and, with "You Really Got Me" and "Ain't Talkin' Bout Love" following one after the other, this was absolutely crucial. I must say, at this point I was really starting to get into it!

With the first guitar riffs it was clear what Marvin's strategy would be. He adopted a wide-legged stance and began to windmill his arm in a grandiose manner. He almost couldn't help it. His own arrogance drove him to it. Joe, conversely, took a more conservative, yet accurate, for that piece, stance: legs closer together with his pick hand playing it closer to his midriff. Yes! This was just what I was hoping he would do.

LOL! At one point, Marvin actually did a scissors kick. It was so out of place for that particular part of the guitar solo. I shook my head pityingly at Sed, who responded with a shrug and mouthed, "WTF?" He didn't even get the blunder. Just like his master, he eschewed subtlety for vulgar showmanship. Joe kept it tight but real, through the end of the track, and I think it slowly dawned on Marvin that Joe had won the round. However the scoring system worked, if there was one. Must be. Oh, who was I kidding? I wasn't sure, but I would certainly mark it down for Joe and argue the point vigorously when the final results were tallied. Even if I was the only one tallying.

When "You Really Got Me" began, Marvin decided to up the stakes. His pace picked up as did his wild gyrations. I grimaced, at least internally. I didn't want to give anything away, but Joe would never be able to keep up this pace. As Marvin finished the later refrains off with a series of scissor kicks, the last of which, he stuck the landing and followed it smoothly through into the splits, I surely thought Joe was out of round 3. But Joe surprised me by going for something to match Marvin's kick/splits. OMFG! *No, Joe!* I wanted to scream. He would never be able to pull off that move. Why, it'd tear his groin out. I could just see the invalid that was my friend, with myself pushing him about his last remaining years in a wheelchair, lamed. Although, it dawned on me, the new motorized scooter chairs were all the rage and much more convenient.

But Joe wasn't trying to duplicate Marvin's move. As it turned out, he executed a little spin, from which he then dropped down neatly to a sitting position, spun once more in that position, then flipped over onto his stomach, stretched full length on the floor. His great bulk proved surprisingly supple, as he let the wave flow the length of his body, and bounced up and down, propelling himself across the floor, doing a classic Caterpillar. With each landing he made, there was a hollow 'boom', and the entire floor shook, which caused the furniture to jump and rock. Heck, even I was bouncing. The 'thump-boom' of his Caterpillar was the perfect accompaniment to the ending of that song. It was slightly awkward, admittedly. Joe was mixing dance styles the way vampire detective stories mixed genres, but we all knew Joe had won that round. And I was certain that I had finally caught on to how this whole dance-dance duel thingy was played.

I glanced over at Marvin, who was furiously grinding his teeth, as Joe dragged himself up from off the floor. I so wanted to help him. He looked in terrible shape, though trying heroically to grit his way through it. But, I also didn't want Sed to cry foul and attempt a disqualification. Joe would never forgive me if that happened.

"Ain't Talkin' Bout Love" began, and Marvin decided to change tack. Completely. He must have been thrown off by Joe's successful one-upmanship, because he now brought his head banging in close. Way too close. Joe matched him move for move. Their chests were bumping, slightly at first, and their heads were close to butting. This was bad. I should've halted it, and called my own foul on Marvin for dirty play, but something stayed me. Perhaps it was the thought of Joe never letting me live it down, if I threw the towel in the ring at that stage of the bout. Yet, I think it was something more. Maybe my own blood lust had been awakened, and I so wanted Joe to K.O. that joker. Whatever it was, I let it go and caught sight of Sed, instead, bouncing up and down excitedly, hollering on his master, "C'mon, C'mon, Beat That Chump!"

"Go Joe, Go!" I shouted a countering encouragement. And then it happened, in the latter half of the track. With Marvin forcing the issue, and Joe refusing to give ground, their heads struck one another with a sharp '*crack*'. Joe reeled back a step. There was a smear of blood on both their foreheads, so I was unable to tell whose it was. Marvin grinned savagely, but Joe manned up with a grim determination, and charged back into the fray. Marvin read his intent and met him, both large bodies slamming chest to chest. It was like the Hungry Hippo mosh pit. Once, twice, thrice they collided, then backed up and did it again. On the fourth such collision, I saw Marvin push off—a clear foul! I guessed. He tried to hide it by using Joe's own backward mo', but he wasn't quick enough. It sent Joe reeling backwards, out of control, with a wail of, "*Yaaahh!*" His full weight fell on a side table, which collapsed underneath him in an explosion of kindling.

"*LMMFAO!!!*" Sed cackled madly, capering about, fisting pumping the air.

"That's it. That does it!" I'd seen enough. I hurried over and clicked the stop button on the tape deck, then rushed back and knelt by Joe's side, where he lay atop the remains of the table, his eyes closed and head bloodied. Did he breath still? I couldn't be sure. I laid an ear to that massive chest, and was relieved to hear the bass-like beating of that great, noble heart, which knew not the word stop.

"You're disqualified," I announced to Marvin, who was being toweled off by Sed, *with one of our blankets!*

"Don't be absurd, *Stan*," Marvin again gave my name that high-pitched namby-pamby bray, which so irked me. "Your man couldn't carry his own water, that's all."

"He could if you hadn't pushed off. I saw you!" I thrust a finger at him.

"Get real, beeyotch, you don't even know the rules" Sed sniffed dismissively. "Marvin won, straight up."

"*No*," I seethed, then was interrupted by a light tug at my sleeve. OMG! I'd forgotten all about Joe. His eyes were still closed, but he whispered through parched and cracked lips, "Help me up, Stanley," I did, with some effort. He needed my support to stand, which I gladly lent him.

"Once again you show there is no depth to which you won't sink, Bals," Joe said, at length.

"I win, you lose. Deal with it, Lopp."

"I shall not. It is you who has lost, sir," Joe said coolly. Marvin glared at him, trying to shoot death rays from his sockets, by the look of it. Joe merely regarded him back with cold, heavy-lidded eyes.

"I say Marvin's the winner," Sed finally broke the silence. He even raised one of Balman's arms up above his head.

"And I say Joe is," I threw in. I couldn't replicate the gesture, since I was supporting Joe on his feet.

"A stand off, is it?" Marvin said, noting, more than asking.

"So it would seem," Joe replied, clinically.

"Well, then, let's call it a draw and let it go at that," Marvin suggested. Joe mulled this over, then nodded once curtly. Marvin continued, "Of course you realize this means nothing has changed. You've still never beaten me, and I'm still going to get you," he laughed. "Happy shopping. Come, Sed." They moved to the doorway, where Marvin turned one last time, and said, "I'll be seeing you around." He winked and they were gone.

"I rather doubt that." Joe whispered to the empty space where his arch-enemy had last stood. "You've got to find me first."

It was the better part of a week before Joe had recovered sufficiently, from the injuries and severe fatigue suffered in his duel with Marvin, to venture out of bed. That time had been hardest for Teffer, on whose thin, crayfish-like shoulders fell the task of trying to nudge or roll over a bed-ridden Mr. Lopp, in order to apply salves and change his bed pan. Teffer's mewling coaxed my assistance on occasion, but only for the first task, never the latter. Joe was a mass of bruises and aching joints after the duel. The unenviable task of picking splinters from Joe's fleshy posterior with tweezers fell to our shrinking doorman as well. On more than one occasion, I had to drag him out from under the bed or back into the room, after he had beat a hasty retreat just ahead of flying bric-a-brac or an alarm clock or anything else within Joe's reach, where he lay sprawled face down on his bed.

I finally removed all items within easy reach, though his tongue could do equal damage, and brought Teffer to tears before the operation was over. But Joe had ever been resilient in body and spirit, and was so, when I discovered him in his study at the end of that grueling week. He was adjusting his cravat in the mirror.

"Is the monocle really necessary?" I inquired.

"The monocle is absolutely essential to the part of Lamont Baskerville," he replied. It made him look like a World War I-era Imperial German dirigible captain, but I held my tongue.

Ever since Marvin's visit, Joe had determined to go about his business undercover, in an effort to outwit his nemesis, and Joe certainly had plenty of aliases, coupled with a wealth of experience playing these roles, to elude even the most dedicated snoop trying to track or uncover him. Yet, why Lamont Baskerville? I couldn't quite fathom it. I searched my mental records for a bio of this alias, but all I could recall about this long unused character was that he had a fondness for absinthe and burlesque. Whereas, Joe couldn't *stand* absinthe and burlesque.

Toward the end of that week, as he was feeling more and more fit with each passing day, Joe had finally accepted a commission for a new assignment. He insisted on taking the bus, something not normally preferred, in the expectation that it would be easier to shake a tail. What with the number of passengers and stops along the way, it was far superior to a cab under the circumstances.

"Do you stop at the haberdashery in the vicinity of 6th and Pinkleton?" He asked the bus driver, as we boarded.

"The what?" The driver shrugged, uncomprehending.

"Bill's Big & Wide Men's Store," I clarified.

"Sure, take a seat," the driver said, and we were off.

Joe, out of old habit, liked to spend the time leading up to appearing at the scene of a Shop, especially when he was in character, as a mini dress rehearsal before the curtain went up for the real show. So it was that, when we arrived at Bill's Big & Wide, he was in full character and raring to go.

Now, different characters have different personalities, obviously. Lamont adopted varying attitudes, opinions, and mannerisms, depending on the type of shopping or store he was confronted with. At least I thought that was part of this character's make-up, which would rank him as one of the most complex Joe had ever devised. The subsequent performance at Bill's served to ratify my memory. If it had been another kind of store, Lamont would have been a pussy cat, or near enough. But, when it came to men's clothing and toiletries, he could be fussy. Very, very fussy.

I think it's safe to say that the staff at Bill's had never encountered the likes of a Lamont Baskerville before. From the very moment he strode through their doors, he put them through their paces. Fetching, measuring, fitting, changing; he had them running from the first, with the crack of his whip-like tongue and droll, haughty sarcasm. Later, once he'd broken them in sufficiently, he only needed administer a frown or slight shake of his head to inspire redoubled efforts to please him. I think of it as putting the fear of the Baskerville in them.

It was nearing the end of the Shop, as Lamont was being fitted with a plush velor cumber bun as part of a 'casual-clubbing' tuxedo ensemble he had artfully concocted, when a familiar and most unwelcome voice broke in, "Good Gawd, Lopp, you look like an enormous Velveteen Rabbit. All you need are some ears." Joe froze. I turned and saw Marvin standing next to a rack of sport coats, pad in hand, and his smirking shadow lurking just behind. "At least, you don't seem to have scarlet fever. Spreading contagion to the general public would result in even further deductions for you."

"Yeah, uhn-uhn, but he's got something." Sed chortled, and shook his head. "Dayum, man, you gonna add some footies to that get up?" The employees who had been hovering like hummingbirds about Joe, froze and looked to one another in confusion, maybe even fearful anticipation. There was a sudden heightened tension in the air, much of it coming from a red faced Lamont. For a moment, I imagined I saw steam rising from his collar.

"So who are you supposed to be today, Lopp?" Marvin made a few notes on his pad. "By the looks of that monocle, I'd say either Baskerville or Throckmorton."

"I'd say he looks like a douche," Sed chimed in.

"Shut up, d-bag," I shot back quickly.

"Stanley." Joe said, with only mild reproach, then told the staff in a calm, steady voice, "That will be all." They didn't budge. *"Leave Us!"* he barked, and they scattered in a whirl and rustle of cloth and were gone. "What is your purpose here, Marvin?"

"You know very well my purpose," Marvin gloated, making some more notations, with a red pen, I realized. "Poor performance, all in all," he sniffed, then grimaced.

"What are you talking about?" I demanded. "He was flawless."

"First of all, *Stan*," Marvin began, I clenched my jaw, "unless your boss took this gig using his alias, he's committed fraud. And even if he did, he's misrepresented himself."

"These are tried and true practices," I countered.

"Nonsense, Lopp, here, is a throwback to another era," Marvin said dismissively. "He's a dinosaur. Nobody does this type of thing nowadays. As to his 'performance', I found it abusive and degrading to the employees of this fine establishment." I gaped, what cruel irony that Marvin Balman, of all people, should lecture another for abusive and degrading behavior towards MS test subjects. He had invented the practice which later became known as 'Toying With The Prey' or, in industry jargon, 'The Hot Shop'.

"Joe is an artiste," I finally managed to splutter.

"No longer." Marvin snorted. "Now he's just a big boob. Oh, you probably aren't even aware of how others in the business laugh at him behind his back. Besides," he shrugged, "he was always overrated. Could've used a bit more polishing in the theater, is my guess. But he was so sure he was ready for the silver screen." He'd been studiously ignoring Joe this entire time, but now fixed him with cruel eyes, "You took short cuts you shouldn't have, and now look where it's landed you." He continued to rub salt in the wound Joe's expression clearly indicated he'd opened up. "All washed up, and no other decent skills to see you through your retirement. Oh my."

"Are you quite finished?" Joe asked at length.

"Quite." Marvin snapped his notepad shut and tucked it away. "The way your star's falling, by the time I'm finished with you, all that'll be left of your career is a smoldering crater. Come, Sed." And they departed.

"Joe, I--,"

"Please, Stan, no words. I just want to be alone for a while." He was struggling mightily to hold it together. I could tell he didn't want me around just then. Or anyone, in case he broke down and lost it completely.

So, I just said, "Sure, Joe. I guess I'll head back home," to which he merely nodded. "Need anything?" I asked. He mutely shook his head. At which point, I left him standing there and returned to our flat alone.

I waited up for him well into the small hours of the morning. I had dozed at about the time the reproduction Louis XIV Versailles clock on the mantle stuck three, and was not out too long, when I was awakened by what sounded like burglars trying to break in the front door. Very clumsy burglars, at that. I crept to the foyer and cautiously peered in, just in time to see Joe stumble through the door.

"Shhhhh," he shushed to no one in particular. He hadn't seen me yet.

"Joe, thank goodness you're back," he whirled at the sound of my voice. In the act of closing the door, he lost his balance again. I rushed to hold him up. I've developed musculature I never knew I had, in Joe's employee. The door was also lending support, with his back leaning heavily against it.

"Ahhh, Stan," he sighed, not sadly, but dreamily instead.

"What's this?" I just then noticed he appeared to be wearing a headband. I plucked it from his brow. It was a frilly woman's garter. "Where have you been, Joe?" I was suspicious.

"Here and there, dear friend. The whole world is green tonight. I feel as though I'm traipsing through a fairy land." He pushed off from the door, did a little dance, and kicked one thick leg up in the air. Uh-oh, I sprang to steady the inevitable loss of balance. It was like supporting the Leaning Tower of Pisa. "Time for bed, my friend," I said quickly, steering him down the hall to his rooms. All the while he babbled about fairies painting the world green, and trying to fling one leg or another up in the air. Thank goodness Teffer had retired to his own room hours earlier. It simply wouldn't do to see his employer in this condition.

Joe persevered, as always. He simply did not hail from quitter's stock. To be sure, it took a couple of days to recover from the fallout of the Bill's Big & Wide fiasco but, afterward, he was back on his feet and Shopping with a vengeance. Unfortunately, the results were much the same. No matter which assignments he took on, or what disguise he assumed, there were Marvin and his pet rat, Sed. Whether Joe was in Bath & Body Works as Chester A. Bittner, the retired voice-over specialist, or at the Cookie Co. picking out some chocolate chips, as Matty Jon Little, the near-sighted, yet wise-cracking, home appliance repairman, invariably Marvin showed up with pad in hand, making notes with his red pen, while tsk-tsk-tsking Joe's performance.

Joe always kept his composure, however, and there were no more incidents like the one with Lamont after Bill's Big & Wide. Perhaps, due to the fact that none of the aliases he chose thereafter had the bad habits Lamont had. I wish I could say I kept my compose, but it was not to be. Sed and I got into a scrum in a bin of Nerf basketballs at a Kmart Superstore during promo night, after his latest bout of beeyotch-calling.

And when I say *in* a bin, it *was* in a bin, where store security had to pry us apart. There were no charges filed, thankfully, but my actions certainly didn't help Joe's rating any. Truth be told, it was already in the toilet, and being flushed, by then.

By the end of another month Joe was, for all intents and purposes, unemployable. Times were hard and resources were running very low. I won't say he was a spendthrift, but he did pursue a much more lavish lifestyle than anything less than full-time, multi-faceted, creative employment could afford. Oh, he had other sidelines which saved us from being evicted, but the MS racket was the real bread earner. So much so that when we were forced to read at night by candlelight, due to our electricity being cut off for failure to pay, it was readily apparent just how desperate things had become.

I really do think things fell hardest on Teffer, as hard things have a habit of doing with that poor man. He was sent out daily during those bleak times, to haunt the loading docks of any store he could find, with direct orders from Joe to beg up any surplus goods or foodstuffs that were going to be dumpstered, due to damage or expiration. He actually did a pretty good job of it, yet I could tell that it wore on him something fierce. There were many a day he would return to the flat with a bag of damaged and dripping hair gel tubes, or spotted tomatoes or the like. He would wordlessly lay his finds before us like a faithful pet, before retiring to the bathroom, where he would run the shower for hours on end.

Since we had no gas or electricity, they were cold showers indeed. That is, until Joe, gently, suggested he cut it short due to a rising water bill we obviously couldn't afford. After which, he took to lathering in a small basin, and scrubbing his skin until it was raw, then powdering himself with some talcum products he had scrounged. Like a chamber servant's ghost, he waifed about the flat, scared the hell out of me on more than one occasion in the dead of the night, just appearing, white and unearthly with candle stick in hand, out of nowhere, as if he'd stepped directly from the set of *Dangerous Liaisons*.

It was in the depths of these dark times that some good news finally emerged. Amongst his other pursuits, trying to make ends meet, and keeping his own spirits up, Joe had entered his name, often more times than allowed by the rules, in any and all contests and drawings he came across. However, for all his efforts to stack the deck in his favor, he came up empty handed every time until one day.

"Success!" I heard him trumpet. Then, the pounding of his feet approaching down the hall preceded his breathless entry into the salon, where I had been doing a touch of writing.

"Oh?" I asked glumly. I'd become so accustomed to our dystopic lives I was unused, by then, to any hint of hope or possibility.

"The Great Grocery Grabfest, Stanley!" he bubbled with excitement. "Where four lucky winners will be able to feast like princes for a month, *and I'm one of those princes!* And high time, too. Can't tell you how many times I've entered. Plum lost track of the count, but no matter."

"What's the deal with this one?" I perked up. Was there some glimmer of hope here, after all?

"I and the three other lucky entrants get five minutes, and as many carts as we please, to fill them up with anything in the store during that time period. This is just the break we've been looking for," he said, with faraway eyes, no doubt already planning the menus, course by course, of the upcoming feasts. I had to smile, this was the best news our little household had had in quite some time, and it was all due to Joe's relentless, if quixotically directed, energies.

On the day of the Grabfest, Joe and I arrived early. He most definitely did not want to miss the start on account of traffic. The rules were clear on that point: there were no do-overs or late starts allowed. Now, you may be wondering, what is the name of this store, and how can I enter their contest? I would name the chain, but as you will see, due to events which unfolded on their premises, I must keep the company's name confidential. Their attorneys were most insistent upon it.

The ride to the grocery store was relatively quiet. Even our usually gabby cabby didn't have much to say. Only once did I mention our current predicament to Joe, I wasn't going to hen peck too much.

"Mutual detestation is generally best," Joe mused, answering indirectly. "It's always a shame when one person despises another and the feeling is not shared."

The grocery store had been cleared of all other shoppers during the hour set aside for the event. The Grabfest contestants needed to be vetted and signed in. Then, after the five minutes of the dash 'n snatch, there would doubtless be pictures taken for the local papers of the happy grabbers and their loaded carts mounded with vittles.

Joe had been putting himself through a mild calisthenics regime all week leading up to this, trying to build up some stamina and increase his breathing capacity. For such a large man, even five minutes of intensive physical exertion could be very debilitating, I only hoped it wouldn't prove fatal. I'd been monitoring his heart rate and blood pressure all during his week-long training regimen, if you could call it that. He was, all in all, in fair shape, so I issued my own informal, if tepid, clean bill of health. It should be obvious to my readers, by now, that such a thing as my approval is often inconsequential to my employer, but someone has to look after him. Fate had decreed the task to me.

He decided to forego his usual dark, double-breasted suit, which always made him look rather like a banker, and had adopted a red sweat suit and bright white sneakers, which made him look more like a pimp. Without the bling, that he left at home. His headband, which on first glimpse I had mistaken for the garter bestowed on Lamont that one unfortunate evening, was pulled lower over his eyebrows. He was taking this event very seriously, indeed.

There were three other participants besides Joe, as I've stated, two of whom arrived before us. While Joe's credentials were being checked, they were introduced to us both. Their names are unimportant here, as they were unremarkable, and, aside from providing some backdrop, are not relevant to this story. One was a mousy, little woman of early middle years, who looked like a bookkeeper, the other was an elderly grandmother type, who looked like she would have even more trouble than Joe, getting around the store and filling her cart. I pegged her as one who would simply go to a few sections selected beforehand, and swipe the shelf off into her cart.

Studying up on this kind of contest during the week, I learned that this sort of pre-planned targeting was standard procedure. Joe had made a list of areas of special interest, and had visited the store a couple of times to map it out and conduct a test run. Highlighted areas included sections of imported soups, seafood, and butterball turkeys. So, there we were, just waiting for the fourth contestant, when I heard something which I had not been at all expecting.

"Well, if it isn't Lopp and *Stan*."

"What's up, beeyotch?" Yep, no need to even guess. It was Marvin and Sed alright, standing there just inside the sliding doors, looking obnoxiously pleased with themselves.

"What are you two doing here?" I blurted.

"What do you think? We're here for the contest," Marvin said, incontestably.

"You--," Joe caught himself before he could say what he really thought, "are the fourth contestant?"

"Correct." Marvin moved closer, lowering his voice. "You can't win, Lopp, not against me."

"This is not a contest with winners and losers," Joe explained with heavy contempt, as if to a simpleton. "We compete against the clock, not one another. The real contest was the drawing to determine the participants."

"Then I still won," Marvin sneered. "You see, Lopp, even if you do manage to harness even a small sample of luck, I'm still there as well, always keeping pace with you. You can't outrun my shadow."

"Who's trying?" Joe said nonchalantly. "First, I would have to give a diddly-damn." He casually checked his watch.

"How's business?" Marvin abruptly changed the subject. "Since your complete absence from any agency's call list, I imagined that things had gotten a bit tight on the old home front. But this?" He looked around the store as if marveling at a new wonder, disbelieving, "This is pathetic. What, are you starving? Have things gotten that bad this fast? Though, I must say," he put a hand to his chin and tapped his lips with his forefinger, as he scrutinized Joe from head to foot, "I can't imagine you wasting away from starvation. You've enough fat on you to keep you going for at least a year."

"Yeah," Sed added, snickering, "and if it came to it, he could just eat Stan." They both cracked up, falling about each other at their own idiotic sense of humor.

"You're no slip of a figure yourself, Bals," Joe observed dryly.

"Oh, I've put on a few pounds, indeed," Marvin patted his round belly. "It's called prosperity. Many cultures consider the more weight a man carries to be indicative of success, and thus esteem. Something that's well in the past for you, so what's your excuse?" Sed crowed his laughter, actually sounding more like a hyena. "Now, if you'll excuse me, I'd better sign in." He and Sed brushed past us and made their way to the registration table.

"What are the chances that Balman would enter and win the same contest as you?" I asked, disbelief clear in my tone. Joe's answer indicated his suspicion had already been aroused. My alert level was raised to orange, or whatever the hell color coded scheme the government used, that was just below critical.

"Not very good, Stan," he replied softly, intently staring at Marvin's back across the distance, as he signed in. "Something is not quite right here."

"You think he cheated?"

"I'm almost sure of it. But how? As yet, I cannot say. It's well known that he will go to any lengths to one-up me. He's been doing it since I've known him, and that's been many years. He's positively pathological, you know." I knew that much to be true.

The store manager arrived then, to give us a run down of the rules. The time would be announced over the stores P.A. System, as the five minutes wound down, every minute being reported, and then the last fifteen seconds would be counted down, as well. Extra carts would be kept in their normal place in the cart queue at the front of the store. Every participant could only start with one, and only have one at any given time, bringing back a full one to the front of the store, in order to retrieve an empty one. That was the real time killer, I hated that rule! They would all be monitored, and, when the final whistle blew, they had to stop filling their carts immediately, or face disqualification and the forfeiture of the cart they had been filling. As a somewhat more generous gesture, in such an event, they would be allowed to keep the contents of any previously filled carts. I cautioned Joe not to get too greedy at the end, but he just waved me off, as if gluttony were an entirely foreign concept to him.

They took their places, carts side by side in adjacent check out aisles, facing the opposite way *into* the store. The store manager said, "OK everyone, remember, on my whistle, and no false starts. Though if you do, we'll just start over," he laughed, and the two female contestants laughed with him. Joe did not, he looked intense, both hands gripping the cart handle tightly. He was in a strange kind of half stooping, sprinters stance, with his left leg stretched out behind him and his right cocked in front. Marvin, in the lane next to Joe, didn't laugh either, though he looked his usual confident and cocky self.

"Okay now," the manager addressed them again, "Mrs. Gambill, are you ready?" The grandmotherly woman, who was on the far end, nodded. "Ms. Clarkely?" The mousy woman nodded with a silly grin on her face. "Mr. Lopp?" Joe gave a curt nod. "And Mr. Blakeston?" *Mr. Blakeston?!* Marvin nodded with a self-congratulatory smile. Joe's head whipped around in my direction, his eyes seeking mine out. When they met I could see the great gears of his mind churning, trying to fit the pieces together, "Alrighty then, on your mark," the manager called out theatrically, as if he were in the center ring under the big top. Why did people have to be so grandiosely geeky when in the spotlight? "Get set ...," and when the manager blew his whistle, they were off.

Joe practically rocketed from his gate with Marvin only half a step behind. The two ladies were somewhat slower, for them it appeared to be merely an enjoyable Sunday drive. But by the looks of Joe and Marvin, it may as well have been an ancient Roman chariot race. Joe took the initiative, steering his cart to the left away from Marvin. He appeared to be heading to the soup's aisle. Oddly enough, Marvin went driving his cart right after Joe, his legs churning to try to match, if not overtake, the surprising burst of speed which Joe had put on.

Marvin made up enough ground that, by the time Joe reached the aisle's entrance, and was making his right hand turn to enter, Marvin was on top of him. He broadsided Joe's cart with his own, sending Joe's crashing into an end aisle pyramid of jars of peanut butter, which went flying in all directions. I gaped, stunned. I couldn't believe what I was seeing. Marvin didn't stick around. Like all cowardly hit and run drivers, he straightened his cart and dashed off down the aisle, while cackling madly, "Bwaahaahaa!!"

Sed cheered on his master, "Yeah, Baby. Yeah!" I did so want to pop him in the chops, but, control ... control.

I overheard one of the store cashiers utter an, "*oh my*," to the manager, who wore a confused frown. This had all the makings of a demolition derby, which was likely to turn the manager's confusion to shock and horror in short order. I now saw the inner workings of Marvin's master plan. It wasn't to gather free groceries, it was to wreck Joe's ability to do so, and feed his household. I could only hope Joe had come to this sudden realization as well. Time was of the essence. I bit my tongue to keep from revealing this to anyone else. It would all depend on how Joe reacted.

He was struggling to free his cart from the peanut butter and cardboard. A surprising number of jars had deposited themselves in the cart, I couldn't recall whether that had been an item on Joe's list. Oh well, there was scant time to clear it all out. I did hope he picked up bread and jelly along the way. Peanut butter and jelly sandwiches would be far from satisfying Joe's gourmet appetite, but eating was eating, after all.

Joe savagely kicked a few remaining jars out from under his wheels, and he tore out after Marvin with his mouth fixed in a rictus snarl. Oh dear ... oh dear, oh dear, oh dear. Since only the participants were allowed in the 'arena', as I came to view the shopping floor, my view of what transpired next was somewhat obscured. I rushed down the outside of the row of cash registers, shoving my way through the other gathered spectators: friends, family and employees, who themselves had caught on that something out of the ordinary was transpiring, and wanted, similarly, to get a better view of the action.

I was just in time to see Marvin turn the corner at the far end of the aisle and disappear, still cackling his, "*Bwaahaahaa!*" *Oh Joe!* I wanted to shout, *don't forget the soups!* But he was seemingly oblivious to the 'grab' at that point, only the dash still held his attention. So be it, I reconciled myself and my hunger pangs. He needed to go on a diet anyway.

Joe was soon lost from view at the aisle's end. The next indication as to the location of the combatants, as I now considered them, was a loud crash, a woman's scream and a veritable explosion of boxes of cereal, which were flung far and wide. Many had burst open, and a showering cloud of what appeared to be Cocoa Puffs, and maybe even some Count Chocula, snowed up into the air and drifted down at the back end of the long rows of product shelves.

People were frozen, unbelieving of what they were witnessing. I myself wanted to sink through the floor and not have to deal with the fallout from this disaster in the making. I heard laughter behind me. I turned and saw Sed, doubled over, and pounding his fists on his knees. I ground my teeth and turned away, fuming. Calm, remain calm, I had to tell myself, over and over.

"Should we call security, sir?" One of the employees asked the manager, who could only shake his head slowly, obviously at a loss as to what to do. The brief bark of a siren sounded. I looked out the large front windows and saw two police cruisers in the parking lot, officers just stepping out. Apparently, someone had already made a call, but who? Oh Lord, I hoped I didn't have to bail Joe out of the slammer. Where would I get the funds?

The rattle of cart wheels snapped my attention back to the action. Joe was the first to reappear at the far end of the store. The crowd of onlookers shuffled down that way, and I was swept along by their mass and momentum. Joe skidded to a halt at a large refrigerated bin, and stooped over to lift from it none other than the large butterball turkey he had singled out on his list. Oh good, I thought, maybe the plan was back on. But no, he hoisted the turkey up over his head with both hands, and flung it with full force at Marvin, who had just appeared in my line of vision. The frozen fowl was like an oversize, oblong cannonball, which caught Balman full in the gut and staggered him, though he kept his legs under him.

Joe was off again in an instant, but it took Marvin a couple of moments to recover. When he did, he pointed his cart at the receding figure of Joe, and set out in pursuit once more.

I pumped my fist in the air and shouted, "YES!" People around cast me odd, sidelong glances.

"*Beeyotch*," I heard the muttered curse to my left, but ignored it. Joe was now charging along the front of the store just inside the row of registers. I could see some tears in his sweat suit, and a cut on his right cheek. He was panting heavily and sweating profusely, but the look of determination on his face kept his legs pumping, as he hurtled along behind his cart, now half full of peanut butter jars and burst cereal boxes, leaving a trail of their contents sifting in his wake.

Marvin came along in hot pursuit. They were headed towards the other end of the store where the bakery was located. The crowd moved to keep pace with them. Almost lost in the spectacle was the mousy little woman, who came staggering out of an aisle without her cart, but with blood on her chin and cereal in her hair.

"*Help me,*" she pleaded weakly. One of the stock girls spotted her and rushed to her side, just as her legs gave out and she collapsed. I, next, heard the front doors swish open, and caught a glimpse over my shoulder of two policemen enter, guns drawn. What the--?! But the crowd bore me along like a wave, and the action on the floor took center stage once again. Oh please don't shoot my mentor. I offered a silent prayer.

Nearing the baked goods, a cart suddenly appeared out of the mouth of an aisle, directly in Joe's path, with the grandmother in tow. Joe quickly swerved to miss her, but Marvin did not. He crashed directly into her cart, sending it spinning, and knocking her backwards and out of sight, as she gave a faint cry of, "*aaahh, I'm falling!*"

Joe's evasive maneuver, however gallant, cost him momentum, which allowed Marvin to make up the distance. He crowned this turn of fortunes by driving his cart directly into Joe's backside, sending him flying onto a table laden with doughnuts, pies, cookies and assorted other pastries. He slid across it's surface, and managed to dislodge most of the contents, before dropping off the other side himself.

"Who's in charge here?" One of the officers asked of the crowd.

"I am, officer. I'm the store manager."

"Do you know if a Gerald Blakeston is on the premises?"

"Why, yes, he's that large fellow over there," the store manager pointed to where Joe and Marvin were busy pelting one another with rolls and cupcakes, firing them at point blank range from opposite sides of the display table.

"The one in the hideous track suit?" The same officer asked, with evident distaste.

"No, the one with the hair," as the manager said this, Joe splattered a cream-filled doughnut directly between Marvin's eyes. The officers moved towards the two overgrown children cautiously, guns raised before them. They needn't have worried. Joe and Messy Marvin were oblivious to all but their own food fight. I caught sight of Sed, trying to sneak away in the direction of the front doors, and had a notion he should stick around. I laid a hand on his shoulder and spun him around.

"Leggo, beeyotch," he pulled himself free from my grasp, but not for long. That was the last time he 'beeyotched' me. I balled my left hand into a fist and swung at his head, as if it were a baseball, and I were swinging for the fence. The connection was so sweet, and sung from my fist up through my central nervous system with ringing tones of satisfaction. Seeing him crumple and laid out on the floor, made me feel like a man, a real man! *I jacked him up!*

Meanwhile, the officers had handcuffed Marvin, and were leading the besmeared scoundrel to the front of the store, "Are you going to tell us your real name? Since you are evidently *not* Gerald Blakeston?" One of the officers asked, the other holding Balman by the cuffs and collar.

"Who is this Gerald Blakeston, of whom you speak?" Marvin was so obviously, to me, trying to play dumb. It was just stupid.

"You have some of his ID on you, though you left out any with a photo," the officer said.

"He signed in for the contest as Gerald Blakeston," the manager pointed an accusing finger at Marvin.

"Well, the real Gerald Blakeston is out there," the officer jerked a thumb towards the parking lot. All eyes followed it. We saw that an ambulance had arrived, and a couple of paramedics were lifting a body out of the trunk of a car, then placed it on a stretcher.

"He's dead, by the way. Much of his personal ID was missing, though he still had his drivers license on him. With photo," the officer produced it and held it up beside Marvin's face. "No resemblance whatsoever." He poked a finger into Marvin's chest, "I take it the bottle of chloroform was yours?" Marvin visibly paled and gulped, but couldn't trust himself to say anything. The officer continued, "When you chloroformed him, you used too much, idiot. Either that, or you suffocated him, when you gagged him. The autopsy will determine which. In any event, you're going to be charged with murder in the first degree. Along with carjacking and kidnapping, very clumsily carried out in broad daylight. Did you not think his neighbors wouldn't notice when you jumped him in his driveway? Now, give us your real name, and that of your accomplice. There was another man spotted with you, by all accounts." Still Marvin wouldn't, or couldn't, speak.

"I think I can be of assistance," Joe stepped forward, coated as was Marvin from head to foot with pastry fillings. He proferred a business card. The lead officer took it and read, "Josef Q. Lopp, Mystery Shopper Extraordinaire and Dabbling Detective." He looked Joe squarely in the eyes, "Are you kidding me?"

"Not at all, Officer," Joe replied stiffly, trying to maintain his dignity under all the icing, "I know this man in your custody to be none other than one Marvin Balman, known career criminal and all around bad person."

"Shut up, Lopp!" Marvin had regained enough of his senses to make a lunge at Joe, but was restrained.

"And there lies his accomplice," I pointed out the unconscious form of Sed. "Sed Letticus, by name."

And so it ended, with Joe victorious over his arch-enemy at long last, and hopefully this time for good. Once Joe had reported all of Marvin's wrongdoings to a mystery shopper and private investigations tribunal, which had been specially convened to review Joe's charges against Marvin, he was ultimately reinstated to his former rank of Master of his Craft. All negative marks levied by Marvin were expunged from the records. It was as Joe had said, Marvin truly was pathological and his compulsion to show up Joe drove him to the ultimate act, whether it was an accident or not.

It came to light that Marvin had made use of bribes to gain access to information regarding the winning contestants in the Grabfest. Now, this may seem incredibly unlikely, but one has to keep in mind that the MS industry is very closely linked with corporate contest administration firms, not to mention all the other avenues available to someone of Marvin's maniacal interest in all of Joe's doings. It proved a relatively easy task to keep himself apprised of my friend's every move, and by his own earlier admission had been doing so for years. Such was the murky shadow world which mirrored the carefully groomed, wholesome sun shiny day public image of corporate America. Oh, the stories I could tell, but another time.

Marvin and Sed were tried together for the carjacking, kidnapping and murder of the unfortunate Mr. Blakeston. Not surprisingly, their defense attorneys tried to argue some absurd extenuating circumstances, or lack of sufficient mental capacity, in an effort to get the charges reduced, or some even dropped altogether. This is unlikely to succeed, but who knows, Marvin and Sed are a slippery, slimy duo. Since the trial has been drawn out by so much legal maneuvering and grand standing on the part of the defense, it still was not concluded at the time of this writing so I am unable to relate to you the outcome.

Joe resolved to largely ignore the proceedings, and has only been kept remotely apprised of the events of the trial by my own avid interest in it. Yet, I didn't want to overburden him with the details, so I kept most of it to myself, and he seemed happiest with this arrangement.

Life quickly returned to normal and as the work began to flow back in, so, too, did our financial situation return to health. It wasn't long before Joe began mentioning his desire for a break, and a possible vacation to 'take the airs'. Though, first, he wanted to complete the correspondence coursework for his private investigator's license, which would allow him to officially wear two hats and raise his prospectus, to further broaden his career by the types of cases he was able to accept. He was already having new business cards printed in anticipation of this, so we shall see what the future holds.

The Pigeon King

In the annals of the unique career of Josef Quillenthorpe Lopp, which I have striven to chronicle as faithfully to the actual events as human memory makes possible, the multitude and variety of cases is astonishing. There are the everyday dramas and run of the mill affairs which may slip by conscious notice due to their more mundane nature, to be sure. Often these are passed over as mere interludes between the cases of grander scale, namely those dealing with a mystery or high crimes such as murder, or the involvement of famous personages, or even the presence of rampant and exotic sexuality.

But, from amidst even this smorgasbord of fascinating tales, come others, more curious of content, that fall, not somewhere in between the everyday and the glamorous, but somewhere outside. On their own they exist in a separate category, due to the peculiarity of the events and/or characters involved, in what may not be officially considered part of the Joe Lopp Professional Canon. This is just one such tale.

Even before I entered the den, I could hear Carly Simon singing "Nobody Does It Better", the theme song from the James Bond movie, *The Spy Who Loved Me*. This told me that Joe was working on his personal/professional website, since that was the song which automatically began playing when the home page popped up. He sat before his monitor with feet propped on a pillow atop a low footstool, with small portraits of England's King Henry VIII embroidered on its cover. When he was in a mood like this, he often complained of a bout of the gout, or some other such malady, none of which he had, so far as I've ever been able to determine. But Joe was a hypochondriacal savant, and, as such, it was the better part of common sense to play along with his encyclopedia of 'ailments'.

The site was officially entitled "Josef Q. Lopp's Investigatorial Abbey Ltd.". Generic enough, right? The byline was, "Clienthood Culled From Good Faith". The sub-byline was, "The Loppster", and this was followed by a small emoticon wearing a fedora, with a smoking cigarette dangling from the corner of it's mouth, followed by, "Has Two Minutes To Save The World". He had all manner of information on his site including, but not limited to: a time line of his various careers with awards of distinction, a blog where he posted musings on subjects which were of interest to him such as theater and 19th century ceramics, as well as a link to a page entitled, "Mama Lopp's Homespun Homilies", where he dispensed advice on all manner of topics under the sun. Such posters as Joe were widely regarded by professionals from any given field as a nuisance, at best. At worst, a danger. But that didn't stop him, or even slow him down.

This is where 'Mama Lopp' was headed when I entered the den.

"Any good one's today?" I asked.

"Let's see." he scrolled. "Ah, here's one from a young girl seeking my wisdom. Listen to this," and he read, as I read along over his shoulder:

> Yo Mama,
> I M to give a class preesentashun @ my skool.
> I wuz wund'ring if U could be so kind to give
> me sum informashun a bout yur wurk, R life, R

anything that could be use full. If not, then may
be how to make stuff up on the spot.
Sinceerly yurs, Mary Sue Draughton

"Adorable, simply adorable," he gushed.

"Are you going to respond?" This was just up his alley, I had to admit, but he needed to be careful.

"Of course. It's my responsibility, as an elder, to help the younger generations in their continuing education of life and the world about them. Just as so many assisted me in my own maturation process. I'll mark this for later." That's funny, I thought, like Mary Sue, that he made much of it up on a whim, as well. He paused for a moment, reflecting, "Of course, since I'm dealing with an elementary school age youngster, I'll probably need to include a disclaimer. I believe I have the one provided by my attorney still on file, eh, Stanley? We wouldn't want a repeat of that most unfortunate incident, which occurred the last time I dealt with such young school children."

No, it's not what you think. Whichever of a number of different paths you're traveling down in your imagination right now, don't go there. But it was very likely the next worst thing. The 'most unfortunate incident' was in fact a PR nightmare, and all of Joe's making. What had happened was this:

Joe had given an interview to a group of budding elementary school journalists for use in their school paper. When the edition with the interview came out, Joe was so incensed, I don't now recall whether it was due to a crack about his professionalism or a derisive observation on his appearance, but he promptly threatened a libel lawsuit, if a retraction was not immediately forthcoming. I should have been paying closer attention, I do handle Joe's public image as part of my many duties to him. I guess I thought this would be a perfectly harmless exercise, which would require zero supervision on my part. Never again.

Well, you can imagine the impact this had on the children behind the article. They were scared to death. The number of wet pants and tears shed over this imbroglio can really only be guessed at from my end. I had to spin the entire affair like a madman, when it became public, just to keep a rampaging mob from running us out of town. I ultimately prevailed upon Joe to drop the matter completely, which he did at the 11th hour.

It's not that Joe's a vindictive person, but he is proud and stubborn. If you let him walk out on a limb, there's no need to saw it off behind him, because he'll just keep going on, of his own accord. Only when he realizes that the limb's about to break and he's liable to plummet to his death, does he begin to inch back again to safety, as happened in that wildly belligerent episode, hopefully never to be repeated. Eternal Joe vigilance is ever my watchword.

"Let's see," he was continuing through his emails. "What else have we here? Oh, this is interesting," he said, finding one that piqued his curiosity. "Listen to this:

> Dear Mama,
> My wife is afraid to leave the bathroom. She takes all her meals in there. She sleeps in there. She lives in there. She's taken to sitting on the commode and even sleeping on it. Now she is stuck to the seat and can't get off. Please help, how do I unstick her?
> Sincerely yours, Delbert McClenehen

"That's thoroughly disgusting," I commented.

"Quite. It's known as agoraphobia," Joe explained, "a fear of leaving a safe place. There may be a particular name for the bathroom variety, though I'm currently unaware of it. This condition is somewhat different from claustrophobia, which is a fear of confined spaces. Agoraphobes may find a confined space, such as a bathroom, most comforting, as long as it's safe."

"That poor woman needs professional help."

"That's just what Mama Lopp is here to provide." *That* wasn't quite what I had in mind. Joe began typing his 'remedy':

> Dear Sir,
> You'd do best to use Vaseline, KY jelly, heck even butter would do. Lubricate those areas attached to the seat of the commode. Really grease her up, mind you. If there are any open sores, which I reckon there are like to be, then be sure to have some antiseptic ointments on hand. Use some leverage. The wall by the john should serve. Brace your leg against it, have your wife grab a hold of you, then give a mighty big push-off from the wall. That should unstick her, and how. If that doesn't work, Plan B is to call the paramedics.
> Best of Luck to You, Mama Lopp

Well, there you have a sample of Mama's homespun wisdom. Personally, I could never tell whether he was joking or not. But then again, I'm convinced neither could any of the people he dispensed his suspect advice to. It's a good thing this kind of informal internet chit-chat didn't constitute legal negligence. Not yet, anyway.

As I was mulling this over, a high pitched shriek came from somewhere in the flat, rattling Joe and me. "What was that?" I asked.

"Teffer?" He looked to me and I to him. Wordlessly, we dashed from the den. We found Teffer standing on a chair in the kitchen, whimpering in terror.

"Teffer, what is it? Pull yourself together, man!" Joe ordered his doorman cum butler cum manservant.

"R-r- r-roach," Teffer stuttered and pointed to the baseboard below the sink.

"Oh, it's just a cockroach," I said with a laugh.

"*Uh-uh, you say*," Joe hissed, "not in this flat. We are cockroach free."

"Well, other than this one, maybe we are," I was somewhat flip, but I just then noticed how deadly serious Joe had become. He stooped down and gasped, when the cockroach scuttled half a foot or so.

"Hello, my *leetle* friend," he said in a voice which was a mix of Peter Lorre and Bart Simpson. "Stan, fetch me the Raid."

"I'm afraid I can't do that, Joe."

"*Wha-a-a-t?*" He drew it out in utter surprise.

"I'm not at all comfortable assisting you in exterminating another life form," I explained as reasonably as I could.

"What are you, a Quaker now?" He seemed to be more dismissive than anything, as if I changed my beliefs like clothes.

"No, I am not, though I do share their general pacifist world view."

"At least it's not the bloody Branch Davidians or some other kook cult," he growled.

"You know, some faiths believe the reason killing other life forms is wrong is because the soul of a deceased person has taken up residence in that creature."

"I'm well aware of that, Stanley," he retorted crossly. "Are you trying to school me today? Lurn me mah lesuns?" He asked this last in an illiterate sounding voice, and a pretty good one at that. "I'm quite versed in matters of religion and divinity." In other words, he'd viewed numerous hours of the subject matter on PBS.

"No, I--," I began.

"It's not like I take pleasure in pulling the wings off of flies."

"But--," I tried again, but he cut me short once more.

"Spare me the holier than thou claptrap. Look at it from another angle, Stan. Who would really want to be a cockroach, hmm?" I could only shake my head. "Exactly. A pretty damned ugly existence I'd say, and so would you. Therefore, by killing said cockroach, I'd be putting the poor soul out of its misery, and possibly ushering it on to a new and better reincarnation as something more suitable than a filthy cockroach, wouldn't you agree?" I nodded hesitantly. This was so Joe, no matter how much I wanted to disagree, he just had a way with his own peculiar brand of logic which could be so very persuasive. "In such a belief system as I've sketched, exterminators would be merely carrying out the tenets of their faith. Hell, the Orkin Man could well be considered a saint. Ha!"

I wanted to point out that history was replete with 'exterminators' who had trouble distinguishing between roaches and people, but, just then, Teffer whimpered and pointed once more. The roach was on the move again.

"Just hang tight." Joe said wearily, going to a small utility closet and rummaging around. Retrieving the can of roach spray, he came back to the sink and dropped to all fours, "Now then, where are you?" I wasn't about to help him, but the roach made its move, scuttling off along the baseboard. Joe scuttled after it, firing bursts of the poison as he went.

"Blast!" He swore.

"What's wrong?" I asked.

"He's escaped. Curse his disease carrying little carapace!" I couldn't help but smirk as Joe lumbered to his feet. He caught this, "Oh, that's the way. You won't find it so amusing, when you wake up with him in your bed."

I couldn't help it. At that point, I burst out laughing. Joe spluttered, "They bite, you know." At that, I laughed all the harder. He shook his head scornfully at me, "It's the age old battle between man and roach, and they intend to win. Maybe someday you'll wise up and join the fray ... on the right side." He gave me one last glare and strode from the kitchen.

The next day started us off at Ihop first thing in the morning. What should have been a relatively short and easy shop, turned into an all morning affair. I should've guessed what was coming, when Joe chose to starve himself the previous evening. Joe ran the servers and cooks ragged, as they struggled valiantly to keep every inch of the table's surface filled with food. He put away enough pancakes and bacon to feed a crew of starving deckhands. At his age and physical condition he was a coronary waiting to happen.

The staff of the restaurant nearly botched the whole deal, and would have wasted all their efforts, had they not managed to fulfill Joe's order for one of his favorites: BBQ scrambled eggs with diced ham and green peppers. This technically wasn't a fair test on which to grade the employees, since the item was not a regular feature on the menu. Yet, if the itch was upon him, Joe would downgrade anyone and everyone for the slightest cause. His was a detail stickler's way of thinking. I'd once seen him downgrade an entire KFC franchise because, when he was greeted in the drive-thru, he failed to hear a 'smile' in the voice of the poor kid who was taking his order over the intercom.

Fortunately, the Ihop crew were able to whip up that which Joe had requested. After only one bite, which elicited a "passable" from him, he called for the check to settle accounts. This was one of the lower tier shops where the agency would normally reimburse the Shopper up to $50, and Joe had used up every penny. Admittedly, he only took on these types of assignments if food were involved.

Mid-afternoon found us at a post office branch within easy walking distance from our rooms. After the Ihop marathon breakfast, we tied up a few loose ends for one of Joe's clients in a private investigation, and he was mailing the client the results. Joe had received his PI license at last. Lord knows he had put it off long enough. Now officially wearing two hats, he might not be the first, but he was certainly the foremost, MSPI in the world. Oh yes, I'd heard of a fellow from Belgium who thought he was hot stuff, but no one could hold a candle to my friend. In the two years of PI practice since, Joe has only had his license suspended once.

For my part, I try to portray the debacle, which led to his suspension, as nothing more than a comedy of errors. Perhaps debacle is too harsh a word for what ultimately went down, but Joe resolutely refused even to admit to any error on his part. A brief run down of the events are these:

Joe had been working a case in a purely PI capacity. Since the details of the case are not pertinent to what happened, I will withhold them here for the sake of brevity. Suffice it to say, it was a run of the mill case, and I was somewhat surprised Joe accepted it in the first place. In any event, Joe was accused of breaking and entering, at a Motel 6, and this is what led the authorities who monitor the PI industry to suspend his license, pending a formal hearing.

He was *not* charged by the police, though they were involved, but only peripherally. The entire matter was made even more embarrassing, by the fact that Joe had entered the wrong motel room. At the wrong motel. In entirely the wrong part of town. I ... was not along on the night in question, and to this day, Joe denies he made a mistake. Instead, he insists he was fed bogus information, and the person who passed it on to him is the real guilty party.

As to the accusation of breaking and entering, well, Joe is always quick to point out the thanklessness of a private dick's lot in life, considering they do many of the things that most others wouldn't stoop to do. In any event, he managed to be reinstated by the simple expedient of shifting the blame to a crowd of teens, who had rented a nearby room for purposes of throwing a kegger. I instantly disapproved of this ploy, but as Joe pointed out, they had been breaking the law anyway, with underage drinking, and as minors, they would only receive a slap on the wrist, as this would be viewed as drunken teenage high jinx.

Thankfully, this is just what happened. Short term probation and light community service in atonement. The teens had at first denied responsibility for the B & E, but in their inebriated states, they came to realize later, they couldn't be sure one of their party hadn't done it, and so, ultimately, they caved in and paved the way for the clearing of Joe's name. They really stood no chance. Even the most practiced rhetorician would be hard pressed to refute Joe, when he was in all-out accusation mode. A party of drunken teens were particularly doomed. However, though he was cleared and reinstated, his official record was not completely expunged of the incident. Something, I know, which niggled him still.

Joe finished his business with the postal clerk and we departed. Outside the entrance, a dirty, raggedy man was panhandling. Joe stopped to fish in his pocket and dumped a handful of change in the man's outstretched hand. We began to walk away, but were arrested by a voice behind us, which croaked in offended disbelief, "*Pennies?!* You cannot be serious?"

Joe turned around. "Sir," he said with stiff formality, "you are begging in front of a post office," as if that explained everything. "Come along, Stanley," and we began to walk away once more, but the beggar wasn't finished with us quite yet.

"*Hey Everybody!*" I heard him call out, "*That guy just gave me a bunch of pennies!*"

I began to look back, but Joe stopped me. "Eyes forward, Stan," he cautioned primly.

"*Can you believe that?!*" the vagrant continued ranting, "*What a Skinflint!*" I didn't turn my head, but from the corner of my eye, I could see people stopping and pointing at us, laughing.

"Keep walking, Stanley," Joe said, in a suddenly chipper tone.

"*Cheap Bastard!*" the beggar kept haranguing the passersby, "*You'd think it'd kill him to help a man down on his luck!*" The attention the man had drawn to us was such that I flushed with embarrassment, but not Joe. He had a small smile on his fleshy lips and carried himself proudly erect, even twirling his cane and tapping it on the concrete in rhythm with his stride. He was like the Music Man. You'd think he'd won a great prize or something. Well, that was Joe, always calm under fire. He never rattled under pressure, appearing to all as if he hadn't a care in the world, and nothing whatsoever was amiss. Because in his mind, you see, nothing was. God, how I admired the man!

The incident with the beggar seemed to whet his appetite, even given his gargantuan Ihop feast, so we purchased a couple of hot dogs from a vendor, and sat munching on a bench in the park near our building. We were both quiet, the only sounds were our gobblings. I noticed that Joe was staring at a fixed spot and chomping, his jowls jiggling vigorously. I followed the line of his gaze, and realized it could only have been aimed at a young couple frolicking in the grass under the shade of a tree. The young man was tickling his young woman friend, who was giggling and playfully resisting, while exposing far too much butt crack.

"Joe?"

"Hmff?" He grunted through bites, never averting his eyes.

"What are you looking at?"

Now he did look away, "What? Oh nothing, nothing." My friend was a keen observer of human nature, I just hoped he wasn't becoming a dirty old man.

"Excuse me, sirs," a voice cut in. We both looked at the source, it was an elderly vagrant. I had noticed the rumpled, dirty clothing and wild gray beard snoring on a nearby bench, when we first arrived. Yet, I had not seen him awaken, and approach us.

"I'm sorry, all out of change," Joe said with forced amiability.

"Sir, if I may--," the vagrant began, butJoe didn't let him finish.

"Here," he thrust his half eaten hot dog at the man, "take it."

"It's not money or food I'm after," the old fellow explained. "It's just that you look powerfully familiar. Like someone I use to know, but haven't seen in many a year now."

"I doubt very much it was a mutual acquaintance," Joe came close to openly scoffing, and was not entirely successful in concealing a haughty disbelief at the man's assertion.

"His name was Archibald Lopp," the old vagrant continued, oblivious. Joe gaped, eyes wide, and he froze like that. "Archie Numbers we use to call him."

"Joe," I waved a hand before his bulging eyes, "wasn't that your grandfather's name?" The name sounded familiar. I tried dredging up what little I had heard about him from my memory.

Joe slowly nodded. "*Ye-e-e-es*," he breathed the word, not quite speaking it aloud, and, for all the world, sounding like Charles Foster Kane pining for Rosebud, when he uttered, "Archie Numbers."

"Whatever happened to him?" I asked. It was the old bench bedder who answered,

"No one knows. He just up and vanished. It was 1957. I recall it very well. My memory's goin', but I remember the year, because he disappeared right at the time the Pigeon King was due to reappear."

"The what?" I asked, thinking perhaps I had misheard him.

"Ain't'cha ever heard o' the Pigeon King, young feller?" he gave me an appraising look, before continuing, "Well, now, come to think on it, only us street folks are ever in tune with that sort o' thing."

"Thank you, good sir, and what is your name?" Joe had suddenly sprung to life and burst to his feet, looking a touch wild about the eyes.

"They call me Grizzle-Gray Mo."

Joe grasped his hand, and pumped it vigorously a couple of times, "Pleased to meet you, Mo. Here, take this, eat it." He handed over the hot dog. Mo hesitantly took it, looking confused. He scratched his matted head. "By the looks of it, you could use it," Joe dug his wallet from his hip pocket and pulled out some bills, handing them over, "and maybe get yourself a roof over your head for a change, eh?" The old vagrant was taken aback and stumbled for something to say.

"Why, thank you, sir," he came up with at last, "but who're you?" Joe proferred his business card. Mo scanned it briefly. A hush fell over the encounter, before, "So you *are* related to old Archie?"

"Come along, Stanley," Joe, for whatever his reasons, chose to ignore the question.

As we were walking away, the old man called out to us, "Y'know, I only brought it up because your grandfather disappeared while searching for the Pigeon King. And the Pigeon King is set to return," I looked back, the old vagrant took a bite of the hot dog, then said around his full mouth what sounded like, *"soon."*

Joe and I didn't return to our flat right away, instead, opting for a quiet booth in the diner which occupied a corner of the ground floor in our building. I took a sip of coffee from my mug. Joe's sat steaming and unattended before him.

"I've always thought you resembled your grandmother, personally," I remarked, for something to say, if nothing else. "Of course, I don't recall ever seeing a picture of your grandfather." Seriously, how many Sydney Greenstreet look-alikes could there be in the world at any one time? Of either gender?

"All photos were destroyed by my grandmother, in a fit of jilted rage, I'm sure you understand." I could only nod.

"Yet, what are the odds your grandparents shared such a striking similarity?" I asked.

"It's not like they were identical twins, Stan. Though there were resemblances, only in more minute ways, which a casual observer might not grasp the significance of right off the bat."

"And yet they stamped you rather strongly, it would seem."

"That's the way with the Lopps, Stan. In some instances opposites attract ... only not with us. In our case similarities seek one another out like iron filings to a magnet," he explained. I needed a moment to digest this, as with most things regarding Loppiana.

"Joe, why did you want to get away from that old homeless guy so quickly?" I finally asked, casually, trying to draw him out. He had been quite distant since the encounter.

"Was I that obvious?" Joe asked, with a rueful smile. I nodded. "Powerful emotions, Stan, powerful memories.

"Would you care to share?"

Joe shook his head regretfully, "You should have seen how my grandfather's disappearance tore up my grandmother, her believing he had run off with another woman. Ate at her soul, it did. She never recovered fully from that."

"What do you believe?"

"I never believed it," he shook his head again, this time emphatically.

"But you seem to have an opinion? A belief?"

"It's only now dawned on me, with what Mo told us. I've certainly carried the pieces of the puzzle around with me all these years, but was simply unable to put them in their natural places, to make it all fit correctly."

"And?"

"Stan, don't you see?" Joe said, almost plaintively. "My grandfather disappeared while searching for the Pigeon King."

"Why would he be searching for some guy who styled himself the Pigeon King, Joe? If such a person existed, what was he to your grandfather? As Mo said, this is a matter of interest only to the homeless. You've never intimated that your grandfather had struck upon such hard times."

"Stan, he wasn't --," Joe began, but I charged on, heedless.

"Was there an opium craze going around at the time?" I asked, innocently enough, I thought, "Oh no, maybe that was the era of *Reefer Madness*?" I was mulling this over out loud, but more to myself than Joe.

"Stanley," Joe's voice turned stern, "consider this a warning."

"Just saying, Joe." I continued blithely on. "Any history of mental illness or sanitariums in your family tree?"

"Oh, you know, the odd electric shock treatment has certainly struck my family's tree from time to time. Hmmm," he rubbed his jaw thoughtfully, "may want to throw in a lobotomy, as well. Dear old Aunt Alma, never was the same, but she sure could play a mean kazoo after that. I think it had something to do with the tonal vibrations of the instrument upon that part of her brain which was affected by the procedure." He caught himself and turned serious once more, wagging a finger at me, "Stanley, you've been warned!"

I changed tack, slightly, "Didn't your grandfather run numbers for the local mobsters? Thus the nickname, Archie 'Numbers'. I vaguely recall you mentioning it, once. Wouldn't that be more likely to explain his disappearance, being involved with the criminal underworld? Cement shoes, and whatnot? Can't quite figure out what he was doing hanging out with this city's down and out bum community, though."

"Now Stanley, I want you to cease and desist this instant!"

"What?" I was taken aback by his vehemence. He seemed to be reading more into my line of questioning than I had ever intended.

"This fancy of yours which pegs all of my relatives as having been either degenerates or ne'er-do-wells."

"I think nothing of the sort," I protested. "You do have a very colorful lineage, of course, but I've never viewed them as you suggest. Well, not all the time," I was forced to add, for the sake of honesty. "Look, let's just drop it. Obviously, the connection between your missing grandfather and this 'Pigeon King' is a very real one in your mind. I respect that." Did I have a choice? "But tell me, who is the Pigeon King, anyway?"

Joe looked around warily at the other diners, then leaned forward over the table and lowered his voice, "Not *who*, Stanley, rather *what*." He lost me with that. "There isn't much known about the Pigeon King, precisely, because not many people even know he exists," he said, darting a glance about him again before continuing. "The Pigeon King's lore is a closely guarded secret within the transient community. He's a powerful totem for those people, one they seek to protect at all costs. I don't even know all that much about it, but I do remember some stories told to me by my grandfather, when I was still but a young lad."

"Let's see if we can clear this up," I was trying to make sense of it all. Call me dense, but I was having a hard time following what he was saying, "Is this Pigeon King, then, some kind of a leader to the homeless peoples. He would have to be pretty old, if he were even still alive. If he's *of* the homeless, well, they generally don't live overly long, given their lifestyle choice," I rambled on, letting my thoughts drift one to the other, connect-the-dots style. "Do you know whether the 'position' is passed on from one generation to the next, like a succession, as the royal title would suggest? Or is a new one elected when the old one dies?" I was getting quite caught up in the whole yarn, which surprised *me* most of all.

"No-no, Stanley, you misunderstand," and here he lowered his voice even further. "The Pigeon King is just what his name describes: a pigeon. But, seemingly, unlike any ordinary pigeon."

I'll say it right now. Here, he not only lost me, but nearly caused me to laugh disrespectfully in his face. "A pigeon? You're not serious, surely?" My interest waned as quickly as it peaked. Who gave a damn about a flying, feathered rat?

"Stan, as I said, the Pigeon King is no ordinary pigeon."

"OK, I'll play along. How so?"

"Why, he's the king of all the pigeons," Joe read my puzzled expression, and added, "He's *huge*, Stan. The largest pigeon ever. At least three times the size of even the largest normal pigeon," I leaned back in my seat, crossed my arms on my chest, and fixed him with a look that said, 'I don't believe a word you're saying', and let him have at it. I was already mentally humming a catchy little number as distraction. "Normal *male* pigeons, by the way. For some reason females just don't measure up in terms of size or pretty plumage in the animal kingdom, unlike the human world. Were you aware of that?"

I skipped his question, and went straight to picking apart the ludicrous story he had just spun. "Uh, Joe, I'm not familiar with the lifespan of a pigeon, but from what Grizzle-Gray Mo said, this Pigeon King would have to be over fifty years old by now."

"As I've said, this is no ordinary pigeon," he was insistent. "Remember, he is regarded as a totem. Like many other tribal peoples through the ages, who have adopted various animal guides and such for their magic or symbolic attributes, in the belief such traits can be conferred onto humans, so too with the transient community." Great, now we were getting into ancient tribal magic.

"Well, a pigeon is certainly fitting," I allowed, trying to keep the skepticism from my voice. I most definitely didn't want to sound as if I was belittling Joe's interest, even though the seeming supernatural turn this thing was taking gave me second thoughts. As well as third, fourth and fifth. While it is true that my interests, and readers of some of our more otherworldly adventures can attest to this, ran more towards the esoteric, even I wasn't buying this one. Surprisingly, Joe appeared to have swallowed the hook, the big beluga. What with his devotion to the twin powers of deductive reasoning and manufactured illusion, it made his sudden infatuation with this all the more confounding.

"Alright, so back to your grandfather," I prodded, trying to keep in mind what was at the heart of all this: Joe's missing grandfather.

"He obviously disappeared at the time of the last return of the Pigeon King in '57," he noted. "Mo pinned the date, and my memory is clear on that point, so I concur."

"Mobsters?" I threw it out again.

He leaned back and shrugged, "Who can say? Yes, it was well known in our family that he did some small-time work for the local mob, so it's certainly a possibility, I'll concede," he sighed. That was something, anyway. Then continued, "But it's also damned curious that the royal bird's name surfaces in his disappearance as well." He frowned, tugging on an earlobe.

"What are you going to do?" I asked.

"Investigate."

Joe spent the following day searching online databases, as well as his own extensive reference materials, for any further information on the Pigeon King. Meeting with scant success, other than a brief mention or two in collections of urban legends, we took ourselves the next morning to the main branch of the metropolitan library. It wasn't that Joe couldn't run the kind of deep web searches he would have the librarians perform for him, from the comfort of his own study, no. And it wasn't as if he had an official shop with the library either. Considering his occupation, having people jump to his instructions was second nature to him. Being waited on so much of one's life could serve to turn one spoiled and jaded, though I doubted this effect on Joe.

"Stanley, what's taking them so long?" He complained to me, looking up from the microfilm viewer in the reference section. He was scanning some old newspaper accounts from the time of his grandfather's disappearance.

"Not sure, Joe, I'll go check." As it turned out the librarians Joe had given the scent to, and aimed in the direction of the trail he wished them to follow, found little, hardly any more than Joe had already. Aside from a few mentions of a mythical nature concerning his quarry, they came across only faint whispers which would pop up from time to time on internet message boards and in forums whose primary themes or topics of discussion usually had nothing whatever to do with the purported Pigeon King. These postings were uniformly cryptic. Indeed, Joe had spent the previous evening trying to make contact with these mysterious posters himself, but just as soon as one appeared on a random thread, to which Joe would respond, they would melt away and disappear as completely and anonymously as they had appeared.

Joe was of the opinion these posters were transients themselves passing along coded information to other members of the transient community, to whom Joe must have stuck out like a sore thumb. Or rather, like a member of the 'homed' community. And unfortunately, Joe hadn't the key to decipher the code and this lack was made glaring in his posted responses. It should not be supposed that the homeless were not internet savvy, simply because they didn't own computers. Far from it. As Joe and I exited the library I could spot them by their dozens, either using the public computers the library offered, or loitering about waiting for their reserved appointment time to arrive.

We did receive one added piece of information not previously uncovered, gleaned from the memoir/ancestry of a local man who's name, even now, escapes me. In it he made brief reference to what could have possibly been the Pigeon King, and linking the great bird's appearance to mysterious disappearances down through the years. Joe took this added twist rather grimly, which forced me to try and allay his current obsession with the Pigeon King and his missing grandfather, by pointing out the cheap spiral-bound packaging of the manuscript and its obvious homemade construction. The man was clearly a local nut job, whose life story the library had accepted and stocked in their genealogical collection, as a community service. Yet, Joe wasn't buying my line. His lips remained pursed and his forehead creased with frown lines.

"What now, Joe?" I asked on the front steps of the building.

"I believe we've exhausted the written records route," he said. "We're going to have to acquire some human intel. Something I'm uniquely qualified to gather," he added, not entirely immodestly.

"Where from?"

"Not so far off as you might imagine." He pointed the tip of his cane to a spot where a transient, if his manner of dress were any indication, sat on a bench in a small park adjacent to the library, feeding pigeons, of all things.

"Let's see what we can get him to divulge," Joe said, starting off down the steps.

"If anything," I remarked, going with him.

"At this point any tidbit of additional information we can get will be beneficial," he said. "These people know more than they're willing to tell, as evidenced by the online forums. There's a virtual bum intelligence service transmitting more secrets than the CIA, MI6, or successor to the KGB combined." I rather doubted that. Joe continued, "They're global in scope, as well, Stanley, and far from stupid. With free access to all the knowledge the public libraries of the world have to offer, and internet access to pass it on instantaneously ... why there's a multinational 'nation' of people whose activities the sheltered world knows nothing about. The fluidity of the transient lifestyle only aids this. And the Pigeon King is Exhibit A of this. *You* had certainly never heard of him before, any more than so many others."

As Joe spoke, we crossed the distance to where the man was tossing small debris and crumbs from a paper bag to the crowd of pigeons round about him. He was talking as well, whether to himself or to others on nearby benches I couldn't immediately tell.

"Time, time, you got the time?" he said. It took me a few moments to attune my ears to what he was saying, as his voice was somewhat slurred, though I think not with drink or drugs, rather with madness.

"What?" A yuppy female on an adjacent bench asked, clearly annoyed. The man had a queer way of looking at a person, yet, seeming not to be looking at them all at the same time, making it difficult to determine just whom he was addressing, not to mention what he was saying. As I said, madness.

"Time?" The yuppy asked. The vagrant bobbed his head from side to side. I couldn't tell if that were a yes or no. She glanced at her watch, apparently taking his bobbing as an affirmative, "It's three-thirty."

But he was already babbling on about something else. I could only make out, "where," from his constant stream of rambles, and presumed he was asking for directions. Either that or something of a more personal nature, which seems to be what the yuppy woman concluded, as she hurriedly gathered up her bags and departed without another word.

"Where's *blah-blah-blah*," was all I managed to decipher from his next utterance, and this directed at an elderly woman with a walker, parked on another bench alongside a young boy in shirt sleeves and tie.

"What?" The young boy responded in some surprise.

"Where's tha' *blah-blah-blah*?" the vagrant spouted off again. This time it clearly seemed to be a question. Joe and I moved closer, and stopped to observe from a vantage point some few yards behind the man on the bench.

"What do you want?!" the boy blurted, his panic rising. The vagrant repeated himself, again somewhat garbled. "I don't know," the boy replied tremulously. It was pretty clear to me the man was seeking directions, to where I couldn't say any more than the boy. Again, more rambling, and the boy's voice rose in return, *"I don't know,"* panic having fully taken hold.

"What's wrong? What's the matter?" Now the elderly woman stepped in, her own anxiety rising in response to the boy's.

"I don't know what he wants!" The boy wailed.

"What do you want?" The woman demanded of the vagrant.

"I jus' wanna know where Brubaker Street is," the vagrant was clearer now. My hearing, and that of the woman and boy, must have adjusted to his manner of speaking.

"I don't know where it is!" The boy cried.

"He doesn't know where it is. Now, leave us alone!" the woman shouted. Grabbing the boy's arm, she wrenched him from the bench, collared the walker with her other hand, and they fled.

"Thank goodness he's a talker," Joe murmured. "Let me handle this. I have copious experience dealing with these types." If his experience was anything like his handling of the other homeless I'd observed him interact with, it would be a wonder if the man stuck around long enough for us to get anything out of him but curses.

"A word with you, my good man," Joe said, tapping the vagrant in a friendly fashion on the shoulder with his cane as we approached from behind.

"Eh? What, what?" He whipped his head from left to right in an effort to see who had accosted him. We moved around to face him in front of the bench.

"We're in search of information only, my friend," Joe assured him.

"I don't know you," he appraised us, shaking his head finally. "Never seen ya before. Look-see, I'm a friendly fellow, sure enough, but you two's no friends o' mine."

"I'll pay," Joe jingled a pocketful of change. The bum laughed. "Very well," Joe allowed, "how about a nice, new crisp dollar bill?"

"Do I look like I'm eight years old?" was the snide reply. "You gonna *ooh-aah* me with gewgaws an' doodads then, mister?" He snorted into his whiskers.

"The whole world's a wise guy, isn't it?" Joe said sotto voce, then groaned slightly, and cut to the chase on the negotiation. "How much?"

"Depends on what yer needin' ta know."

"We seek information on the Pigeon King." The man's eyes instantly widened. I took this as a warning sign, but Joe did not, and continued obliviously on. "Anything you may know, however trivial it may seem, I assure you it will not be to me. In particular," Joe put a hand on the back of the bench and leaned closer for confidentiality, took one sniff of the man and quickly straightened back up, though he lowered his voice, "we seek the most likely date, time, and place of his reappearance."

The bum sat absolutely immobile for the space of five or six heartbeats, then suddenly snapped out of his trance, hastily gathered up his grungy rucksack, and sprang to his feet with surprising speed and agility, making to hurry off.

Joe adopted a distasteful look, as his hand shot out to grab the other's arm, "Wait!" The bum shook him off, scurrying away.

"Have ta go," he mumbled, "don't know nothin'."

"We're friends of Grizzle-Gray Mo," Joe hastily added, taking a couple of steps after him.

"Don't know no one by that name," the bum called back over his shoulder.

"Here," Joe said, taking out his billfold and removing a business card, "contact me if you hear anything." Well, that was patently absurd, I thought, watching the man scuttle into a crowd and disappear from sight.

"That ... could have been handled with more tact," I suggested cautiously.

Joe shook his head, "No, Stan, these people are great keepers of secrets. To get them to divulge fully, would require a good deal of time and a torture chamber of scientifically, diabolical cunning," I caught my breath, only hoping he wasn't planning on going *there*, "neither of which I have the patience or inclination to invest," I let it out in relief.

"That man appeared more fearful, than anything," I noted.

Joe squinted, nodding slowly, "Perhaps, perhaps," he paused, pinching his lower lip, deep in thought. "Come along, Stanley, there are more where he came from." Sadly, from a societal health standpoint, he was correct.

Yet all of our approaches to the homeless citizens of our community produced much the same results: a hasty denial of any knowledge, and a rather frantic scurrying into any crowd or up any alley at hand. We called it a day after half a dozen of these futile encounters. Clearly, the vagabond volk were more loyal to their own community than any other.

Please recall, it was not in Joe's nature to give up the chase when he had the scent of the hunt fresh in his nostrils, or even if he only thought he did, that is. The next morning I found him rummaging through the rags bin in our dust closet.

"Stanley," he told me, "if we ever hope to come into possession of the required information, we are going to have to eat like them, drink like them, talk like them, think like them," he paused for a second, considering, then added, "shoot, shit and sleep like them." He lost me there. Sometimes I wondered if Joe didn't fade briefly in and out of his own life on occasion. "We're going to have to *become them,*" he finished with great vigor and urgency.

His plan, as he unfolded it to me, was to dress like mangy vagrants and hit the streets slumming with the homeless. Or, as he put it, "hangin' with tha' homies an jivin' for tha' chitchat." I would not have given us very good odds of pulling it off, if not for Joe's extensive experience in the theater, as well as intendant expertise in the art of make-up and costume. He would play the leading role, as always, I, a mere bit character.

We outfitted ourselves in old, ragged slacks, me in a holey undershirt and zippered hoody, while Joe chose an Oxford style shirt with frayed collar, over which he wore a moth-eaten Cardigan sweater. He hadn't shaved, forbidding me from doing so as well, and looked like a skid row grandpa. And, most definitely, not one you'd want to look after the kids. But there was something missing.

I mentioned this to Joe, and he replied, "Ah, that something is none other than dirt, for the most part. There are a few other minor tweaks as well, but, we are, quite simply, too clean truly to pass the litmus test for vagrancy. You haven't applied deodorant, have you?" I shook my head. "Good, the smell test is a key hurdle which must be cleared. I suggest we spend some small time on the treadmill before we go out in public. Let's let our sweat glands ripen us up a bit. Teffer!" he called.

Our doorman stuck his head around a corner, "You called, Sir?"

"Would you be so good as to fetch the potted rhododendrum from my den and bring it to the kitchen?"

"Yes, Sir."

We were waiting in the kitchen when Teffer returned, lugging a huge potted plant, struggling to keep from dropping it. "*Back*," he squeaked, face red and strained from the effort, "*my back*."

"Over by the sink will do," Joe casually gave directions. "Now, Stanley, we apply the make-up."

He scooped some dirt from the pot and began rubbing it into his face, appraising the application in a lighted mirror he had brought from his spacious wardrobe closet, what he termed his 'dressing room'. This was professional stuff and Joe had all the tools of the trade.

"Go ahead, Stan, dig in and make sure to grind it into your clothes as well. Teffer," he caught our doorman who was just in the act of slinking from the kitchen almost doubled over, "best lay some newspaper down, we're liable to create quite a mess."

We were about dirtying ourselves up for some minutes, Joe directing me whenever he noticed a patch of my clothing not soiled suitably. "I would have preferred actual commercial make-up, but there is simply no way we would go without detection. In order to take on a role fully, one must authentically get in and *stay* in character."

Once sufficiently filthy, Joe swatted my hands away, when I reached towards the faucet to wash them, purely out of habit. He wagged an admonishing finger, "The dirt under your nails is exquisite, best not mess with perfection. Now, let's get some *booooooze*." He took down from the common liquor cabinet (he kept the good stuff in his study and den), a bottle of undistinguished whiskey, with which he plied his less illustrious guests. Then, much to my surprise, he began splashing me with a shower of whiskey, I soon reeked of it. I tried to dodge out of the way, reflexively, but he stayed my movement, "Stand still, too much is going on the newspapers and not enough on you." He had emptied much of the contents on me already. "Here, gargle with what's left, but don't swallow, mind you. Rinse and spit. You can't hold your liquor, and I want you with your wits about you."

For himself, he took down a pint of gin and began dabbing it to his pulse points, as if it were perfume. "Why aren't you bathing in it, like you did me?" I asked him, a trifle offended.

"Because your character is an out of control alcoholic, who can't hold a job, after being kicked out of his home by the wife and children he violently abused. You have repeatedly alternated between rehab, jail, and halfway houses, and would be smoking meth and offering your ass for pocket change, if it weren't for me. My character, on the other hand, is a formerly distinguished college professor, who lost his tenure and was evicted from the ivory tower due to academic politics, and has never been able to get back on his feet at this stage of his life."

"What happened?" I asked in full sympathy, getting caught up in the background story. Joe was a master storyteller.

"Oh, you know, it involved accusations of plagiarism concerning some medieval manuscripts, which had never been previously translated, much less published. They were accusations only," he said with some heat, drawing on his character. "Nothing was ever formally proven, but I was quietly forced from my position, with less than adequate compensation. I do have a wee bit of a drinking problem," to which he tipped his bottle of gin vertically and guzzled half of it, before recorking it and smacking his lips in satisfaction. I noticed he hadn't spit. "But, I've taken you under my wing out of the goodness of my own heart. Also, you're a good do-boy. Now then, let's hit the treadmill, ten to fifteen minutes each, and then we hit the bricks."

So it was, that fifteen minutes later we were just about to exit the flat when he stopped me, before I could open the door, "Remember, Stan, always stay in character. If you get confused about your part, just follow my lead. I'm professionally trained, after all. Never succumb to stage fright, it will wreck your career." With that final piece of advice, he rolled his great head around on his neck, then threw it back and climbed the octave scales with, *"La-la-la-la-la-la-la."* He went up and down the scales a couple of times, then, "Curtain's up very soon now," he said, "let's both break some legs," and we set out.

A quick dress rehearsal took place on the sidewalks and in the alley entrances, leading to the first of the principal destinations Joe had identified as 'optimal targets'. These were, as it turned out, the cardboard boxes and dumpster residences of his quarry.

"I wish to corner them in their own homes," he had explained, adding, "bait them in their lairs. People are much more likely to let things slip when they feel most comfortable, and that is usually on their own turf. Besides, if that doesn't work, a dash of threat of encroachment may serve the same purpose. If they're too busy protecting the fort, as it were, we may get lucky by the distraction. A man's home is his castle, after all, and it is only there that one can rummage through another's medicine cabinet, and uncover the Valium and genital warts ointment they would so like to hide."

Our progress was relatively brisk. Whenever we encountered one of the transient community, we would stop for a brief exchange or to bum a smoke. Joe desired to run through the script, free flowing as it was, just to make sure I had my lines and delivery down before the real performance began. It was his concern that should we, meaning me, slip up and be uncovered, whilst grousing for Pigeon King info, word would spread faster than our feet could shamble (in character) along the homeless wino-vine, thus making our task practically impossible.

Our first stop turned out to be a small commune squatting under a highway overpass. The cardboard structures were converted packing containers and the like, with wooden pallet slat floors, tied together with bits of rope. It was all rather ingeniously done, I had to admit. There were maybe a dozen residents, mostly lying about. A couple were boiling something in an old pot over a small fire. We were introduced to the woman who ruled over the community, shortly after making our entrance. She came rolling out of one of the cardboard structures, mussing herself and proclaiming her midday nap was "beauty sleep time," then immediately began ordering the other members of the community around with all the imperiousness of a queen bee.

Going by the name, Molly Dolly Sticks, she was anything but. A stick, that is. She was easily the fattest homeless person I'd ever seen, and she must have seen a kindred gorging spirit in Joe, for she took to him at once. Joe introduced himself as Professor Ernesto Mackleberry, bowing over her hand to deliver a gallant kiss to her ham hock knuckles, which elicited the giggles of a silly girl. He introduced me as Hank Zipp, and she'd given me a sympathetic look and a pat on the head, when Joe explained my severe DT's as the reason for my refusal of the gruel I had been offered. I'd completely forgotten Joe's stern admonition never to refuse the offer of hospitality or food. It would be a dead giveaway, since beggars cannot be choosers.

Joe accepted the dubious chow in my stead, and shared his bottle of spirits with Molly Dolly in return. Watching Joe shovel down the gruel was bad enough, it even aided my DTing act by causing me to blanch and shudder. But I did so hope he wasn't going to drink from his bottle after Molly had. Her mouth housed the worst looking set of teeth I'd ever encountered up close. Yet, *Ugh*, he did. Knowing Joe, he would never allow an insignificance such as oral disease to stand in the way of a performance.

"So, Molls, tell me," Molls? Joe had a knack for becoming easily familiar with a person once he gained their confidence. Very few people had the skill set to pull it off successfully *and* consistently. Those that did generally could not be trusted, however. Politicians come readily to mind, and any kind of successful salesman. "what's your estimation of time and place of the PK's return?" PK? Now he was *really* being familiar.

"Hrrm, as to His Majesty's return, Professor," she began by way of reply. Evidently they *all* took the oversized fowl seriously. And yet, what struck me, was the seeming utter impossibility of this belief in the mythical bird. I mean, this was the second person who had spoken of the PK (to follow Joe's example), as if they actually believed it existed. Mass delusion, plain and simple, as far as I was concerned. It had happened before. These delusional fits were often characterized by imitative behavior, easily enough achieved in such a tightly organized society as the vagrant underground, where outsiders were vigilantly guarded against.

I didn't even need Joe to tell me this, though I had probably picked it up from him, during one of his self-assigned, intermittent psychological internships, where he would set out for days on end to just observe people going about their daily lives. Sometimes he was prone to overstep the bounds of propriety in privacy, but really only skirted the perimeter of a Peeping Tom's territory, without ever venturing fully into that icky realm. He had no formal training, but this kind of study greatly aided him in his professional career. He also had contacts at the local loony bin, who provided him access to observe their patients capering madly about and painting with urine and feces. These little jaunts, regrettably, I suspect are more for entertainment purposes than clinical study. What can you do? We all have our quirks.

Of course, the other thing that was revealed by her response was that Joe's scheme of blending into the vagrant underground was succeeding. She showed no hesitation in acknowledging the existence of the PK, as she saw it, and the first to do so since Grizzle-Gray Mo, "opinions vary, mind you," she continued, "but the best figures I've been quoted to date puts the Royal Return and Procession anywhere from one to three days from now." Procession? Just how much more absurd could this wild goose chase become? Still, I kept my peace.

Joe, on the other hand, was gleefully rubbing his hands together, "And as to the *where*, dear lady?" He did that saccharine coo which always made me want to wretch.

She simpered. I was sure she had developed a crush on him. Ye gads, this could quickly spin out of control. The thought did occur to me that, if I vomited, I would be keeping very much in character.

"Well, now, as to that," she took a swig of the gin and wiped her mouth with the back of a dirty hand, "my money's on one of three places."

Joe-- excuse me, the professor, leaned forward expectantly. "Yes, yes," he nearly salivated, and wasn't to be disappointed.

"The small park by the old Woolworth's store, the spot on the corner of Main and Chimney where the guy with the taco cart always is, or the bank of the creek by the bicycle path just off Epoch Avenue closest to Fairweather neighborhood."

"Aaahh," he sat back with a satisfied sigh. "Now we're getting somewhere."

"What's that?" Molly Dolly asked quickly.

"Nothing, nothing, dear lady," Joe beamed at her, she simpered again, and I nearly retched again. Joe hastily made our excuses for departing so suddenly. Molly implored him to come back anytime for a 'visit', complete with a wink and a leer, as we made our farewells. It was too much like the Nina affair. Anytime a treacherous trollop made advances on Joe, I confess I exhibit the same reaction. It was the protective mother need in me, after all. We all have it, even if we won't all admit it.

Our next stop was adjacent to a food distribution warehouse, around back at the loading dock, to be exact. There, we came across two fellows, Ferris McCoy and Slammy Juniper they were called, who were engaged in a spot of dumpster diving. Joe quickly earned their trust by helping them fish some packages of lunch meats, whose sell by date had long since expired, from the dumpster. The data they provided correlated well with what Molly Dolly had told us. They gave Joe a couple of locations close by the areas Molly had named, and their date ranges were within her parameters, as well, with Ferris and Slammy predicting two days and three days hence, respectively. Or was it Slammy at two days, and Ferris at three? Well, no matter. We bid farewell, before they could offer to share any of their rancid turkey or bologna with us, and sought out further leads.

Surprisingly, to me, but seemingly not to Joe, every other vagrant we spoke with gave us virtually the same answers. The same general areas of town in the same three day window. It was all adding up rather quickly, and tightly, which is what made me nervous. I was actually beginning to believe in the cockamamy thing, Joe couldn't have been more pleased.

An hour later, and Joe had just finished crossly rebuffing a man trying to bum a smoke, where we had parked ourselves at the entrance to an alley. Of course, we had been doing the same thing ourselves for much of the day.

"Damned cigarette moochers," he groused, "worse than money moochers." For some unexplained reason he had always held the smoke moochers in particular contempt, in fact they literally made him angry. He tended to ignore things like that when the shoe was on the other foot … *his* foot. I diverted his attention to the remarkable similarities in the information we had spent the day obtaining, and from such diverse sources.

"It doesn't surprise me in the least," he remarked. "In fact, it's just as I suspected. And these sources are not as diverse as you might think. They're all part of the same community network, therefore, they all know what's goin' down, as they say."

"Yet, not exactly the where or the when," I pointed out.

"Most likely, no one knows for certain, but the one's we've spoken with have narrowed down our stakeout positions quite nicely." he said, then added more fiercely, "We're close to finding the truth of this little mystery, Stan!"

"This Pigeon King, if it exists, isn't going to bring your grandfather back," I noted, a hint of sadness in my voice. Joe took it for condescension apparently.

"I never claimed he would do anything of the sort," he shot back haughtily, then softened his tone. "I realize you don't really believe in the Pigeon King, and, my word, I'm not sure I can fully credit it either." This was news. I perked up. "But, there's still something not quite right here. Remember what that little mouse told us outside the plasma donation center?" Wrong rodent, I thought. She struck me more as a rat. I could go with weasel, but that would have been too high a praise.

So I said, "About disappearances?"

"Precisely, and it was more than just my grandfather. Others have gone missing as well, if our little mouse is to be believed." She wasn't. Appearing rather faint, her stare and her speech were vague, as if they'd pumped her well nigh dry. "We've come across this information before, remember?"

"With the homeless," I pointed out, "I'm afraid this may be all too common. They are rootless, coming and going as they please."

"But there appear to be historical spikes in the rate of disappearances when the Pigeon King returns," he insisted.

"Joe, almost none of the people we interviewed were even alive fifty years ago, the last time the Pigeon King purportedly returned. Yet, we heard tales about returns going back well over a hundred years. It's all pretty far-fetched, if you ask me."

"Well, I'm not asking you, Stanley," he retorted primly. "But, from what I interpreted, perusing all the old newspaper microfilm at the library, taking it at fifty year intervals, which seems to be his appearance cycle, the accounts very much meshed with what we've heard with our own ears."

"Joe, you can't have gone back very far."

"Late Eighteenth century, Stanley. Mark it down," he licked one finger and swiped it in the air, indicating he'd scored a point. It was his way. "At least, that's how far back the oldest newspaper in the city dates to." I really had no idea our metropolis was that old. "No, the patterns are clear."

"Just as it's likely that a disappearance could have any number of explanations, all unrelated to the Pigeon King."

"I would merely ask that you keep something in mind in your haste to be dismissive," he said earnestly. "Even myths and legends contain elements of truth. The stories related to us today may sound like nothing more than garbled retellings of superstition and fairy tales, but the reality is that, while the details may have blurred with time and telling, the fundamental historical reality often remains. Thus, the human need for telling such tales, to pass on our past."

A sound, which began as a vibration just on the edge of my perception, now grew in volume until it caught both our attentions. The noise continued to grow until it was a roar, the roar of a crowd, at that. It was coming from further up the alley. Joe and I exchanged a questioning glance. He shrugged and led the way deeper into the alley in the direction of the noise. The alley took several twists and turns, yet, it was easy to follow the noise, as it continued to increase in volume the further we progressed.

At last, we came out onto a paved lot where a large crowd had gathered. The throng appeared to be almost exclusively made up of the homeless, though there were a smattering of pimps and prostitutes sprinkled throughout. As we neared the edge of the gathering, we had to stand on tiptoes to see what all the attention was focused on. There was a clearing in the middle of the crowd with two men, evidently bums themselves, grappling with one another, while a couple of young, college age men were video recording the action at the edge of the clearing. Those young twits!

I'd heard about this sort of thing. "My God," I couldn't help but exclaim, "it's a bum fight!" I tried to keep my words for Joe's ears only, not wishing to attract notice from the crowd, though they seemed oblivious to us, being firmly riveted on the action in the 'ring'. *"This is illegal!"* I hissed to Joe.

"I'll take the one in the plaid overcoat. He's a fighter," Joe observed clinically. I gaped. "I'd put a C-note on him, if I had one on me."

"You cannot be serious?!" I was flabbergasted.

"No, probably not." he conceded, then, "It's unlikely any here would have that kind of money, excepting the pimps, that is. Even the 'ho's would more than likely only be able to pay off a stake with 'favuhs'."

"Joe, were you even listening to me? This kind of thing has been outlawed." I was floored by his attitude. "Someone should notify the authorities. I--,"

Joe clapped a meaty palm over my mouth and whispered insistently in my ear, "For the love of God, Stan, never even joke about contacting 'The Man', in company such as this. Understood?" I nodded sullenly. Joe released me. "Look, I'm not up on recent laws or legislation governing this sort of thing, so, if it's not illegal, it's certainly unethical, I'll grant you that," then added, "I only say this to prevent both of us from getting capped in the ass," giving my arm a reassuring squeeze.

"You look nervous about somethin', old time," a deep, smooth voice spoke from Joe's opposite side. I peered around--, uh-oh, it was one of the pimps, gold chains, toothpick, and one of his bitches draped over an arm. This was potentially big trouble. He was regarding the both of us with heavy-lidded, suspicious eyes. Fortunately, Joe was quick as a cat on his feet and coolly defused the situation, "Naw man, jus' chillin', jus' chillin'." Most others from Joe's station in life would have been out of their depth, but not Joe, never Joe. The pimp slowly turned his attention back to the fight, as did we. I let out a sigh of relief.

The fight, as I made brief mention, wasn't much of one. Almost without exception, the homeless were simply in no condition physically and/or mentally really to stage a competitive contest. This particular contest consisted largely of wildly thrown roundhouse punches which, invariably, hit only air, choppy missed kicks which seemed to unbalance the attacker more often than not, and clumsy grappling which was the featured element of the match.

This one soon ended, when one of the exhausted and disoriented combatants charged Joe's pick, the man in the plaid overcoat (the fashion sense being a crime in and of itself), who stepped, not aside, but, directly into the path of his opponent, and delivered a vicious nut kick. The other man howled, clutched his crotch and crumpled to the pavement, where Plaid Overcoat was able easily to pin him down for a long enough count to cause one of the young film makers to holler, "Ding-Ding!" signaling an end to the barbarous affair.

"We have a winner!" the college puke crowed, lifting Plaid Overcoat's arm in the air, in what struck me, as a sick caricature of a victor. I so wanted to wipe the insipid grin from the punk's face. Good grief, the law of the jungle atmosphere was even beginning to infect me. We needed to get out of there. I turned to Joe to voice just these sentiments, when,

"Next challenger!" the kid called out. There followed a good deal of murmuring and discussion amongst those assembled, but no ready takers, as everyone was suitably impressed by the 'skill' displayed by Plaid Overcoat, who began to taunt the crowd,

"C'mon, you cowards! Ain't no one got the stones to take on nutkick?!" Nutkick? Was that his name, or handle? He did have a rather devastating one as his last opponent could attest. It was about the only thing he had demonstrated any skill at, and a cowardly one it was, in my opinion.

"Here's one right here!" The call came from the pimp opposite Joe, and he was pointing *at* Joe.

"No-no, nope, not me." Joe tried to avert attention from himself. "I'm just an old retired professor. Street fighting is not my line. If you'd care for a translation of the works of the ancient Hurrians, then we'd be in business." he chuckled self-deprecatingly. But, those around us were having none of it, beginning with the pimp who gave him a shove in the back, which propelled the modest professor into the arms of others in front. And it was these others who were not about to let go, as Joe's struggles to free himself increased. Someone had to be fed to the shark, better Joe than themselves, they must have figured.

"Joe, no!" I called out in a panic, trying to make my way towards him, but was rebuffed as the crowd closed ranks around him, clutching onto his person with eager talons like a flock of vultures.

"You're making a tremendous mistake." I heard Joe say, as he was passed along through the crowd towards the ring. "I'm a man of peace, *violence never solved anything!*" His voice ended in a hoarse shout, as he was flung off balance into the ring, barely managing to keep his feet. I tried to force my way through the crowd, but they held me off, forming an impenetrable wall which I could not breach, though I scouted the entire perimeter, frantically looking for a weak point.

"Don't be such a baby, old man," I heard the kid who was running the show say disparagingly to Joe. "We'll make you a star," he told Joe, snickering.

"Now you listen to me, you little snit," Joe said. I could tell he was going to deliver a scathing lecture in true professorial fashion, but the brat didn't give him the chance,

"Ding-ding, fights on!" he called out hurriedly while scampering to the edge of the crowd, leaving Joe stranded alone in the middle of the ring with only Plaid Overcoat for company. I had stopped my probing of the outer wall of spectators, and could only stand on tiptoes, at that point, and watch in anxious helplessness. I saw the brat and his friend slap palms, and he cried out, "Roll cameras!" Then, more to his friend, though his voice carried, "YouTube is gonna love this shit," he nudged his friend, who nodded enthusiastically.

Unfortunately, Joe was more intent on following the kid and continuing to deliver his lecture, and wasn't aware of Plaid Overcoat running up behind him, until the man pounced onto his back. Joe staggered briefly under the weight, but quickly regained some semblance of balance. PO (as I'll refer to Plaid Overcoat, from here on out) rode him piggyback style, while crooking an arm around Joe's neck in a crushing choke hold. Joe's face reddened, then purpled, as he staggered about trying to dislodge his aggressive passenger.

It wouldn't be long before he began to lose consciousness. He needed to do something quickly, or he would lose the fight. What am I saying? He could lose his life! I was so frustrated, and wanted to tear through the crowd before me, to go to my friend's aid, but then suddenly, with one great burst of strength, Joe leaned back, his attacker holding on even tighter, no doubt thinking Joe was going to flop on his back on top of him, pinning and crushing PO. That's what I would have done, I reflected, but instead Joe unexpectedly sprung his upper body forward. The man in the plaid overcoat was caught entirely by surprise, and went hurtling over Joe's shoulders and tumbled to the ground, rolling over and over before coming to rest in a heap. Joe bent over, hands on knees, gasping for breath. His opponent recovered somewhat more quickly, regaining his feet, and shaking his head to clear it.

"Joe, look out!" I cried. Joe's head snapped up. His opponent was pawing the blacktop with raggedy-sandaled feet, preparing to charge. Joe scanned about quickly, I assumed looking for an avenue of escape. No shame in that, retreat can sometimes be the better part of valor, given the circumstance, and this would certainly fit that. Only, that wasn't what he was after.

Darting quickly to one side, he snatched a faded red shawl from a crone in the front row, "Do you mind? Thanks." He didn't wait for a response, instead dashing back to the center of the ring, he flourished the shawl like a matador with a cape ... at which point, PO charged.

Joe spun away at the last moment, leaving PO grasping at air. With a howl of frustration, he turned, pawed and charged again, and again Joe was slippier than trying to catch smoke in your hands, as he whipped the shawl away and pirouetted out of PO's reach. Over and over again, PO charged with rising frustration and rage, as Joe managed to elude him, while, at the same time, putting on a masterful performance of makeshift bullfighting at its finest.

The crowd gasped in wonder at Joe's flourishes and footwork. If they'd known of his training in ballet, as part of his stage days, and his fondness for Hemingway, they wouldn't have been so surprised. Unfortunately, it was bound to happen eventually, one too many passes by PO allowed him to finally clip Joe and knock him off balance, at which point PO managed to close with his elusive opponent and wrestle Joe to the ground. PO had Joe on his back in a flash, this his preferred style of combat, and he was good at it.

Just as everyone was counting down the seconds aloud in unison, for the winner to be declared, "one, two, three, four--," Joe suddenly rose up and head butted his opponent, whom Joe quickly rolled aside from off atop of himself, and climbed to his feet, while PO lay dazed. Joe had a great head for head-butting, but he was wearing down, the signs were evident to all. Hands grasping his trousers at the knees, accompanied by ragged, gasping gulps of air, were bad signs, no matter how much he may have wanted to win.

Taking a cue from Joe's teaching that improvisation and cheating were not mutually exclusive in almost any given situation, I cast about for some further 'teaching' aid for my dear professor. I saw the perfect lesson tool propped up next to a dumpster by one of the surrounding buildings. Racing to it, I grasped it and dashed back to the ring.

"Joe!" I called out. He looked around and saw me, giving a wan smile. "Catch!" and I launched the five foot long piece of wood at him like a javelin. He expertly snatched it out of the air, and turned it over in his hands, inspecting it. The wood was not a rounded broom handle or some similar kind of rod, it had square sides, but with the benefit of being thin, like a long stake. He looked back to me and winked. Nervous energy coursed through me. I could see his confidence and energy returning.

PO had just regained his feet, rubbing at the spot on his forehead where Joe's head had contacted his. He was, by all appearances, in no mood for any more play. "I'm gonna kick you a new one," he growled, intending to serve up the specialty which had earned him his name, though to me he would always be PO. Joe stood the stake up, and was casually grasping it, with one hand behind his back. PO was oblivious, in his fury, to the calls from the onlookers, warning him that his opponent had a weapon, which he hadn't seen me toss to Joe, being too preoccupied tending to the after effects of my friend's head butt.

I noticed the two 'film makers' and the pimps all eagerly relishing this. Even most of the homeless, though they were being victimized by this travesty, were drooling for more violence. The blood frenzy of a crowd is an incredibly disturbing and shameful aspect of the human makeup. There were no rules, this was bum fighting, an even lower form than the more run of the mill street fighting: it was brutish and vicious. PO charged, Joe whirled the stake around from back to front, then spun it like a propeller over his head, waiting patiently for his opponent to come within reach. He was a rock of calm in that sea of shouts and cheers, all feral emotion crashing over him, though he let none of it penetrate his zen-like mask of seeming peacefulness. PO, meanwhile, was too committed to his charge to notice this. He came at Joe with his head down, barreling directly at him. *"Win at all costs,"* Joe's voice sounded in my head from an earlier teaching, *"then you won't have to complain. Only losers complain, they are likewise accorded the status of annoyances, and aptly so ignored."* So true, so true.

Joe adopted the horse stance, one of the four basic karate stances, which he must have learned from an infomercial martial arts DVD series he'd once purchased, and lashed out at the last possible moment, connecting with the back of his opponents knees. Pop-pop, in rapid succession, the contacts sounded like gunshots, as he danced out of the path of PO's charge. He was a fearsome fighting machine just then, continuing to twirl the staff, overhand, underhand, watching with studied disinterest as PO struggled back to his feet, after that last take down.

Sirens erupted from out of nowhere and the crowd froze, but only for a split second, before all bedlam was unloosed and everyone scattered in a hundred different directions at once. I forged my way through the tide to Joe, and grabbed him by the arm. He seemed not himself at all, still wearing the warrior's guide in his own mind. I needed him to snap out of it, "Joe, come on." The sirens sounded again, louder, they were definitely headed our way. "Drop the staff, we have to get out of here." He looked at the weapon in his hands, as if he'd never seen it before, and finally flung it away with a look of distaste. Not surprising, really. Joe's was a placid, good-natured personality, not normally given to bursts of violent activity. We could all learn a great deal from him in that regard, I'm sure.

As we were about to exit the lot, I saw that the only other people still left were the two kids, hastily packing up their camera equipment. "Just a moment," I told Joe, and approached them. "Hey, Punk?" I called out. The one who had done the talking turned to me.

"What do you want?" His tone was scornful. By way of reply, I launched and landed a crunching nut kick that sent him slowly to his knees, and then to a fetal position, in which state, I could only hope the police would find him and his videos. But Joe and I didn't wait around, we ran to the nearest alley opening and vanished.

Later that evening, Joe was pouring over a map of the city, tacked to his sketching easel. He had hot and cold compresses strapped to his back and neck.

"How are you feeling?" I asked, strolling into his den with a tray of mai tais. This was normally Teffer's task, but he had been given the night off, to serve as a judge on an awards panel at a local film festival, featuring animated spaghetti westerns.

"I've no time for pain, Stan," he replied, without looking up from the map, where he was carefully measuring off some distances with a ruler and precisely marking a line with pencil, tongue between teeth. I set the tray down and offered him a glass when he had finished. "Cheers," he lifted it to my health and promptly downed it.

"How goes the search?" I asked.

"There are three clear locations, according to the data I've correlated from what we received. Take a look," he beckoned me over to his side of the easel, "here, here, and here. These were the spots most commonly referred to by our informants." Nice way to recategorize the destitute, but true enough. "Would you agree?" The places he had highlighted and connected with lines on the map seemed to correspond with what I could recall we were told by our 'informants'.

"Okay," I allowed, "but the real question is, when?"

"Obviously within the next three days, Stanley," he retrieved another mai tai from the tray. I always made sure to include at least four when we were having drinks. This one he sipped, however. "No other dates fell outside of that range."

"Tomorrow, then?"

He nodded, "Bright and early." He toasted again. I followed suit.

"The game is afoot, then, eh?"

"The game is a three-legged race being run by amputees, Stan. No way we lose this one."

"Do we go in costume again?"

"Not necessary," he said. I gave a sigh of relief. "We confront the Pigeon King, and his followers, as we truly are. To do less would be a blatant falsehood to His Majesty." There were a couple of things which disturbed me about that statement, though I couldn't decide whether it was the verbal slippage into referring to this, most-most likely, mythical flying rat as His Majesty, or his view that the imagined encounter would be a confrontation. Nevertheless, I looked forward to our coming hunt with eager anticipation.

When the next morning found us taking our rest on the sill of a fountain in one of the city's parks, I reveled in the lovely morning sunshine, and the suspense. The invigorating anticipation caused me to blurt out, "Don't you just feel like Linus and Sally awaiting the arrival of the Great Pumpkin?"

"No, Stan, the Great Pumpkin was pure fiction, a hoax," he shook his head at my gullibility. Lighting a cigar, he blew on the cherry, carefully cultivating a satisfying glow. "The Pigeon King, on the other hand, is quite real. You will see."

Over the coarse of the next two days, however, I most certainly did *not* see. We spent all day and late into the evenings of both days staking out the prime spots Joe had identified, and for all the effort? Nothing.

"Maybe they were the wrong spots?" I offered hopefully late the night of the second day of futility, as Joe feverishly poured over his map, making notes and consulting reference books stacked beside his easel. "Or the wrong days?" I offered again. "Or maybe he just isn't coming," I said, subdued.

Joe was shaking his head at every one of my bleak prognostications, "No, Stan, zilch on all of the above. What is most notable about our past two day stakeout is, the dog that barked in the night. Or in this case … didn't."

"What dog, Joe?"

"Precisely my point. In this instance, the dog would be a euphemistic stand-in for the very people most keen on the Pigeon King."

"The homeless community?"

"Exactly. And where were they?" Come to think of it, I couldn't remember seeing any homeless, and voiced this to Joe, "Quite right, there weren't. Not a one. That, in and of itself, is highly significant, and suspicious."

"Do you feel we were fed false leads?"

"Possibly," he allowed, yet frowned, "though I really can't see how they could have 'made' us. My costume and performance were flawless, and you weren't too bad yourself." I beamed at the high praise, especially coming from one of the greatest virtuosos of the day. "I do believe the dates were a legitimate range, but the locations seem to be lacking," he continued puzzling over the map, squishing his lower lip between thumb and forefinger.

"Maybe we just missed him," I offered.

He gave me a pitying look, "Don't be absurd, Stanley. Had the Pigeon King made his appearance at any time in the last two days, the outpouring from the society of the indigent would have made the 'Who's down in Whoville' blush in embarrassment, at their own pious presumptuousness."

"What, then?"

"Come take a look," he bid me peer over his shoulder at the map, which was now a crazed connect the dots schematic, resembling more the product of crafts time at a special education program than any serious coordinate vector search. "These are the three areas we have been monitoring the last two days," he indicated the spots. They were hard to pick out under all the subsequent notations and doodlings he had made. In fact, I thought I could make out a duck playing a grand piano in one spot near where city hall was located. I shook my head to clear the fatigue which no doubt was causing me to hallucinate lightly. Joe always preferred to draw miniature dachshunds, anyway. "What do you find significant about them?" I had to admit there was nothing whatsoever I could decipher from it all.

"Observe the areas of the three locations," he said patiently. The professor was in and he was in full teaching mode, "In particular, their sides."

"Well, one is square shaped," I began cautiously, looking to Joe who nodded encouragingly, "one is more trapezoidal."

"Go on, go on."

"The third is a kind of odd, squashed pentagonal shape."

"And? What do you deduce from that?" he was brimming with eagerness.

"I ... I don't know. What *do* you deduce," it was less a question. I was too thoroughly confused.

"Count the number of the sides, Stan,"

I did as he bid, "Four, four and five." Where *was* he going with this?

"And what do they add up to?" Hadn't I seen this at some sort of political rally a few years ago?

"Thirteen," I answered tentatively, starting to dread his destination.

"Exacto mundo!" He exclaimed. "Don't you see?"

"I'm afraid you've lost me, Joe," I had to confess.

"Thirteen, Stan. What is the significance of that number?"

"Other than it's generally considered very unlucky, I don't--,"

"There you have it!" He cut in, bouncing on his stool like the class dunce who suddenly got one right. I was growing tired of this.

"Have what?" I asked crossly.

"Numerology, my dear chap," oooohhh, *great*, "thirteen, an incredibly unlucky number to be associated with an incredibly unlucky people. Namely, the homeless."

"Is this scattered dissertation nearing it's conclusion?" I hated to be led around drunkenly through a fun house of distorted mirrors. It gave me a headache.

"The conclusion is this, my friend," he seemed not to take offense at my sudden rudeness. "Notice the leading edges of the three spots I've highlighted," again, he indicated the places we had been loitering the last two days. "See where they all point inwards, towards one another?"

"Okay," I allowed.

"Now follow the lines I've drawn and see where they intersect." I did, and saw the three lines all cross one another at a spot which he had emphasized with a bold 'X'. "X marks the spot, Stan!"

"There?" I pointed, unsure if I had the right spot. There were numerous other X's littering the map.

"There," he corroborated, with a self-satisfied smile. It seemed an unremarkable location, not quite a park and not quite a vacant lot. I knew the area well enough, it was surrounded by apartment high rises and office buildings. But if that's where he had his heart set on …

"Tomorrow?" I asked resignedly.

"Tomorrow," and a fierce gleam alit deep within his eyes, "we learn the truth."

Tomorrow turned out to be a long day. Joe was determined to forego the previous spots we had staked out and focus solely on the location he had pinpointed, using his own peculiar brand of numerology. We arrived early and, as it turned out, had a long wait in store for us. Over the intervening hours of our lonely vigil, I grew more and more pessimistic of anything out of the ordinary happening. Coupled with my skepticism to begin with, and the previous two day's futility, this should not be surprising. As the day wore on towards late afternoon, I had entirely given up hope and voiced this to Joe.

"I'm beginning to agree with you, Stan," he, surprisingly, admitted in a glum voice. "Heretofore, I had taken the absence of the homeless as a sign we weren't looking in the right place. Only now, I have to take it as a sign that this entire venture has been nothing more than a fool's errand," he blew out his cheeks heavily, "a wild goose chase, if you will." He squinted up at the westering sun, now beginning to dip towards it's bed over the horizon. "Let's call it a day," he heaved himself to his feet, "and try to put this episode well behind us."

I solemnly agreed, secretly pleased it was over, yet remorseful for the disappointment it was causing my friend. We strolled from the bench on which we had been rooted all day. At first, Joe had thought to have us both camouflaged and nested away in a tangle of bushes with binoculars, like two overzealous ornithologists, but thankfully decided against it. He felt our best posture would be to do nothing more out of the ordinary than find a quiet bench, break out a bag of seeds, and feed the pigeons. A sort of libation, to curry favor with the Pigeon King. Well, it hadn't worked, but a good idea anyway. I guess.

It was as we were making our way from the 'not quite a park', when I saw something which has burned it's image into my memory and I know I shall recall it vividly until my dying day.

"Joe," I grabbed his arm and turned him in the right direction, pointing, *"Look."* I breathed in awe. He gasped when he saw what I had seen. A great winged monarch fluttered down from the sky, alighting on a swath of green grass directly in the center of a patch of late afternoon sunshine. He dazzled my eyes with his presence, like a star in the spotlight. He was just under a yardstick in height, I'd swear, his proud head calmly tilting from side to side, as he surveyed his realm

through brilliant orange eyes. The great bird's soot gray, pus and dirt brown plumage reflected a beautiful sheen that such colors had never exhibited before. *My word, but he was a stunning sight to behold!!*

Other pigeons arrived in his wake, and many others came from all points of the compass to crowd about that majestic bird: robins, jays, larks and a plethora of other species I couldn't begin to name. They appeared for all the world to be forming a court where the Pigeon King stood regally as the center of attention. It was more than just a parliament of fowls, it was a splendid royal court of fowls with all the others filling in the roles of courtiers and supplicants, the Pigeon King's loyal subjects.

"Joe, do you see, do you see it? Isn't it magnificent?!" I stood transfixed, and actually had tears in my eyes, watching the Pigeon King strolling about his inner circle, bestowing regal pecks and feather ruffs upon his followers, who had begun to chirp and warble so ecstatically their tiny voices combined to form an intoxicating melody which drifted upon the breeze, forming, as it went, a single chorus raised in praise at the glory of the return of the Pigeon King.

Riveted as I was, and unable to take my eyes off the scene, I only distantly noted that Joe didn't respond. Well, I thought absently, he must have been as awestruck as I. "Joe?" I turned my head. Joe was in a shooter's stance, right arm outstretched with a massive chrome-plated revolver in his hand. He was aiming directly at the Pigeon King. *"Joe, NO!!!"* I screamed, lunging at him. My hands caught the wrist of the hand holding the gun, and forced his arm upwards just as it went off with a deafening roar, far too close to my left ear, leaving it ringing. But I faintly heard, a split second after the report, the sound of breaking glass and a scream.

I held on for dear life, both of us struggling, Joe to lower the gun and myself trying to keep it pointed straight up in the air, "Stanley, let go! I can get off another shot!" I half turned my head and saw the Pigeon King just then taking flight, with most others of his court, who seemed to be forming a protective screen around His Person.

"No you can't, Joe, he's leaving!" Still we struggled, our arms locked together, both of us with very different purposes in mind for the firearm.

"I can hit him on the wing, let go I say!" He shouted, renewing his struggles to free his gun arm.

"But, Joe, why?!" I wailed, clinging to his arm all the more fiercely.

"For my grandfather! For taking him from us!!" His voice came out as a hoarse, choked sob. How could I get through to him that the Pigeon King couldn't possibly have been responsible for his grandfather's disappearance? Could he? No, no, it was too absurd, and yet I'd seen him with my own eyes. But no, he was still nothing more than an overgrown pigeon. A study for a piece in National Geographic as an avian oddity, but nothing more than that. "Besides, Stan, he would make an ideal new trophy for my collection on the mantle in my recreation room," Okay, he was beginning to rave, here it was, the great white hunter was at it again, "What am I saying?" his struggles slackened. Now, maybe he was coming around. "The mantle would be too small. I'd build a special case for him, and all the while, he would be imprisoned therein, and his beady little dead eyes could take in the view of his new lord and master, whether I be at work or at ease." He began to giggle, and his violent struggles resumed. I had to find some way to snap him out of this fit of madness,

"Joe?!" I raised my voice, pleading, in an effort to clear away his sudden mania. Although, I just then realized, maybe it wasn't so sudden. Evidently it had been building for some time. I hoped the loony bin was not his final destination. "Would Linus shoot the Great Pumpkin?!"

"Linus Be Damned!!!!" He roared, flinging me about, yet I hung on tight. Somewhere in all of it, I became aware of a

presence, palpable, as if something was close and watching us. Joe must have felt it as well, for his struggles subsided until they gradually stopped, just as mine did. I relaxed my hold and we both slowly turned and saw a large crowd of homeless, who had assembled not ten yards from us. I couldn't possibly explain how that many people had gathered so quickly and silently, except to say that Joe and I had been so engrossed in our struggle over the gun that we had been oblivious to all else. There was a long, drawn out silence.

"You tried to shoot the Pigeon King," one raggedy man at the forefront of the ranks finally said, a dirty, accusatory finger pointing directly at Joe.

Joe looked down at the firearm in his fist, with a curious expression as if he had no idea how it had gotten there. "What? This?" He quickly holstered the elephant gun under his voluminous coat and buttoned it. "No. No-no," he spread his hands in what he must have hoped to be a reassuring manner and shook his head, "you've got it all wrong. There's been a terrible misunderstanding." He smiled. They read it as false.

"Misunderstandin' nuthin'!" A withered crone spat, "you tried to kill our Right Royal Monarch!" The crowd rumbled dangerously. The situation was tense and right on the verge of--

"*Get Em!!*" someone yelled. They surged forward.

"*Run for your life!*" Joe bellowed, and we turned and fled. The army of the homeless shambled after us, looking for all the world as if they were in a stage somewhere between their last methadone treatment and *Night of the Living Dead*. We'd gone little more than a block, running for all we were worth, when I took a look back over my shoulder and saw that about half their numbers had broken ranks, collapsing onto the sidewalk or wandering dazedly off of it into oncoming traffic, where vehicles were swerving wildly to miss them. Still, the remainder were a determined bunch, and continued shuffling along on our trail.

Unfortunately, Joe was in little better physical condition than many of our pursuers, at least where extended outputs of energy were required, so that, before we reached the end of the next block, he pulled up lame. He collapsed against the side of a building in such a manner that it appeared either the building was holding him up, or he the building.

"Stanley, I can go no further," he wheezed, loosening his tie and undoing his collar.

"Joe, we must! They're gaining on us!" I was frantic. I couldn't leave my friend to their less than tender mercies, nor did I want to experience such myself. I looked back. The vanguard of the remaining pursuers were within half a block of our position.

"Go on without me, Stan!" he cried. "Let them have at me. It's all my fault anyway. It will give you time to make your escape."

"I'm not leaving you," I reached out and unpeeled him from the wall. "Lean on me. I'll support you," and he did, allowing us to continue up the sidewalk with a hopping, hobbled gait. I cast another glance back over my shoulder, and was relieved to see the ranks of the homeless mob had further thinned. Yet, there were still enough keeping up the hunt, and these were perilously close now.

"Joe, there!" I nodded my head to where a city bus was just pulling over to a bus stop, directly ahead of us.

"Ohm, huff-huff," Joe puffed, "chariot of deliverance."

We made it just in time and quickly climbed aboard. Our pursuers, the one's still active in the chase, milled about outside the doors, trying to bum enough change from passersby for the bus fare. Joe collapsed in a nearby seat.

"Hey!" The bus driver called out, "Be a gent and let the lady sit down, will ya?" We both looked around and saw a pregnant woman standing pensively nearby. The bus was crowded and many others were standing as well.

"*Why is it always women and children first, Stan?*" Joe gasped. I helped him from the seat. "Why can't an eminent man be spared the unenviable task of going down with the ship?" Passengers close by laughed and shook their heads at my friend. He wasn't finished. "Oh, you laugh now. Just wait until your time comes and you're called upon to make the ultimate sacrifice. There will be no laughing then, I'll warrant," he admonished, obviously still light-headed from our recent exertions.

"Come on, Joe," I guided him down the packed aisle to the rear of the bus. Once there, we took up places right next to the back door. Two of the bum cohort had managed to scrape up enough change for the fare and boarded just before the bus departed. They were tough looking hombres, clearly shock troops. They zeroed in on us and began slowly to squeeze their way through the crowded aisle, coming our way.

"We've got company, twelve o'clock," I whispered. Joe nodded grimly. "What are we to do?" There was an unsteady tremor in my voice.

"Leave it to me," he said softly, his right hand sliding slowly inside his coat. I quickly grasped his wrist and pulled his hand out.

"*Are you insane?!*" I said in a strangled whisper. "*You can't fire that thing on a crowded bus!* In fact, you shouldn't fire that thing anywhere, outside of a firing range or a war zone."

"What would you call this?" He asked petulantly. This galled me even further.

"No, Joe," I said with finality. Then, I had a sudden idea. I reached over and pulled the bell cord, requesting a stop at the next bus stop, which our bus happened to be virtually on top of. The bus decelerated rapidly and swerved quickly to the side of the street, the driver, frantically but professionally, trying not to miss the stop.

I was ready for this maneuver, and grasped the overhead hand rail to lend both Joe and myself support. Our two hunters, contrarily, were not prepared and lost their balance, spilling onto laps in adjacent seats.

"Now, Joe!" I barked, and he didn't hesitate, for he hopped down the short stairwell to the back door, threw his shoulder into it and flung himself through, I close on his heels.

"This way, Stanley!" He ordered, back in command of the situation. Although I questioned his command decision to abandon the sidewalk and dash out into oncoming traffic, as we hurried across the street, it was only briefly and in my head. We raced across the multiple lanes of traffic, as it zoomed by in both directions. Cars swerved and skidded to avoid us, honking horns and showering us with curses.

"There," Joe panted, and began shouting, "Taxi! Taxi!" I looked back in time to see our two remaining pursuers finally exit the bus, and immediately set out after us.

Inexplicably, one of them shortly veered off, as a car skidded to a halt right in front of him. He approached the driver's side, removed a small spray bottle and rag, and began cleaning the windshield. He thrust his free hand through the open driver's side window, cupped, as if expecting a gratuity for his services. The woman driving the car quickly rolled up the window, forcing him hastily to extract his arm before it was ensnared. The car then sped off in a squeal of tires. *"Bitch!"* I heard him curse.

But the final man had not given up the chase. "Stanley, quickly, inside!" Joe had the door of a cab open, and was making rapid ushering motions. I didn't need any further encouragement and practically dove through the open door, Joe briskly following.

"Lock the doors!" He ordered the cabby, who was quick to comply, as so many are instinctively wont to do, when Joe issues commands. It came not a second too late, for just a breath after the automatic locking mechanism clicked, our final pursuer was at the door, scrabbling for the door handle. When he failed to open the door by that means, he began banging on the window and trying to claw the door open at it's edges.

"*Hey!*" The cabby exclaimed, alarmed at the beating his vehicle was taking.

"Just drive." Joe told him calmly. The cabby put the vehicle into gear and we started off, leaving the last homeless soldier to run some short distance after our departing ride, trying to keep pace with the rapidly accelerating taxi before falling behind, and finally giving up the chase.

"Where to?" The cabby asked. Joe gave some roundabout directions to our building. He explained to me he wanted to make sure we weren't followed.

It was dusk, as we were deposited at the entrance to our building, hugely relieved we had escaped, and thoroughly exhausted by our exertions to effect that escape. Imagine our collective dismay, when we were startled by yet another ragged figure, who popped out from behind the steps leading to our building's entrance. I sucked in a tense breath, really not sure if either myself or Joe had the energy for a confrontation. How had they followed us here? Yet, he appeared to be alone ...

"What the--," Joe began, but the man quickly cut in,

"Greetings, gents." He sounded familiar. "Prob'ly thought you'd not be seein' me again."

"Mo?" Joe was the first to recognize Grizzle-Gray Mo.

"That'd be me. I just stopped by to give you something." He reached into his tattered coat. We both stiffened, Joe's right hand inching inside his own coat. But what Mo removed was some sort of disc-shaped object dangling on a loop of string. "Here," he held it out for Joe, "for you." Joe tentatively took it from him. I leaned in to get a better look, as Joe turned it over in his hands.

It was an old, old metal cap of some kind, larger than a regular bottle cap. It had the curious look about it that was peculiar to some nineteenth century antiques, or even older relics. There were worn markings stamped on one side that read, almost indistinctly, "Philmore Gas Co.". But it was on the other side that proved the most intriguing. On it's surface was etched an exact likeness of the Pigeon King himself, underneath of which was inscribed "His Sovereign Majesty, may he reign feathered forever".

"What is this?" Joe asked at length.

"One of our most prized possessions. It goes to whoever is first to spot His Majesty at each and every return," Mo explained. "I've held onto it for fifty years and now it's time to pass it on. It's a great burden," he went on, "a great responsibility. But also a great honor. The next time the Pigeon King returns, you will have to pass it on in turn."

Mo made as if to go. "But what if I'm not around then?" Joe asked. Mo turned back.

"Will it to your heir." He cocked his head to one side, a mischievous twinkle lit his eyes, then added, "The hunt for the Pigeon King is generational, it don't recognize the boundaries of time." He made to move off again.

"Mo," Joe stayed him one final time, "what happened to my grandfather? Was it the mob?"

Mo thought for a moment, then shrugged and said, "Don't rightly know. Coulda been. Just as he coulda retired to Rio, if he made off with the Mob's money, as had been rumored at the time." Joe opened his mouth to say something further, but Mo waved him off. "Mister, it's just as likely that your grandpappy lived out a long and eventful life, than not. No use frettin' over it. And one last thing," he laid a finger aside his nose, "I'd stay away from the community of the free winds for a spell." The what? Is that what they referred to themselves as? Well, it made more sense than referring to themselves as bums. "Plenty of folks'll be angry with you for your actions today, but they'll get over it." then   he laughed, "The time limit for most long term memory amongst our kind, short of the instinctive recollection of the return of the Pigeon King, is roughly a week," and with that he shuffled away down the sidewalk, quickly becoming lost in the growing dark.

I checked Joe's police scanner that night, relieved to hear that the bullet Joe had fired had passed through a woman's bedroom window, and lodged harmlessly in a wall. The woman had been frightened, of course, but totally unhurt. I was equally relieved that there were no suspects identified as to who had fired the shot, and no one had come forward to point any fingers. I found Joe in his study, seated at his desk. He was spinning the cap Mo had given him by it's string necklace. He seemed hypnotized by it.

When I gave him the news of the woman and his off-target bullet, he nodded, still transfixed by the twirling Pigeon King gas cap. "Good, good," he said, never really willing to let on to such things, but I could tell he was deeply relieved.

"I hope you've learned a lesson from all of this about passion and obsession?" I remarked.

"I certainly have, Stanley." he said, before concluding in a tone which sounded as if he were quoting an old saying from *Poor Richard's Almanac*, or something, "Never mix the two when packing heat."

Well, it was a start. Joe just needed to begin applying some critical thinking to those situations in his life where the fantasy land in his mind began taking over. Time would tell, as will I.